CW01496327

MAYFIELD

Graham Sutherland

authorHOUSE®

AuthorHouse™ UK Ltd.
500 Avebury Boulevard
Central Milton Keynes, MK9 2BE
www.authorhouse.co.uk
Phone: 08001974150

First published by AuthorHouse 9/8/2009

ISBN: 978-1-4389-8426-1 (sc)

This book is printed on acid-free paper.
First published by knowle villa books
Warwick cv34 4bt
www.talksandwalks.co.uk

Other Books by Graham Sutherland

Dastardly Deeds in Victorian Warwickshire
Leamington Spa, a photographic history of your Town
Leamington Spa, Francis Frith`s Town & City
memories
Around Warwick, Francis Frith`s Photographic
memories
Knights of the Road
Warwick Chronicles 1806 - 1812
Warwick Chronicles 1813 - 1820
Felons Phantoms and Fiends
North to Alaska
A Taste of Ale
Wicked Women
Fakes Forgers & Frauds
Warwickshire Crimes and Criminals
Midland Murders
English Eccentrics
Edward`s Warwickshire January - March 1901

Joint Author:

Policing Warwickshire, a Pictorial History of the
Warwickshire Constabulary

To Mo, Claire, Jo, Ally and Clara

PROLOGUE

June 1840 near Aylesbury

Once more, the watcher in the bushes, eased his stiff limbs. It had turned into a long wait tonight. He looked again at the upper part of the house, but it continued mocking him by remaining in darkness. The only visible lights were still downstairs. "Would the maid never go to bed?" he asked himself.

The stillness of the short June night was broken, by a nearby church clock striking half past two. He knew it would be getting light in little more than two hours, and the knowledge did not suit him. Darkness was essential for what he had in mind. Then, as if in answer to his silent question, all the lights, except one were extinguished. The remaining one finally moved from what he knew to be the study. For a few seconds the house was in darkness, until the light reappeared, albeit briefly, on the mezzo landing, as the carrier continued on her way to bed.

At last the light moved into the maid`s attic bedroom. The old man had gone to bed sometime earlier, but the maid had no such luxury. She did not have an easy job. Before going to bed, she first had to see to the final clearing up after her master`s late dinner party, and laying the table for breakfast. Several minutes later, the light went out. Unlike some he could name, the watcher knew the maid was not allowed the privilege of sleeping in a lit room: the usual reason given being the risk of a fire happening. In reality it was down to penny pinching. The watcher slowly counted to one thousand before he moved.

Firstly, he opened his breeches and relieved himself against a tree. He knew it was partly nerves, but, in his kind of work, an empty bladder was essential. Having finished, he bent down and picked up a bag near his feet, and looked up at the sky. A large cloud had almost reached the waning moon, and it would be worth waiting for a few more minutes, until it was completely covered. Once a greater depth of darkness had stolen over the grounds and house, it was time to go.

Being naturally cautious, he kept to the darker shadows under the trees, for as long as possible. Not that it really mattered, as the waning moon cast very little light through the clouds. But he did not believe in taking unnecessary chances. He avoided the gravel drive and ran lightly across the lawns to the side of the house. Tiptoeing, he followed the outer wall and made his way to the kitchen window. Here he paused and listened.

The only sound he could hear, came from a wild animal in a nearby field. Only when he was completely satisfied, did he put down the bag. Stooping, he opened it and took out a long thin bladed knife and several pieces of raw meat, which he laid carefully on the window sill. Picking up the knife again, he pushed it between the two casement windows, and slid it as far as the catch. Applying steady, but gentle pressure, he felt the catch spring back with a slight click, as the window was unlocked. Holding the knife between his teeth, he pushed open the lower window, and waited.

Almost at once, he heard the expected menacing growl, as a large dog appeared and placed his forepaws on the window sill. He saw the animal`s muzzle was drawn back in a snarl, exposing his very strong white fangs.

"Easy boy!" the man whispered, and held out one of the pieces of meat.

The dog ceased snarling and his nose quivered, picking up the scent of the meat, which the man dropped onto the kitchen floor and waited. Almost at once, the dog stood down and resumed his sniffing of the meat, for a few seconds. Deep down he knew his primary duty was to see off the intruder, but the meat smelt most inviting. The dog decided the intruder could wait whilst he swallowed the meat and looked up for more. It came quickly as the man threw the other pieces into the room, where they were soon eagerly swallowed by the dog.

By now, the dog was shaking his head, feeling strangely muzzy, as the drug quickly took effect. He opened his jaw to bark a warning, but no sound came. Slowly his legs buckled and he collapsed in an untidy heap on the floor. Only when the man heard the dog collapse, did he consider it safe to climb through the window and into the house, taking his bag with him.

Opening the bag again, he removed a lantern and a candle. The lantern had been altered to show only a small beam of light, just enough to guide him around the house. Lighting the candle from his own tinder box, he set it into the lantern. Putting it down for a moment, he returned to the unconscious dog and pulled him back to his rug in front of the dying fire. Having made the animal as comfortable as he could, he patted the dog`s head and whispered, "Good boy."

He moved through the kitchen and into the hall, picking up every item which appeared to be made of silver or gold. Checking them for the appropriate assay mark, to prove their authenticity, he rejected any that were not so stamped. He put the genuine items into his bag, having first wrapped them in pieces of cloth, specially kept for that purpose. This was not to protect them, but to lessen the risk of their making any noise, and possibly disturbing someone in the house. Next he moved to the dining room, drawing room and study, putting items into his bag on the way.

Having checked out every room downstairs, he returned to the kitchen. The bag was almost full and it had not been a bad night`s work. It was far too risky to go upstairs. If his employer did not like it, then that was just too bad. But, it was not his employer who was carrying out the burglary: he would not dream of doing such dirty work himself. Still, he mused, the pay was not bad, and there was only one golden rule. He must not help himself to any other goods in the house, except money. It made sense. Such items could always be traced. Whilst that was true of the gold and silver, he knew that was quickly melted down.

Acting on a sudden whim, he went back into the study and picked up a small jet and jewelled snuff box, bearing the initials **W T**. He hesitated only for a moment before putting it into his pocket, knowing it was strictly against his employer`s precise rules. "One for me," he chuckled. "They`ll never notice it`s missing. And its got my initials on it."

Passing the deeply unconscious dog, he knelt beside the animal and fondled his ears. "You`ll be alright," he whispered. "Just a thick head

3

in the morning. I hope they don`t take it out on you too much."

Leaving the dog, he made his way back to the window and climbed through it. Reaching back inside, he picked up the bag and pulled it through. Putting it down for a moment, he reached up and closed the window. It might delay discovery of the burglary for a while longer.

He stood and listened. As he hoped, all was quiet. Picking up the bag, he went back into the garden and moved quickly across the lawn to the boundary wall, relieved to see the rope was still there. Already the sky in the east was getting lighter, and he knew it was time to go.

Several seconds later, he had climbed the wall, hauling the rope up behind him. Dropping the rope over the other side, he slid down it, with a practiced ease, into the lane which ran by the house. He was relieved to see his horse was still there, contentedly grazing at the grass. It was risky, but he needed his horse nearby in case he was discovered and chased. Whilst he always chose the quietest parts possible to hobble the animal, there was always the chance someone else might find it. After all, he chuckled, there were always thieves about!

After waiting for a few moments, in case anyone was about, he quickly checked the saddle girth and bridle. Satisfied he fastened his bag to the saddle, then went to a nearby bush and retrieved another bag, which contained his cavalry tunic, shako, sabre and spurs. Minutes later he had been transformed from a nondescript type of man into a cavalry corporal of horse.

Gathering up his other clothes, he put them into the bag, which he placed alongside the other one, on his saddle. Taking a last look around, he was satisfied nothing had been left behind. Climbing into the saddle he trotted off towards the nearby town, confident no Night Watch Patrol would ever stop anybody wearing a military uniform.

The journey to his lodgings passed without incident, although it was light by the time he had stabled and groomed his horse. People were about in town already, and suddenly he felt hungry, but that would have to wait. He returned to the inn, where he had rooms, treading quietly, careful not to wake anyone. Once inside his room, he locked the door behind him.

Taking another key from his uniform, he opened a large strong box kept under his bed. He carefully put the contents of the bag into it, where they joined several other similar items. After closing and locking the box, he pushed it, with his empty bag under the bed. It had been a good night's work. During the morning, other members of the gang came and gave him their takings.

For the next few days, there was a feverish amount of activity by the magistrates and parish constables, in and the around Aylesbury, which achieved nothing. Several houses had been burgled.

Two weeks later, when the town returned to normal, he packed all the stolen silver and gold into three travelling trunks. Where necessary, he wedged more cloth into all the spare spaces in the trunks. When he had finished packing, he gave each trunk a good shaking. Only when there were no sounds from them did he double lock the trunks and attach labels to them.

With the assistance of two of his colleagues, he took the trunks to a nearby carrier company, and consigned them to the usual address in Warwick. Giving a small sigh of relief, he returned to his lodgings and began to pack. New instructions had arrived, and the gang was on its way to Bicester. He wondered if they would ever get to Warwick.

That idea appealed to him. They had all been lucky so far, but, as he knew only too well, luck could and did run out. He was getting to the stage of having had enough of this particular enterprise, and looking forward to retiring; for a while at least. Almost sub-consciously, he touched the snuffbox in his pocket. He knew why he had kept it. The snuffbox had some value, and being inscribed with his initial, *W T* was a bonus.

For a moment he was tempted to throw it away, wondering if it might bring them all bad luck, but decided to keep it.

CHAPTER ONE

Arrival .....Late October 1840

As the crow flies, the road from Leamington Spa to Warwick is no more than two miles. Yet to John Mayfield, it seemed interminable, as he strove to curb his impatience, whilst the Telegraph stage coach covered the short distance.

Fortunately the weather was still fine or he would have had a cold wet journey from London. All the inside seats on the coach, had been taken, so John, along with seven other passengers, had spent the journey sat on the roof. In reality, he preferred being on top as it was not so claustrophobic as the interior. John had scarcely acknowledged his fellow passengers as he had too much on his mind. Sleeping had been out of the question, and not just because of the risk of falling off the vehicle. This journey was the beginning of a new life for him and he was looking forward to it.

His elderly parents had seen him off at the start of his journey, from London. It had been by coach as the railway had not yet arrived at Warwick, John`s destination. Even after a lifetime of being married to a soldier, John had seen his mother`s eyes glisten as she kissed her son goodbye. His father was more reserved and had shaken hands firmly with him. John had tried to persuade them to come with him, but they had refused to move to the Midlands. It was understandable as their friends still lived in London, but they would not stand in their son`s way.

Suddenly, John felt a twinge of loneliness and regretted not having married. Somehow, he just never seemed to have found the time. For a start, it had been difficult to form relationships when you lived in regimental family quarters, with scant privacy. Then, there had been the problem of always being on the move. Matters had improved once his father had risen from the ranks to the dizzy height of lieutenant. But, without a private income, a handy war or other sponsorship, he had remained in that rank. As such, he was neither accepted as an officer or a ranker. It had been a lonely existence for them all. By then, John had followed his father into the Army.

He had tried to become a soldier, but it was not really to his liking. It was not that he had found the life or discipline too trying, it was just somehow he did not seem to fit in. He was capable enough, and proved it on several occasions. But as the son of an elderly retired lieutenant, he faced similar problems to his father. Being unable to purchase a commission, he had remained as a corporal.

One thing the army had taught John, was how to look after himself. Being slightly built with fair hair and boyish looks, he had quickly learned to defend himself with his fists and a variety of weapons, as some men had discovered to their cost. On his Regiment`s return to England, John had declined to sign on for a further period of service with the Colours, and left the army. His next move had been to join Mr Peel`s Metropolitan Police.

He took readily to the work, and wearing the regulation top hat made him look much taller than his six feet. The streets of London held no terrors for him, thanks to his army training. By sheer hard work, coupled with ambition, aided by his schoolmistress mother, John had reached the rank of inspector. Like his father, he expected to progress no further, and began to get frustrated.

Although never short of ideas, he was restricted by a top heavy command system, which moved quickly in times of emergency, but when it came to administration, was slow to make decisions, being bound by rules and regulations. By the time he received an answer, the opportunity had been lost. To his way of thinking, it was the army all over again, and he was becoming disillusioned. John was not sure how much longer he could put up with it.

He had discussed the matter with his father, who, although sympathetic, had asked the unanswerable question. "You`ve been in the army and now the police. Where will you go next?"

John had no answer and so he stayed in the Metropolitan Police and tried to make the best of it. In spite of his comparative youth, he was well respected and trusted by his men. The advertisement for a superintendent to manage the newly proposed Warwick Borough Police, had appeared out of the blue. Perhaps, just perhaps, this was the chance he needed. With nothing to lose, plus a considerable amount of support from his senior officers, John answered the advertisement and was pleasantly surprised to be selected for interview. Even now he still could not believe what had happened.

It had been the hardest afternoon he had ever experienced. The interviewing panel had consisted of five magistrates, five members of the Watch Committee, and the Earl of Warwick. To be fair, the Earl had acted as chairman and mainly steered the interview along. Although he seemed in favour of the idea of a proper police force for the town, his views were not universally supported.

John`s main antagonist, for want of a better word, had been James Cooper who was both a local industrialist and member of the Watch Committee. No matter how John replied to the questions, Cooper always found a way to belittle him. At first, John had thought the man`s antagonism was all part of an act, put on for the interview, to see how he coped under pressure.

However, he soon discovered the antagonism was for real and like nothing John had ever encountered before. He could not help but wonder why the man had taken such an attitude. Yet, somehow John had kept his temper and won the day, albeit only just. It had been the Earl`s casting vote, in his favour, which gave him the job.

At the end of the interview, most of his opponents had accepted the vote graciously and congratulated him on his appointment, but not Cooper. He had left without a glance in John`s direction. It was not an auspicious beginning as the man, in his official capacity, could make life difficult for John. At the time John did not realise just how difficult that would be. He would soon find out.

In the following days, as he finished his time, in London, John was dismayed to receive next to no information from Warwick. All he had was a terse confirmation of when his appointment would take effect. There was no information concerning recruitment of staff, arranging the purchase of uniform, equipment etc. Whenever he queried these, John was told "The Watch Committee has it all in hand."

John suspected, correctly as he would discover, James Cooper was behind making life difficult for him. To make matters worse, the Metropolitan Police would not let him go earlier because of his involvement in a complicated trial at the Old Bailey. They were determined to get their last pennyworth of work from him.

The coach clattered into Warwick Market Place, as the cold October afternoon was drawing to a close. A mixture of excitement and trepidation greeted John Mayfield as he arrived at his new home.

For a few moments his sense of loneliness returned, and he felt envious of the young couple holding hands, sitting in front of him. John knew it was his own fault and he could not blame anybody else. He was the proverbial rolling stone, but, there was always a ray of hope for the future, no matter how small. The police were not everyone's friends, and they tended to socialise amongst themselves. However, John had always preferred to spend his spare time in bettering himself, in more ways than one, and it paid off. Yet, unlike the young couple in front, who were waving to some older people, waiting by the *Green Dragon Inn*, John had no one to greet him. He would write to his parents, but it was not the same.

His thoughts were interrupted as the coach drew to a halt and passengers alighted. John waited until everyone else had left the roof before climbing, stiffly, down on to firm land once again. It was good to be able to stretch and move his legs, having long since lost the feeling in his buttocks, and his back ached. Going to the rear of the coach, he waited as the guard handed him down his large carpet bag. It contained most of his clothes. The remainder and his other few belongings, were somewhere between London and Warwick, on a carrier's waggon.

John Mayfield had arrived in Warwick.

"Superintendent Mayfield? Superintendent John Mayfield?" came a voice from behind him.

John turned and saw a man standing behind him. He was slightly shorter than John's six feet, but more broadly built and some five or six years older. The stranger sported a dark moustache and bushy sideburns, like his hair, such as John could see escaping from under a top hat, was also dark but streaked with grey. In addition to a loosely knotted tie, he was wearing the typical dark coat and lighter trousers, which had once been fashionable, a few years ago, but were now somewhat dated. For a long moment, both men studied each other, liking what they saw.

"I am sir," John replied. "Although I do not actually take up office until next week."

"Tish, man! As far as I`m concerned, you are our new superintendent of police. I daresay though, you`ll find Warwick town somewhat different to London."

"You seem to know all about me," smiled John. "But, I must confess, I know nothing about you, sir."

The stranger held out his right hand. "I`m forgetting my manners. Waldren. Thomas Waldren."

John took the outstretched hand and returned the firm grip. "Pleased to meet you, Mr Waldren."

"Actually, it`s Doctor Waldren, if you want to be really formal." His blue eyes twinkled mischievously.

"I do apologize," came John`s slightly formal reply. "I didn`t mean to cause any offence."

"None taken," laughed Thomas. His laugh was infectious and eased the sudden slight tension. "It`s my fault. I should have introduced myself properly. Where are you staying?"

"Over in the *Woolpack*."

"An admirable choice until your new police station is finished. You can even see it from the *Woolpack*. What are your plans for this evening?"

John shrugged. "Nothing specific. I was going to book in at the *Woolpack* and then take a walk round the town, just to get the feel of it and start to find my bearings."

"Good. I`ll have someone take your luggage there. Your walk around the town can wait until tomorrow. Tonight, you will come and dine with me and my wife. I`ll show you some of the town as we go."

John tried to protest, but Thomas held out his right forefinger.

"It`s no use saying no. Sarah, my wife, will never forgive me, if I leave you all alone on your first night."

"I really don`t want to put you to any trouble.........." began John.

"Think nothing of it," smiled Thomas. "Anyway, if I don`t take you home, Sarah`ll never speak to me again."

Thomas looked at a nearby porter, who was eyeing up the two men expectantly, and beckoned him over. "Take this bag to the *Woolpack*, please."

11

The porter picked up John`s bag and waited whilst Thomas dug into his pocket, and pulled out a 3d piece. He tossed it to the porter, who caught it deftly in his right hand, and, at the same time knuckled his forelock. The man turned quickly and made off towards the nearby *Woolpack*.

"Jenkins!" called Thomas after him. "Keep the change and buy your wife a present."

"Yes sir. I`ll do just that."

"He`ll not buy her a thing," commented Thomas, sadly, as the man vanished. "He`ll spend it on drink. Just like all the others."

"Warwick`s no different to anywhere else, then?" queried John.

Thomas looked at him and shook his head. "No its a problem everywhere, as you know only too well."

"Perhaps, one day........?"

"Not until the water`s fit to drink: there`s full employment and everyone`s had the benefit of education. Then, and only then, perhaps, we might see a change."

"Amen to that," came John`s solemn reply.

"Amen to that," Thomas agreed. "Enough of the miseries. On behalf of our dear, thoughtful and considerate Watch Committee, of which I happen to be a member, and from whom the Good Lord, please deliver us: Welcome to Warwick."

Thomas led John on a short tour of the town. He explained how there was a market every Saturday, complete with two hiring fairs in mid October. John looked at the bustling Market Place. Some market men were still trading, whilst others were in the process of dismantling their stalls. If he shut his eyes for a moment, the noises reminded him of the busy markets back home in London, or even India, where he had spent some military service.

Shaking his head at the thoughts, he reminded himself: This was his home now.

Finally, Thomas stopped outside a large double fronted Queen Anne style stone built house, in High Street, near the Unitarian Chapel and almost opposite the Lord Leycester Hospital. John looked up at the imposing house.

"Built soon after the Great Fire of 1694," explained Thomas. "It took out most of the town centre, and St Mary`s Church. The good thing is it led to the rebuilding of the town as it is today."

He paused as a red painted carriage drew up alongside the two men. As they turned, the window was lowered and an angry red face appeared. Thick steely grey eyebrows emphasized the cold, fish like grey eyes which glared over the bulbous nose. John recognised him immediately as James Cooper, from the Watch Committee.

"So you`ve come, Mayfield?" The voice was harsh, like a file being drawn over metal. "I didn`t want you, or anybody else, and I still don`t. I thought you would have realized that?"

John made no reply, but coolly returned Cooper`s stare. The other man was the first to break eye contact.

"As for you, Waldren," Cooper snarled. "I suppose I shouldn`t be surprised to find you in the company of this man." He indicated John with a jerk of this right thumb. "But, knowing you and all your radical ideas, I would have expected nothing less."

Cooper returned his full attention to John and waved a large gloved finger at him through the open carriage window. "One mistake! Just one mistake! And I`ll see you`re finished. Finished for ever." He turned his face to the coachman, who had sat impassively whilst the exchange was taking place. "Drive on!" he hissed.

The coachman shook his reins and the horses moved forward. At the same time, Cooper withdrew into the carriage and slammed the window shut. The carriage moved down West Street in the general direction of Stratford. John and Thomas watched it go.

Thomas turned to John and shook his head. "My apologies for that, he said. "He is the rudest and most ignorant individual I have ever come across. Yet, he likes to think of himself as being a gentleman. He doesn`t even understand the meaning of the word. And, would you believe, he has ideas of receiving a knighthood? And he even has at least one very influential sponsor. At least, so I have been told."

"I`m James Cooper, of the Watch Committee. And don`t you ever forget it!" John mimicked. "We met when I was interviewed. I must admit, I`ve met nicer people in this town." He looked at Thomas and grinned.

"Thank you." Thomas, returned the grin. "At least he`s not my patient. If he was, I think I`d poison him."

Both men laughed. John followed Thomas to the front door. However, before they reached it, a small man, suddenly appeared out of a neighbouring house and hurried towards them. He looked straight at John and smilingly held out his right hand. "Would I be right in thinking you are Mr Mayfield, our new policeman?"

John took his hand, "I am sir, but you have the better of me."

"Tish! Trust Waldren here to forget his manners." He kept his smile and looked at Thomas.

"John, this is my esteemed next door neighbour, William Slattery. He`s a rogue so don`t believe a word he says," replied Thomas, laughingly.

"Don`t believe a word he says!" replied Slattery in the same bantering tone. John could see the two men were the best of friends. He had also noticed how the doctor had called him by his Christian name.

William Slattery was not really a small man, but he had a very pronounced stoop, coupled with a thin body. He was dressed formally in black, and John noticed his face looked drawn and pale, and was framed with a shock of grey hair. Clearly he spent much of his time indoors. A pair of fairly strong lensed pince-nez perched on the end of his nose, gave him the appearance of being an academic.

"Afraid I can`t stop," continued Slattery. "But I`ll see you around, Mayfield. The best of luck in your new post. Yet I fear, with people like Cooper about, you`ll need it." Slattery touched his hat and walked away towards the town centre.

"Don`t be fooled by him," said Thomas. "He has a very shrewd brain and is an expert jeweller. What he does not know about gold and silver is not worth knowing. Even the Bank of England consults him from time to time."

By now they had reached his front door, which was opened by the Waldren`s butler, who had clearly been watching for their arrival.

"Thank you, Redman," acknowledged Thomas as they entered the house. Thomas handed over his hat and coat. John did likewise and followed his host into the drawing room.

It was a pleasantly large room, with a fire burning away under a marble mantelpiece. A large gilt framed mirror fastened on the chimney breast gave the room a feeling of being much larger than it really was. The lamps had already been lit. A maid was in the process of closing the shutters and drawing the curtains.

John saw a small, plump woman sitting by the fire, sewing. She was wearing the standard long, full dress of the period in greenish gold and blue with full length sleeves. Her dark hair hung down in ringlets, topped with a small white lace cap. John could not help but notice the shorter fashions of London had yet to make it to Warwick.

"My wife, Sarah," introduced Thomas.

"How nice to meet you, Mr Mayfield," said Sarah. John noticed there was a slight roll to her voice, emphasizing her Gloucestershire upbringing. She held out her hand and John took it. "I hope you had a good journey?"

"It was tiring, Mrs Waldren."

"Oh do call me Sarah. I cannot abide all this formality."

"Only if you agree to call me John."

"Willingly. Did I see you talking to that dreadful James Cooper, just now?"

"Being spoken at, I think would be more accurate," chuckled John.

"No," interrupted Thomas. "Being barked at. The man`s insufferable. Just because he owns an iron foundry down by the canal, thinks he owns the place."

Thomas walked over to the sideboard as he spoke, and took the stopper from a decanter. "A glass of Madeira John? I know Sarah will."

John noticed the use of his Christian name again and smiled.

"Yes please." He liked this couple who had gone out of their way to make him welcome.

"Cooper`s an upstart," continued Thomas. "He thinks his money can buy him everything he wants."

"But it does, dear," said Sarah. "That`s the problem. How else did he get on the Watch Committee?"

Thomas grunted something unintelligible in reply.

Later, after they had dined, the three of them sat in the drawing room. "Are you married, John?" asked Sarah.

"Typical woman`s question," muttered Thomas.

"No," replied John. "I suppose I`ve never really thought about it, though I`ve always been fond of children. Do you have any?"

John sensed the sudden change in the friendly atmosphere.

"We lost our only son at birth," explained Thomas. "Sarah can`t have any more."

"My apologies," said John. "I should have thought before I spoke."

Sarah reached out and touched John on his arm. "You weren`t to know. I`ll look forward to helping you with your children, when the time comes."

John put his hand over her`s. "That`s a promise," he said, and meant it.

At last the evening broke up, and John reluctantly left Thomas and Sarah, and made his way back to the *Woolpack*, in the Market Place. He would stay here for a few days until the new police station was ready. When it was, the living accommodation would become his home for the next few years, and he would be expected to live there. That was always provided James Cooper did not manage to have him removed.

John began to like the feel of this town. He had done so at the time of his interview, but now he was really here. Having never really expected to be offered the position, he still had difficulty in believing his good fortune. Yet, James Cooper apart, it would not be the easiest of jobs. His entire force would consist of one sergeant and four constables, whom as yet he knew nothing about. Although they had already been appointed, he had not been involved in their selection.

By any stretch of the imagination, it was very few men to police a busy county town, complete with weekly markets, race meetings, the Assize Courts, the Quarter Sessions and a nearby military barracks. At least he had the power to call on special constables if need be, provided a magistrate would swear them into office, for whatever period was necessary.

If those problems were not enough, he would also have to deal with the likes of James Cooper, whose sole aim in life, seemed to be the undermining of John`s position. He wondered why. Cooper seemed to have plenty of money, and should, in theory, be welcoming the new police, not opposing them. It did not make sense.

John shrugged. It was not an unusual attitude. Not that long ago, people had once feared Peel`s new police. They had acquired the nicknames of *Raw Lobsters* and *Blue Devils,* from their coats, modeled on the military style, but being in navy blue rather than red. The names were meant as an insult.

As a town, Warwick had only just agreed to form its own Borough Police Force. It was a reluctant decision, forced upon the town by outside events. Like almost everywhere else in the country, for many years the town had employed a single professional police officer, who was assisted by the outdated system of appointed ward constables, who tried to avoid the duty if at all possible.

These constables were appointed annually, but it was an unpopular duty. Most of them had their own businesses to run and could ill-afford the time. For them, it was a long year in office. The temptation to turn a blind eye, and not become involved in anything, was very real. Some actually employed substitutes to do the work for them. To make matters worse, the town's original professional officer, although very capable, was ill and unlikely to return to full duties again.

In reality, he should have been the man to lead the new police, and not John. True, there were also the night watchmen, most of whom were getting on in years and should have been in their beds, not out patrolling the streets.

This grossly inefficient system had finally been exposed by Peel's new police and the idea was spreading throughout the country. It was not a popular move and legislation, passed the previous year in 1839, began to force local authorities to accept their responsibilities for operating a proper and regular police system. Such was John's inheritance.

St Mary's Church clock was striking midnight as John climbed into his bed in the Woolpack. He blew out his candle and lay for a while in the darkness and listened to the various noises in the town. Soon he would be able to call Warwick his town.

CHAPTER TWO

Settling In

After he had eaten some breakfast, next morning, John walked over to the new police station, in the Holloway, which still had to be completed. He was surprised to find nobody was working there, and wondered if this was another one of James Cooper`s tricks. As if in answer to his unspoken question, St Mary`s Church bells began to peal and he remembered today was Sunday, which explained why nobody was working.

He spent the remainder of the day walking around the town, just to find out where places were and generally get the feel of the place. But, he still found it to be a long and somewhat frustrating time. He had not been given any keys to the police station, so could not get into the building. As he had no idea who his new officers were, there was no chance of going to call on them. It really was not how he had imagined his welcome would be.

In spite of his frustration and loneliness, John resisted the urge to go and call on the Waldrens. When they had parted the previous night, he had been given an open invitation to call any time he wished, but he did not like to abuse their hospitality. Nevertheless, he was very grateful for their friendship and hospitality.

At last Monday dawned, and after an early breakfast, John made his way over to the police station once more. This time the door was unlocked and he could see workmen scurrying about. He breathed in and enjoyed the smell of new paint and freshly cut timber, but wondered just how long it would retain its freshness.

From somewhere upstairs, in his future living quarters, John supposed, he heard the sound of banging. Looking round the entrance hall, with its small counter and enquiry hatch for members of the public to use, John pushed open the door to the side of the counter and walked into what would be the charge office.

"Can I help you sir?" A voice greeted John.

He saw the speaker was a big man, sitting at the desk, whose dark hair continued down the cheeks of his slightly round face, as thick bushy side whiskers. These were linked by a similar coloured moustache to a broken nose. His dark eyes, twinkled, yet held John`s gaze without faltering. Although he was dressed in casual clothes, the man was too clean to be a workman.

"I was wondering when this would be finished," replied John, indicating the police station. He did not have the financial resources to stay too long at the Woolpack. Clearly there was at least another week`s work before this old house was properly converted into a police station.

The other man laughed heartily. "So do we." His eyes narrowed slightly. "I don`t think I know you, sir, do I?" he quizzed.

"No. I only arrived on Saturday." The man was inquisitive and John recognised the signs.

"Staying long, are we sir?"

"Many years, I hope. It all depends on how this venture goes." John waved his hands around the station again.

"Ah!" exclaimed the man, getting to his feet. "You wouldn`t be Superintendent Mayfield, would you, sir?"

"Indeed, yes; and which of my officers are you?"

"Mathew Harrison, sir. Sergeant Harrison, that is." He drew himself smartly to attention whilst speaking.

"At ease, sergeant," replied John, and held out his right hand, which Harrison took, in a firm grip. "I`m very pleased to meet you."

"My apologies, sir. I did not know you had arrived."

"I came up on Saturday by coach."

"I do apologize, sir. Nobody told me you were coming. As it happens, I was out of town, but it would have been a simple matter to have re-arranged that appointment."

"Don`t worry. I was met by Dr Waldren, who took very good care of me."

"He would do. He`s a good man, fair and a damn good doctor, if you`ll pardon the expression."

"Tell me: why the delay in finishing the police station?"

Mathew grimaced. "It`s being done by James Cooper`s men, and they come and go as they please. They are a law unto themselves."

"I thought he was an iron founder?"

"Correct, except that he has the necessary connections to become involved in anything he puts his mind to. Slowing down the building of the station, is but part of a day`s work to him," came the bitter reply.

"There must be somebody else whom I can see, isn`t there?"

Mathew shook his head sadly. "I wish there was. Basically James Cooper runs this town, or rather his money does."

John nodded his agreement and then accepted his sergeant`s offer of a tour around the station. By London standards, it was not very big. Besides the parts he had seen already, there was only his own office and uniform room on the ground floor. The basement of the old house had been converted to make just two holding cells.

Sergeant Harrison saw the look on John`s face. "At least we are fortunate in having both the County Gaol and the House of Correction only a few yards from here. We won`t have to keep our prisoners for very long."

During the day, John discovered his sergeant was married to Margaret and they had two sons called Edward and James. He had spent ten years with the Royal Warwickshire Regiment, including some time in the Provost Marshal`s Department. In 1840, he had left the Regiment to join the police.

At first he had been tempted by the new Knightlow Hundred Police which had started earlier that year. But the new police force, whilst having responsibility for parts of Warwickshire, excluded Warwick. Being Warwick born and bred, Mathew had jumped at the chance of being a police officer in his own town. With his background, he had been an obvious choice for the rank of sergeant.

They finished off the tour with a quick inspection of John`s living quarters, which were upstairs. To say the least, they were not very large. He would have a bedroom, living area and a small kitchen. It reminded him so much of military living quarters. Grimacing a little to himself, he could not see these quarters appealing to any wife he might marry in the future.

The one privy, in the small yard, had to serve the needs of all occupants of the building, John included. He wondered, yet again, if this was another example of James Cooper`s work, or was it just coincidence. But as his men would come to know, John did not believe in coincidences.

After the tour, both men went for a walk around the town. John was surprised just how many people spoke to Mathew. They all knew what he was about to do for a living, but still joked with him about it being time he started work again. Where possible, Mathew introduced John to some of the more influential members of the town`s society. The more John saw of his sergeant, the more he was impressed by him. It was a help their both having similar military backgrounds and John hoped all the other police officers, under his command, would be the same. In his heart of hearts he knew it was a forlorn hope.

He had no reason to doubt they would be any different to the men he had left behind him. There would be inevitable questions regarding the honesty of at least one of them, and drunkenness would be another problem. Hopefully they could each take care of themselves, as some people still saw policemen as fair game and would attack them given the slightest opportunity. True, things were getting better, and for the most part, policemen no longer went about in fear of their lives, but hostility towards them still existed.

Mathew broke in on his thoughts by reminding John of the drain on their resources whenever the Assizes and Quarter Sessions sat.

"The races will also be another problem," he added. "It has long been the custom for assistance to be given by the Birmingham Police and I dare say we will be glad to have it."

"Is that with Mr Cooper`s approval?" asked John, sarcastically.

"I know you will have met him. He has to be treated very carefully, but even he will not dare to cancel the Birmingham Police from coming to the races. You see, most of the troublemakers come from Birmingham. Their own police know who they are, and are best placed to recognize and deal with them."

"What do we know about Mr Cooper?" asked John. "I must admit he intrigues me somewhat. He just does not appear to be acting in the way a responsible member of the Watch Committee would be expected to behave."

Mathew explained how Cooper was a comparative newcomer to the town. He was very wealthy and had succeeded in buying just about everything he wanted, including being a magistrate. Here his reputation was one of a harsh punisher, and most people were terrified at the thought of appearing before him. His very glance was enough to fill them with dread. This made his anti-police attitude all the more difficult to explain.

Cooper owned a foundry by the canal, which sometimes operated at night. Popular rumour said he even stripped off to the waist and worked alongside his employees. However, Mathew stressed this was only a rumour.

The man was unmarried, but never seemed to have a shortage of women in his life, not that he kept the same one for very long. He was a vicious and unscrupulous individual, who allowed nothing to stand in his way. Home for James Cooper was a large detached house, set in its own grounds, off the Birmingham Road, called the White House. It had been specially built to his own specifications.

"I'm told it looks a bit like an old castle inside, with suits of armour and swords all over the place. He's desperate now to get a knighthood so he can justify living in such premises," concluded Mathew. "Generally speaking not too much is known about him. His real love appears to be wealth and power. He has them both and is hated for it."

John knew only too well how such men quickly rose to power in small towns and cities. James Cooper was obviously such a man and would cause no end of problems for John and his men.

"Being the County town," said Mathew, breaking in on his thoughts once more. "Sometimes there will be public executions to oversee."

John had not thought about that extra unpleasant, but necessary duty. Fortunately, he did not have to arrange the actual hanging, but he would be responsible for any rioting or other disorder which so frequently accompanied those occasions. By now, they had returned to the police station.

"I believe all the men have been chosen. Is that right?"

"Aye," replied Mathew. "But, haven't you been given any of their details?" He stopped as John's tight lipped expression quickly answered the question. "It was mainly done by Mr Cooper, although some members of the Watch Committee didn't let him have all his own way, although I think it was just for form's sake."

Mathew crossed over to the desk and took out a leather bound ledger from one of the drawers. He turned it round for John to read. Each page was dedicated to a specific officer and was numbered consecutively, with John at number one, and Mathew number two. Each man's personal details were recorded, including his date and place of birth, description, current employment and details of any previous police or military service.

John looked at the next four names of the people who would comprise his whole little Warwick Borough Police Force. Just six men, including Mathew and himself. It was not a lot by any stretch of the imagination.

"What else do we know about them?" asked John. "Though I suspect not a lot."

Mathew sighed. "As you suggest, not a lot. I haven't seen them yet. But I am working on it. Once I know, I'll pass the information on to you."

Finally, they walked down by the river and stood for a while on the impressive bridge over the Avon. "Built by the Earl of Warwick, some sixty odd years ago," explained Mathew. "Not out the goodness of his heart, but all part of his struggle to gain more land."

"Seems like a good place for suicides."

"It is."

Yet, the view of Warwick Castle, from the bridge, was one John would remember for all time. He knew of nothing to rival it. In spite of all the apparent problems he faced, John knew he would enjoy working here.

John intended spending the next day acquiring furniture, for his living quarters over the station. His needs were simple and he was not too worried about what to buy. However, he had reckoned without Sarah, who took great delight in choosing his furniture, linen, cutlery and so on. For his part, John was quite happy to allow her a free hand She was aware he did not have too much money to spend, but she had experience of managing on a tight budget, albeit many years ago, before she met Thomas.

When she had finished, John had to admit his quarters would definitely have a woman's touch about them. Somehow, she had even managed to make them feel like his home, even in their unfinished state. Reluctantly, he locked up the still unfinished police station and returned to the *Woolpack*. He still had another week to go before being sworn in and taking up official residence, provided the building work had finished.

On entering the *Woolpack*, John heard Cooper`s voice coming from the tap room, as the man strode out into the hall. "I heard you were staying here," he snarled. "I didn`t want you here, and I still don`t!" He moved to brush past John, who stood his ground.

"I cannot see why you are so antagonistic to me," said John, mildly but firmly. He was now aware of just how big a man Cooper was, having only really seen him before when he was seated. He was a good half a head taller than John, and much broader, and powerfully built. John could see no fat on him, and knew the man would be a formidable physical opponent.

"Also," he continued. "I would appreciate your men completing the new police station as quickly as possible. Otherwise, I shall demand they are changed and more reputable builders be used."

Cooper stopped and John saw his eyes glitter dangerously. "You demand what?" he shouted, and began to jab John in the chest with his right forefinger. "Don`t you ever dare to speak to your betters like that!" He punctuated every word with another jab at John`s chest. "You are just a public servant!"

"Please don`t do that," came John`s quiet reply.

His eyes blazed too, complete contrast to the the mildness of his voice. He was aware that conversation had stopped in the tap room, as the drinkers were now too busy watching the drama in the entrance. Only those nearest to John saw him stiffen slightly and clench his fists as Cooper stepped forward aggressively.

Cooper saw it too and hesitated. For the first time, he realised this policeman, unlike everybody else he had encountered, was not afraid of him. He had not even flinched when jabbed in the chest. Like all bullies, Cooper did not know how to deal with someone who stood up to him. It was a novel experience.

Suddenly, he turned on his heel and strode out of the *Woolpack*. John watched him go and then walked into the tap room. The spectators made way for him as he made his way to the bar, where he ordered a tankard of ale.

"This one's on the house," smiled the landlord. "You've just made history by putting that bastard in his place."

"After that, I'll buy you one," said a voice behind him. John turned and found himself face to face with a grinning William Slattery. "It's time you met some of the other, more reputable businessmen in the town."

John liked the jeweller and had no hesitation in accepting his invitation.

The following morning, John was not so sure it had been such a good idea. His head was throbbing relentlessly when he had his morning meeting with Mathew Harrison. The burly sergeant quickly presented him with a mug of tea when he arrived. "A little bird tells me you might be glad of his," he chuckled slightly.

John muttered his thanks and gratefully accepted the drink. "How did you know what I did last night?" he added.

"There's not much that happens here that I don't know about. But you were in good company. Mr Slattery is our chief magistrate, and probably Warwickshire's greatest humanitarian benefactor, who provides a lot of money for the relief of the needy. And, he's very fair on the Bench. He really ought to have received a knighthood ages ago."

Their conversation was interrupted by the arrival of the builders.

They looked at John carefully, touched their forelocks and went straight to work. Much as John's head did not appreciate the banging and other building noises, they were still music to his ears. It seemed his little confrontation with Cooper was starting to bring results.

By the time they left, that evening, Mathew commented on the progress that had been made. "That's the most they've ever done, in a single day," he stated, clearly impressed. "Let's hope it will continue."

CHAPTER THREE

Swearing in

The next few days passed in a flurry of activity and meetings. It seemed as if John`s altercation had done some good, as the work on the police station definitely speeded up. Yet, John still had some concerns.

True to his word, Mathew had made enquiries about the new constables and expressed his reservations to John. To be fair, the men were a mixture, as he explained. He promised to give John all the information before everyone was sworn in, as there were still some enquiries he had to make. By now, John had learned to trust the big sergeant.

On the night before their swearing in, the long awaited uniforms arrived and both men unpacked them. Each set consisted of a navy blue swallow tail coat, complete with a button up collar around the neck. As it was approaching winter, there would not be any white trousers until the spring. Meanwhile, trousers were supplied in the same navy blue serge as the tunics. These were held up by braces and a stout leather belt went round the coat. Each man would also be equipped with a long staff and a small lantern. They were expected to provide their own boots. But, no uniform hats had been delivered.

"Where are the hats?" asked John.

"They should have been ordered. I made that quite clear to the Watch Committee. There was no reason for them not to be. They should have come from the same supplier."

"Who was responsible for ordering them?" John stopped as he saw the look on Mathew`s face. "Oh, no! Let me guess. Mr Cooper?"

"I am afraid so, sir. But I never thought he would do this to us. He`s been out to cause us problems right from the beginning."

"Whatever is wrong with that man? No, don`t answer that."

For several minutes John was lost in his own thoughts. "James Cooper isn`t going to win. Here`s what we will do. Get a message to the men that they must all come here tomorrow, in their own hats and be prepared to wear them for a while. If anyone objects, then warn them they`ll not have a job. It`s not ideal, but better than having no hats."

"Leave it to me, sir," chuckled Mathew. He had been impressed by the new superintendent right from their first meeting, and with some justification. His respect had grown when he heard about the confrontation in the *Woolpack*. If anyone could tame Mr James Cooper, he thought, then Superintendent John Mayfield would be the man to do it.

John watched Sergeant Harrison as he left the office, and felt his spirits rise. The man was a capable police officer, and John was happy to have him as his deputy. Somehow, he doubted if the same could be said for his constables.

❧

By 8.30am the next morning, John`s little police force had assembled together. When they changed into their new uniforms, he had a chance to study them for the first time. As Mathew had said, they were a mixed bunch.

Firstly, there was Robert Andrew, a single man, who appeared to have avoided matrimony. He was not as tall as John, and permanently looked in need of a square meal. Women fell for his helplessness, and he made the most of it. John had a feeling they would fall for him all the more, when they saw him in uniform. Clearly he had worn uniform before, and John soon discovered he had been a police officer for one of the railway companies.

Originating from Aylesbury, he regularly wrote to his elderly mother. In return, she often sent him copies of the local newspaper, so he kept abreast of what was happening at home. He made no secret of it being his ultimate ambition to return to Aylesbury. John would soon learn and come to value his thoroughness and first class memory.

"Everything alright, constable?" he asked.

"Couldn`t be better, sir," came the confident reply. "It`s good to be back in uniform."

"I know exactly what you mean," smiled John. He felt confident in this man.

However, the next man, Elijah Snow, was a complete contrast to Robert Andrew. The man was broadly built, but spoke and moved somewhat slowly. John knew he had previously been employed as a labourer. From an educational point of view, he could write his own name and a few basic words, but that was all. Clearly he had been recruited for his brawn and definitely not his brain. Although he had stood to a form of attention when John approached, he permanently rocked on his feet.

"Stand still!" hissed Mathew.

"Ah, well," came his rambling reply. "Do you see, it`s not that easy for me. I`ve never done anything like this before, do you see, and me old darling wife.........."

"I couldn`t care less about your wife," snapped Mathew. "Stand still when the superintendent is speaking to you!"

Snow reddened and open his mouth to reply, but seeing the look on Mathew`s face he thought better of it.

"Do you have any questions, constable?" asked John.

Snow looked at Mathew before answering. His prudence was well rewarded when he saw the look on the sergeant`s face. Snow shook his head. Mathew raised his eyes to the ceiling. The man should never have been recruited, but he knew who had been responsible.

The next officer was Samuel Perkins who was by far the youngest member of the Force. John was aghast to see how young he looked, still only in his teens. Being slightly built, he looked even younger. How ever would he cope with fighting drunks and other violent prisoners.

"How old are you?" asked John.

Perkins chuckled. "I`m twenty four, sir, and much nearer to twenty five. And I know what you are thinking. Don`t have any worries on my account. I am more than capable of looking after myself. I learned wrestling and fighting when I was at school, and I still practice regularly. If you doubt me...." he smiled. "Then I`m sure we can arrange a challenge match."

"You wouldn`t stand a chance against me!" sneered the last man, Patrick Monk.

"That`s enough!" ordered Mathew.

John turned to look at Monk. "I wasn`t speaking to you," he said mildly. "I`ll let you know when I am."

Monk snorted derisively. As he did so, John`s nose began to twitch as he could smell alcohol on Monk`s breath.

"Have you been drinking?" he asked, still deceptively mildly.

"Well, if I have, what`s it got to do with you?" retorted Monk, falling into John`s trap. "The answer is yes. I`ve been celebrating becoming a crusher."

John studied the other man, without replying, and he was not impressed. Monk was scruffy and made Elijah Snow appear a fashion plate by comparison. He saw Monk was of medium height and build, but with a dark complexion, and deep set eyes and eyebrows to match. Complete with dark hair and sideburns, he looked quite threatening and his whole attitude was one of surliness and obvious contempt for John.

"Now listen to me, everyone," instructed John, addressing his men. "I need to make one thing very clear, before we go any further. I will not tolerate any officer coming on duty smelling of drink. Neither will I tolerate anyone getting drunk on duty. Do you understand?"

"Yes sir," replied Mathew and three of the men. Monk remained silent, and just stared straight ahead.

"Did you hear what I said, Monk?"

Slowly, the officer turned to face John. "What I do in my own time, is my own business. If I want a tot before coming on duty, then I`ll have one, whether you like it or not."

"If you do so," came John`s icy reply. "Then it will cost you your job."

"Oh no it won`t!" smirked Monk. "Only Jimmy Cooper can do that, and I`m far too useful to him for that to happen."

"I suggest you listen to me." John`s voice was icily quiet. "Do not argue with me. Otherwise you might just find I have other courses of action available to me, which do not involve Mr James Cooper."

Suddenly, Monk looked less sure of himself. John turned on his heel. "Carry on sergeant."

"Yes sir!" Mathew snapped to attention and saluted. John returned the salute and moved away.

Mathew produced a ledger, which he opened and proceeded to read. "Listen here. These are the Rules and Regulations for the Observance of the Police Force. One: Constables are to devote their whole time to the police service, acting under the direction of their superintendent, and keep their uniform in a clean state and condition." He paused and looked pointedly at Snow and Monk. "Two: On no account are they to drink at any inn, public house or beer house while on duty, nor enter into conversation with anyone except on matters relating to their duty. Three:..........."

John listened as Mathew outlined the seventeen rules and regulations approved by the Watch Committee, for the running of the force. In addition, as superintendent, he had his own responsibilities which included overseeing the general conduct of the force; arranging the men`s duties; keeping proper records; watch potential trouble makers in the town and so on. These were in addition to his general duties as a police officer.

At last Mathew stopped and John looked at his watch. It had once belonged to his father, and his grandfather before, and kept excellent time and showed the hour to be 9.30am. He had another half hour to get the men to the Court House, where they could be sworn in and become authorized to carry out their duties.

"We`ll be leaving for the Court House in five minutes," announced John. "So spend the time making sure you`ve got everything."

"Haven`t we got any hats?" asked Monk. "We can`t work if we`re not properly dressed, can we?" He added with a smirk.

"Nobody asked for your opinion!" snapped Mathew. "And you address the superintendent as sir."

"Why do we needs an `at?" queried Snow.

"To stop birds nesting in your hair," quipped Robert Andrew.

Snow`s astonished look caused everyone to laugh, including Monk.

"Quiet now," smiled John. "As the Watch Committee have seen fit not to give us any hats, you will have to wear your own, until they come."

"That`s not right," called Monk. "We need proper hats. You know, the heavy reinforced leather ones. We ain`t got any protection else."

"Say sir!" snapped Mathew.

"Sir," came the surly reply.

"You`re wearing your own hats for the time being," John replied sharply. "If you don`t want to, then take off your uniforms and leave the Force for good."

John knew it was a gamble, if they all left, he was out of a job. He waited, but nobody moved, and even Monk seemed lost for words. John let out a quiet sigh.

"Now listen," he said. "It`s time to leave for the Court House. So fall out and form up outside."

The men filed out of the charge office, and made their way towards the main door.

"A moment please, sergeant," called John. "What do you know about Monk? Am I right in what I`m thinking?"

Mathew nodded. "He`s Cooper`s man through and through. He was a gamekeeper and quite violent with any poachers he came across. Cooper thinks highly of him, and I`ve not the slightest doubt he`s here on Cooper` instructions. He`s totally untrustworthy and is a born trouble maker."

"And Snow? Whose idea of a joke was his appointment? Mr James Cooper by any chance?"

"Snow`s fairly harmless, although he too worked for Cooper. He doesn`t have the intelligence to be anything else."

"Were these the only candidates? Surely there must have been some better ones?"

"There were several, but Mr Cooper decided on the short list. I thought you knew?"

John shook his head. "Not really, but it`s what I suspected." He paused. "You`d all been chosen by the time I arrived. All my requests to get their details have been ignored."

"Andrew and Perkins tend to make up for them. Somehow I get the impression Perkins was a mistake on Cooper`s part. He`s not as helpless as he looks."

"Let`s hope so."

John had taken out his watch whilst they were talking. He opened the cover and looked at the time. "Fall the men in, please!"

"Yes sir!" saluted Mathew.

Both men left the police station and moved into the Holloway where the men waited. Already a small crowd had gathered to watch them.

"Fall in men!" Mathew called them to order. He watched as they fell into a single line and stood to attention. Already the jeering and catcalls had started. "Ignore them," came his quiet instruction. Snow had already turned round and was grinning at the crowd, but quickly stopped when he saw Mathew glowering at him. Mathew looked at John and saluted. "All correct, sir."

"Thank you, sergeant." John returned the salute. "Carry on."

Mathew moved them off to the right, in single file and they marched, in a fashion, into the Market Place. Andrew and Perkins maintained their step, but Snow was totally incapable of doing so. Monk just ambled. John marched with them keeping one pace behind and to the side of them. A fresh barrage of catcalls greeted them in the Market Place. This new crowd merged with the original one and escorted them all the way down Church Street to the Court House.

Among them was Kate Whiting, with her young son, Edward. As John passed her, she found herself staring at him, unable to look away. At the same time, she felt her heart beat rise. "What am I thinking of?" she asked herself. "I`m a mere foundry worker. He`d never look at me twice. And I`m married."

She turned and walked away, totally unaware how this chance encounter would change both their lives. Although she never knew it then, John had seen her, and was attracted by what he saw.

He would discover Kate was only two years younger than he was but life had not been so kind to her. She stood slightly over five feet tall, with a round face, high cheek bones and slightly turned up nose, deep dark brown eyes, all framed by a mop of thick brown hair. In spite of her lowly status, Kate was an attractive woman, albeit terribly thin. Later she would discover he felt the same way as she had. He too had no idea of how she would change his life.

Slowly the crowd backed off as the new police arrived at the Court House and the men were able to enter without any further hindrance. An angry James Cooper greeted them on the steps.

"I hope this damned noise isn`t going to follow you everywhere?" he snarled, indicating the dispersing, though still noisy crowd.

"Of course it won`t," replied Thomas Waldren who had just arrived at Cooper`s side. "It`s just high spirits. They`ll soon get used to seeing them about town."

"Damned unnecessary expense, Waldren, if you ask me. Can`t see why we couldn`t keep the old system. I`m still against the whole idea!"

"Is that why you insisted your man, Monk, joined them?" Thomas asked innocently.

"Be careful!" glowered Cooper, his face reddening. He held Thomas`s gaze for a few seconds, then stormed away, into the Court House.

Thomas looked at John and winked.

John and his men entered the Court House and made their way upstairs to the Ballroom, where the swearing in ceremony would take place. They were instructed to wait on the stairs, where he took the opportunity to say a few more words to his men.

"In a few minutes, we will be called in to take our oaths, empowering us to be police constables. I know this is a ballroom, and not a court, but it will be treated with the same degree of respect. Do you understand?"

"Yes sir!" came their reply.

"Just remember, you should be proud to wear this uniform. Also, be proud of your appearance and the job you are about to do. If you have no pride in your appearance, behaviour and uniform, now is the time to leave. There will be no disgrace at this stage. However, if you disgrace your uniform and calling, after you have been sworn in, then you will have let down your families, colleagues and town, and there will be no place for you in the police. And lastly, no matter if the populace call us crushers, I do not want to hear any of you using that term. Is that understood?"

John looked pointedly at Monk as he said the last few words. It was one of the longest speeches he had ever made.

Snow`s face began to crack into a grin and his mouth twitched, until Mathew interrupted him with a ferocious glare and the grin vanished.

"For the last time," said John. "Does anybody want to leave now?"

Nobody moved.

"Thank you."

At that moment, the doors opened and an usher appeared. He looked down his nose at the police officers and impatiently beckoned them forward with his right forefinger. John looked at Mathew and nodded. Mathew called the men to order and they all marched into the Ballroom, with John at their head.

The Ballroom was filled with most of the town's businessmen and other leaders and their wives. This was why the larger Ballroom was being used instead of the court. John turned left and moved to the end of the room where several magistrates sat on a rostrum. He quickly instructed the men to halt and had them turn to face the magistrates. A sudden hush fell over the room.

"Who presents these men for swearing in?" asked William Slattery, the Chief Magistrate.

"I do, your worship" announced Cooper, slowly getting to his feet. John thought the man's face was redder, and the scowl even greater than usual.

"However," he continued. "I seriously wonder if they should be accepted, as they are improperly dressed and are not wearing regulation hats. I find this very insulting, and it seems to me to justify the suspicions and beliefs, that this whole idea is a waste of time and money." He looked triumphantly at John.

Slattery held up his hand to silence the sudden outburst of talking in the room, and looked directly at John. "Is there a reason for your not wearing proper headgear?"

"There is, sir. Apparently the order for their purchase was not sent by the Watch Committee."

Slattery held up his hand again to still the renewed outburst of talking. Looking over his pince-nez, he asked his next question. "Is this correct, Mr Cooper?"

"I`ll....I`ll have to look into it," he stammered and glared at John.

"But, Mr Cooper," continued Slattery "Is it not the function of the Watch Committee to provide all items of uniform?"

"Yes," came the mumbled reply.

"Then I cannot consider your objection to be valid," continued Slattery. "Clearly the lack of correct hats is the fault of the Watch Committee in not ordering them. The ceremony will continue."

The usher gave each man a copy of the New Testament. "Hold the testament in your right hand and repeat after me," he instructed.

The men obeyed him and the swearing in passed off without any further incident. When it was over, the usher retrieved his bibles. The men remained standing at attention whilst Slattery gave them his congratulations and best wishes for the future. When he had finished, Mathew ordered them to turn right, prior to leaving the Ballroom. There was great amusement when Snow turned left instead.

"I`ll get it right one day," he laughed out loud. His laughter quickly stopped when he saw the look on Mathew`s face.

John heaved a sigh of relief. His little Force was now official, in spite of Cooper`s efforts.

Why was the man so antagonistic?

CHAPTER FOUR

First Patrol

Back in the police station, the duty men were marched out on to their beats, whilst the others were sent home. John went for his first official patrol around the town. He had become a familiar figure already, but this was his first time out in uniform.

Towards the early afternoon, he found himself in the Market Place and confronted by a mounted major of the 87th Regiment of Dragoons. The major was accompanied by six mounted troopers. Riding his grey mare closer to John, he tapped him on the shoulder with his crop.

"You there! Fellow!" came his upper class drawl. "Take my horse!"

John ignored him and kept on walking.

"I said take my horse! How dare you ignore my command!" The voice was harder and John felt the crop tap his shoulder again.

He stopped, slowly turned and looked up at the major, whom he judged to be in his fifties, with a reddish face and grey bristling moustache. It was impossible to see the colour of his hair which was hidden under his shako.

"Are you addressing me, major?"

A pair of pale cold blue eyes focused on John. "I don`t see anybody else," came his languid response. "And stand to attention, fellow, and salute when you speak to me."

"I will afford you the same courtesy as you give me, major. My rank is superintendent, not fellow."

"You are a mere servant, not a gentleman and you will do as you are damn well told. Take my horse!"

"I am a superintendent of police," repeated John quietly. "And it is not my job to tether your horse. Your own men can do that for you."

"You dare to disobey me?" The major`s voice was now hard, and full of menace.

"It is not a question of obeying or disobeying you, major," John paused. "I will repeat: It is not my task to take your horse and you know it."

As the exchange was taking place, John had been aware of a small crowd gathering. Whilst this confrontation was not of his making, he could not afford to back down. He saw the riding crop rise again.

"If you hit me once more with that crop, major, I will be forced to take action." John looked the major squarely in the face.

The man glowered. Yet, at the same time, he realised the policeman was no coward and seemed quietly confident. And he could sense, rather than see, the smirks on his men`s faces. Meanwhile, the crowd had grown. Here was some unexpected entertainment with a confrontation between the police and the military. Whilst the townspeople might not exactly favour the idea of the new police, the military were even less popular.

Like John, the major could not afford to back down. With his crop still raised, he knew he had committed himself and saw John had moved onto the balls of his feet and was flexing his hands. A sudden silence fell on the crowd, as they waited to see who would strike first.

Strangely, the incident was resolved by the sudden appearance of James Cooper`s carriage, which drew to a stop beside the two men. Cooper`s head appeared out of the window.

"What the devil are you doing, Charles?" he hissed. "Brawling in public is not fitting for a gentleman in your position, even if its alright for him." He indicated John with his thumb. "Put down your crop!"

Major Charles Pearson glared first at James Cooper and then at John. Slowly he lowered his crop and leaned over his horse`s neck. "If you were a gentleman," he sneered at John. "I`d call you out and soon carve you to ribbons."

"You`re welcome to try."

"But he`s not a gentleman, Charles. I doubt he even knows the meaning of the word," interrupted Cooper. "That`s the end of it. I`m going home now, so follow me. Your men have their billets arranged in the *Green Dragon* and Thompson knows where to go."

Pearson looked at Cooper and slowly nodded. Then he turned

back to John. "One day, gentleman or not, we will sort this out between ourselves. My name is Charles Pearson and don`t you ever forget it."

"One day," agreed John.

The carriage moved away with the major following it. The other soldiers rode off, following Corporal of Horse Thompson towards the *Green Dragon,* on the opposite side of the Market Place. Slowly the crowd melted away, realizing there would be no fight to watch today. Yet, in spite of themselves, they were impressed by the way the slightly built policeman had held his ground.

Slowly, he was starting to get the reputation being someone who was not to be crossed. The last ones moved away, nodding to John as they did so, and a tall well built man detached himself from the shop doorway, where he had been watching the incident.

"Well handled, John!" he said.

John spun round, on hearing the familiar voice, with a large grin on his face. "Daniel Roberts! What are you doing here?"

"Same as you, old friend. Police work. And I need your help."

"You`d better come back to the station then. It`s only round the corner."

A few minutes later, John took Daniel into his office. Robert Andrew soon appeared with two mugs of tea and left them alone.

"You`ve done alright for yourself," said Daniel, looking around the office. "I`m impressed. Superintendent in charge of your own force."

"True," John looked back at his friend. "But as an Inspector in the Birmingham City Police, you`ll still have many more men than me under your command."

As he spoke, John studied the other man, noticing how the years had been fairly kind to him. His sturdy figure had not run to fat, although his dark brown bushy hair was beginning to show flecks of grey. John was glad to see Daniel`s dark brown eyes still held their mischievous twinkle.

"You seem well informed about my current posting," smiled Daniel.

"I`ve watched it with interest. We`ve both come along way since we walked the beat in London. And, after today, its good to see a friendly face."

For a while the two friends spoke about old times. John told Daniel about his problems with Cooper, Snow and Monk, and now Major Pearson. The other man was sympathetic.

"I just cannot understand the way Cooper is so antagonistic and deliberately trying to undermine everything I do."

"It`s time you got married and settled down," suggested Daniel, with his brown eyes twinkling.

"How are Emma and Benjamin?" asked John, changing the subject.

Daniel`s face lost some of its smile. "Emma`s fine, but we do worry about Benjamin. He`s a sickly child and, I fear he`ll not make old bones."

"I am sorry to hear that."

For a few moments, neither man spoke. Finally, John broke the silence. "Now, what is the police work you want to discuss?"

"Counterfeit coinage."

❦

Daniel related how one of his officers had become involved investigating a case of counterfeit coinage. He had traced it to Warwick Races, in September. But, there the trail went cold. The money was supposed to have been paid out on a winning horse during the meeting. However, when questioned, the suspect maintained he could not remember the name of the horse or even which race, even though it only happened last month.

"But, it`s not that simple," continued Daniel. "The man is absolutely terrified."

"Perhaps he doesn`t relish being transported?" suggested John.

"No. It`s much more than that. He`s far too scared to be innocent. We feel he knows full well what this is all about, but is too scared to talk. My Chief has offered him the chance to turn Queen`s Evidence, but he won`t. I tell you John, I`ve never seen a man so scared. Clearly, he knows much more, but is even more frightened of what might happen to him, than being transported. He won`t admit it and we can`t prove anything against him, other than having counterfeit coinage on his person."

"Are they good counterfeits?"

"Yes, and damned clever. They`re mainly crowns and guineas, and they`re made of a base metal, but plated in real gold and silver. You really have to be an expert to tell the difference. The size and weight are fine, but the Queen`s head is not quite right. On its own you can`t spot it, but you can when put alongside the real thing."

"Real gold and silver?" John was incredulous. "Are you sure it`s not just a bad batch from the Mint? No, forget I asked that. You wouldn`t be here if that was the case."

Daniel smiled. "No offence taken. I know, it sounds unbelievable, but it`s true. The Bank of England and the Royal Mint are involved. They both agree the coins are not their`s!"

"An illegal mint!" said John. "That`s quite novel, but also expensive. I suppose the materials are all stolen? They`d have to be to make the venture worth while."

"They have to be."

"I can check this area for any such losses recently, but apart from that, what do you want me to do?"

"Mainly to be aware of the problem. I have to say, there`s no evidence to suggest they are even being made in the Midlands. The sole link is the races, here last month. It seems the Mint has been aware of the problem for some time as the coins have been turning up all over the place."

"Have you come across William Slattery?" asked John.

"You mean your man, here in town, the jeweller?"

"That`s the one. I`ve only met him a couple of times, and everyone speaks highly of him."

"Oh yes. He`s been consulted regularly by the the Mint and has given us some useful information.  He`s a first rate contact."

The two friends discussed the case further for a while.

$$\infty$$

Later, John changed out of his uniform and took Daniel across to the Woolpack, where they enjoyed a pleasant supper together, talking about old times. The general atmosphere in the tap room was friendly. John was secretly quite pleasantly surprised when several of the inn`s customers acknowledged him as they entered. They remembered how he had stood up to Cooper, and had now heard about his confrontation with Pearson.

"You`re doing alright," commented Daniel. "I`m impressed! The fact they`re acknowledging you, is a big step forward. And very much in your favour."

All too soon the evening ended, and John escorted his friend across to the *Green Dragon* to catch the Birmingham coach. They stood talking whilst the newly arrived passengers disembarked. John was only vaguely conscious of a young woman getting off, who seemed to have a large amount of luggage. Daniel climbed aboard.

"Remember," he said. "If you need any help, at any time, I`m only just up the road."

John nodded his thanks, and watched as the coach clattered out of the Market Place, and he turned to go back to the police station. As he did so, John became of raised voices coming from behind him.

"Take your filthy hands off me!" came a woman`s sharp voice.

CHAPTER FIVE

Harriet

John turned towards the voice. By the flickering gas lamps, he immediately recognised the back of the young woman who had just left the coach. She was quite tall, only two or three inches shorter than he was, slim, and smartly dressed, although her dark travelling clothes were now looking crumpled. Her most notable feature was a thick shock of golden red hair, which hung down over shoulders.

"I won`t tell you again," she snapped. "Take your god damned hands off me!" Her voice had a slight colonial accent.

John saw that a man had his hands on the woman, appearing to help her into a cab, which had drawn up alongside them. However, he seemed to be taking more time than necessary, whilst the cab driver still sat on his seat, clearly ogling the woman`s now exposed legs.

"That`s a pretty pair of legs," he chortled. "Hitch her skirts up higher! Let`s see some more!"

They laughed, and the one holding her, moved his hands higher, raising her skirts as he did so.

"You heard the lady," John intervened. "Take your hands off."

"Mind your own damned business," snapped the cab driver.

"I`m a police officer!"

The two men burst out laughing. "Oh yes? We`ve heard all about you. What, no hats and can`t tell the difference between left and right," chortled the driver.

Ignoring John, they turned their full attention to the young woman. But, their laughing ended abruptly as they saw the small revolver which had suddenly appeared in her right hand. Pointing it at the man nearest her, she fired a shot over his head. Then she lowered the still smoking weapon until its muzzle pointed directly at his face.

The man swallowed, as his brain registered the fact the revolver was now pointed at him, and it was not wavering. Clearly this woman knew how to handle it. For a moment he hesitated and licked his lips, which had suddenly gone very dry. In the silence, he heard the click as she cocked the weapon once more.

"Apologies ma`am," he mumbled, letting her go.

Without another word, he sprang into the cab, which was already gathering speed as it moved down Swan Street.

"Are you alright, ma`am?" asked John.

The woman nodded and slipped the revolver into her bag.

"I really am a police officer," continued John. "In fact, I`m in charge of this town, and I do not approve of anybody carrying firearms. This isn`t the Colonies. We can`t have bullets flying around." Even as he said the words, John realised how pompous he must sound.

"If you really are a policeman," she retorted bitterly, her green eyes flashing. "Then it`s a pity you don`t keep better control of creatures like that. I keep a gun for my own protection. And I know how to use it. But, you needn`t worry about bullets flying around. You`ll find the one I fired over there." She pointed at the beam, just below an upstairs window of the *Green Dragon*. Her voice faltered, but she quickly recovered. "If you want to make yourself useful, get me another cab."

"Are you staying here long?"

"That`s my business and nothing to do with you," came her curt reply.

Any further conversation was prevented by the arrival of another cab. John helped her load the luggage, but she steadfastly ignored all his attempts to engage her in conversation. Neither did she reveal her destination to the cab driver, until she was out of earshot. No one saw the few tears which welled up in her eyes as the cab departed.

John watched the cab out of sight, and then returned to the police station. As he expected, there was nobody there, but he found a letter, under the door, addressed to him. Opening it up, John saw it was an invitation to dine with Thomas and Sarah the following evening.

Quickly he penned an acceptance and took the letter to their house, before going to bed.

When he arrived at the Waldrens' house, John did not want to disturb anyone, so he just put his reply through the letterbox. As he did so, he heard the sound of happy laughter and voices coming from inside, and felt a twinge of loneliness sweep over him. There was nobody waiting for him back at the *Woolpack*. Neither would there be when his living quarters over the police station were finished.

❧

The next day passed by without any major problems, and John found himself looking forward to dining with his new friends. Time hung heavy on his hands, but finally he was able to return to the *Woolpack* and change out of his uniform for the evening. Not having the luxury of a vast wardrobe, it did not take him long to choose what to wear. Stopping only to purchase a bunch of flowers for Sarah, he quickly made his way to High Street. Redman, the butler, opened the door, took his hat and coat.

"How about a drink before the women arrive?" greeted Thomas as he guided John towards the dresser. "A glass of Madeira?"

John happily agreed and wondered who else was dining with them as he took the proffered glass. The two men discussed how John's first days had gone. Thomas had just refilled their glasses, when the door opened and in came Sarah and a young woman.

John looked up in amazement and acute embarrassment when he saw she was the woman whom he had met, albeit briefly, the previous night outside the *Green Dragon*.

Sarah took his hands. "John, how nice to see you again. I want you to meet our niece, Harriet Foxton. She's just arrived from Australia!"

For a moment, John was unable to speak. The evening was quickly turning into a disaster. Feeling his face redden, he acknowledged Harriet. As he did so, he saw her green eyes light up with a mischievous twinkle.

"But, of course! We've already met last night. How are you Mr Policeman?"

John felt the sudden heat on his cheeks and tried to stammer some sort of answer, only too glad Thomas and Sarah seemed to be suddenly preoccupied. Then Harriet broke the silence by bursting into

45

peals of infectious laughter, which he would come to know so well, and felt himself relaxing immediately.

"I`m sorry," she said and held his hand in both of hers. "I really didn`t mean to embarrass you. Am I forgiven?"

"Of course!"

The meal was a happy and enjoyable affair and the evening passed all too quickly for John. The only drawback for him was the fact Harriet wore a wedding ring, although no mention was made of her husband. John assumed he had remained in Australia, whilst his wife had come over to England on her own, for whatever reason.

It was a lengthy journey at the best of times, and even more so for an attractive woman on her own, although John had seen how capable she was at looking after herself. Nevertheless, he thought, it was not the sort of journey he would want his wife to undertake on her own.

The evening came to an end, when Harriet stood up. "You must forgive me," she announced. "But I really am exhausted. It has been a long journey for me. Good night!"

The two men stood as Harriet left the room and John began to make his own farewells, but Sarah put her hand on his arm. "Stay awhile," she said. Clearly she had something to say.

They waited until the servants cleared the table, and Thomas had refilled their glasses with port. "Harriet told us you had already met," said Sarah. "But she wanted the chance to meet you properly."

"Sarah!" chided Thomas. "You`re matchmaking!"

"Seriously, John," she continued. "She needs male company."

"I wouldn`t have thought that was a problem," he replied.

"Careful!" warned Thomas.

"You have to be told," continued Sarah. "I can see you`re smitten. But, please don`t expect too much."

"It`s not for what you are," stressed Thomas. "Please don`t ever think that. I`m her guardian, as well as her uncle and I would be truly delighted for the two of you to get together. But.." His voice tailed off.

"I could see she`s married," John began, feeling uncomfortable, not knowing what the Waldrens were trying to tell him.

"She was," replied Thomas.

Sarah took John`s hands in hers. "We should have told you sooner, but, you see, her husband`s dead. That`s why she`s come back to us. It was lovely to hear her laugh once more."

John`s mind was in a whirl. He had always enjoyed the company of women, but somehow, his way of life had not really allowed him any time for long term relationships. At least that was what he was always trying to tell himself.

But, deep down, he knew that was not strictly true. He had not wanted any long term commitment, which might interfere with his career. In fact, such thoughts had frightened him, and he was the poorer for his selfishness, knowing he had broken one or two hearts along the way. Now, it was different, and he had got where he wanted to be, and it was time to think about settling down. He was brought back to the present as Thomas took up Harriet`s story.

Both her parents were dead and she had been brought up by Thomas and Sarah. Her mother had been Sarah`s sister. Harriet had met Edmund in London, and after a short romance they married. In truth, both Thomas and Sarah had not considered him to be the best of husbands for their niece. But, Harriet had pleaded with Thomas, and against his better judgement, he had agreed to the wedding.

Soon afterwards, the newly wedded couple emigrated to Australia. Edmund was a perpetual optimist prepared to try his hand at anything to make money. During the voyage, he had lost no opportunity to practice his skill at cards. To be fair, he was a successful player and made a considerable amount of money.

He was careful to invest his winnings in property, and never carried excess amounts of money on his person. Although he received many offers from members of the opposite sex, Edmund only had eyes for Harriet and she for him. It was too good to last.

One evening, Edmund had taken part in a game of cards where he started to lose money unexpectedly. It did not take him long to realise one of the others was cheating. Edmund aught him out and exposed the man for the cheat he was.

The man was very apologetic and offered to pay back his winnings, which he did. Edmund pocketed his money, shook hands with the cheat and walked away. Before anyone realized what was happening, the cheat drew a pistol and shot Edmund in the back. After clinging to life for the next two days, he died in Harriet`s arms.

Meanwhile, the card cheat had fled, but was soon arrested. His trial was a farce in which he claimed to have acted in self-defence. His conviction and hanging followed quickly. But Harriet was oblivious to all this.

Her beloved Edmund was dead and she did not know what to do next. In an environment where women, especially attractive ones, were few and far between, she soon experienced the unwanted attention of several would-be suitors. One, in particular, would not take no for an answer.

He bombarded her with flowers and all manner of gifts including offers to share his fortune and his bed. Harriet was not poor and did not want or need his money, or any other favours and told him so, on several occasions. But, he still persisted in his advances, which she continually refused.

Finally, he was prepared to wait no longer and made the almost fatal mistake of trying to abduct her. Neither he nor anyone else realized, Harriet was a first class shot. Edmund had insisted she learned how to shoot properly, and had taught her, quickly discovering she had a natural talent for it.

Harriet was walking home one evening, when a carriage drew alongside her, and seemed to be passing. Suddenly stopping three men jumped out of it and ran towards her. She was just able to see her would-be suitor inside, and realized what was happening. Without hesitating, Harriet drew the small revolver which she had started carrying, even before Edmund`s death.

The men were not deterred by it or by several passers-by, who stopped to watch. She pointed the revolver in the direction of her attackers, who started laughing, although they stopped momentarily. Some of the passers-by started to move towards Harriet`s assistance, but her attackers ordered them to keep away and, at the same time produced heavy cudgels.

Totally undeterred by Harriet and her revolver, they came towards her. She shouted to them to stop or she would shoot. Her command was treated with more ribald laughter, which quickly stopped when she opened fire.

She shot the first man, where she had aimed, in his right kneecap, and he fell down screaming. Her second shot smashed into the cudgel bearing hand of the next attacker, and his screams added to those of the other man. The third man stopped, watching her warily, and undecided what to do.

At this moment, the suitor chose to leave his carriage and shouted at the man to do his job. Harriet immediately changed her aim and shot at his hat, which flew away back into the carriage. She then lowered her revolver slightly, so it pointed straight at his face. Tensely, she told him the next one would be straight between his eyes. Meanwhile, her third attacker had fled and the suitor retreated back into his carriage, and she never saw him again.

Her reputation spread overnight and Harriet never experienced any further trouble with any other hopeful suitor. But, she also realized Australia was not for her, and returned to England.

"When did all this happen?" asked John.

"Early last year when Edmund was killed. The problem is she misses him dreadfully and is still in mourning, and is not yet looking for another man in her life," replied Thomas. "One of the problems is she is such a strong character, and hasn`t yet let herself go and have a good cry. And she will continue in mourning until she does just that."

"Be patient with her, John," added Sarah. "I know you`ll be good for each other."

"As you can well imagine," concluded Thomas. "A good looking and wealthy widow, has to be able to look after herself. Harriet can do that. Don`t be too hard on her for the revolver. I can assure you she knows how to use it."

John chuckled. "Just don`t let her shoot anybody in Warwick," he warned.

CHAPTER SIX

The White House

Whilst John was being entertained by the Waldrens, James Cooper also had a guest to dine at the White House, where he lived, Major Charles Pearson. However both men awaited the arrival of another visitor, whom they knew would be late.

Cooper watched rather impatiently whilst his butler filled their glasses with cognac, and asked "Will there be anything else, sir?"

"Just leave the bottle. Is Monk in the kitchen?" came the curt reply.

"Yes sir."

"I`ll call him when I`m ready. You can go to bed."

"Thank you sir. Good night gentlemen."

Cooper turned away and waved his hand angrily. As far as both men were concerned, the butler had ceased to exist. The butler scuttled away. When he had gone, Cooper threw another log on the fire and pushed it into place with his foot, ignoring the sudden shower of sparks. They stood on either side of the hearth, looking at the flames.

"Reminds me of being in the field," commented Pearson, wistfully.

"In the field? In the field? My dear Charles, you know as well as I do that you weren`t in the 87th that long, let alone going on active service!" Cooper laughed.

"It wasn`t my fault I was cashiered for cheating at cards. Look what they`re missing!" Pearson laughed. Both men raised their glasses to each other.

"Your health Charles and here`s to the continuation of our very successful enterprise."

"I'll willingly drink your health James, but I'm not so sure about continuing with the enterprise. That's why I wish he'd hurry up and get here!"

Cooper said nothing for a while, but swirled the cognac round the inside of his glass. Pearson did the same. It was good cognac and both men knew it.

"What do you mean?" Cooper finally broke the silence. "The enterprise is going well. We're already rich and getting even richer. What's wrong with that?" He sat down by the fire and watched Pearson do likewise.

"That's the problem. It can only be a matter of time before one of these new police forces somewhere, ties in my recruiting drives with the burglaries."

"The police!" sneered Cooper. "They're not exactly very intelligent. Nobody with any brains would even consider doing that job."

"I don't underestimate them, James, and neither should you. Anyway, I didn't know you'd agreed to have them here. We'll be operating right under their noses, and that could be quite risky."

"I had no option. My hand was forced, although I opposed the idea. I would have won, but for the Earl. Mind you, even if I had succeeded, it would only have been a matter of time before they arrived. But that would have been enough." Cooper paused and sipped his cognac. "Why did you go out of your way to pick a confrontation with that idiot Mayfield?"

Pearson grimaced. "On reflection, that was a mistake. But, how was I to know he was their chief? I'll have him one day for speaking to me like that. Clearly he's not a gentleman."

"It could be argued I'm an industrialist and not a gentleman," Cooper commented quietly.

"My dear James! Of cause I wasn't referring to your status by birth. You've become a gentleman, now, by your own efforts. How is the knighthood progressing?"

"Starting to gather pace, I hope. I've gone out of my way to cultivate the right people, and its starting to work."

"And the judge?"

"Just like a fish being nicely reeled in. His lordship has huge debts, thanks to his gambling son and his own losses at cards. I've encouraged him to invest, what little money he has left, in my company," Cooper paused. "My legitimate company," he chuckled.

"Not the other one, or at least that`s what he thinks. In return he receives a good dividend. So he`s already making the right noises in the right places. If he wants the money to keep coming in, then that`s what he has to do. My money is now his lifeblood. He puts most of it back into the company, hopefully to increase his returns. If it comes to an end, he will be ruined. And he can`t afford to let that happen."

Cooper paused and refilled their glasses. "Never mind all that, Charles. Get to the point. What`s the problem with our current scheme?"

"I think it is becoming too dangerous to keep burgling houses, and shipping the gold and silver to you to be melted down. Sooner or later one of the men will get caught. He`ll probably turn Queen`s Evidence and we can all look forward to visiting Australia, courtesy of Her Majesty." He mockingly raised his glass in a toast to the Queen.

"I don`t think any of the men would dare to do that," Cooper commented icily. "My staff here all know what will happen to them should they think of doing that. That`s not a worry."

"Possibly not, but someone, sometime will discover I`m not a real major."

For a while they discussed their past successes. Basically, they worked to a simple plan. Pearson and his six troopers arrived in a town or village for a few days. They were supposedly on a recruiting drive, but never seemed to find any suitable men. During the nights the men burgled nearby houses stealing only gold and silver, which was all handed to Corporal of Horse, William Thompson.

He packed them up, waited till the hue and cry had died down, then sent the packages off to Cooper at Warwick. Once he had a reasonable amount, Cooper arranged a late night session at his foundry, using only specially hand-picked men. They melted the gold and silver down, and used it to plate the counterfeit coins, which had been made out of base metal.

The moulds had been supplied by their other partner who normally kept a low profile, because of his position in the town. Once they had asked him where he had acquired the moulds, but he refused to tell them.

In reality, it was his enterprise, as he had provided the plans, and the means to set up the whole operation. Afterwards, the coins were eased into circulation in and around large or busy centres of population or trade. Warwick Races, twice yearly, were regular disposal points.

Once exchanged for real coins, the profits, less the handler`s payment, were returned to Cooper, who arranged their distribution between the three of them. He kept meticulous records, in small note books, of his day-to-day dealings, carefully putting them in his safe when they were full. His records went back several years.

Cooper was right about commanding loyalty. He had only needed to make one example. All the men who worked in this enterprise were well rewarded. But one of them had made the mistake of trying to blackmail Cooper, into paying him more. The very next day, he had met with a fatal accident, after having, apparently, fallen into one of Cooper`s vats of molten metal. There were no more problems.

The unfortunate Bunny Robbins, now languishing in Warwick Gaol, knew all about the vat incident. Unbeknown to Daniel Roberts, this was why he would not turn Queen`s Evidence. He had already been promised an assisted passage to Australia for his wife and children, provided he kept quiet. Faced with a new life for himself and his family, or an unpleasant death, he had no alternative but to keep quiet. And he was right to be scared. Cooper was utterly ruthless.

Their scheme had been running now for almost six years and only recently had the first counterfeits been discovered. But, with Cooper`s rule of fear, there was little or no chance of them being traced back to their source. Cooper enjoyed the extra income and had raised his life style accordingly. The White House, where he now lived, was such an example of his wealth.

It was a large house, set in its own grounds, just on the Birmingham side of Warwick, overlooking the Common and the Racecourse, and was accessed via a long drive. On a clear day, it was possible to see the Cotswolds. In reality, it was far too big for just one man, but he had never succeeded in finding himself a wife.

Cooper was interested in women, but marriage did not figure in his vocabulary. He had his pick of the better looking women from his foundry and paid them well for their services. But, the money did not really compensate them for the savage beatings they often received from him.

However, running such a house, and the estate that went with it, was expensive. Having acquired the taste for good living, he was in no great hurry to abandon it all, and so was not particularly pleased to hear Pearson`s doubts and now returned to the subject.

"I would remind you, Charles, I have invested heavily in this operation, and have no intention of giving it up."

"I don`t disagree. I enjoy the money too. All I am saying is our current methods of obtaining gold and silver, have got to be changed. We`re tempting fate too much otherwise." He held out his hand as Cooper started to speak. "No, James, hear me out. I want this enterprise to continue, but not in its current form."

"Yes, I can see some sense in that. What do you suggest?"

Before Pearson could reply, they heard the sound of a horse trotting up the drive. Minutes later, Monk showed the newcomer into the drawing room.

"Apologies for being late. But I had a dinner function I could not get out of and I thought our guest would never leave."

Cooper handed him a glass of cognac and refilled the other two glasses.

"Charles is worried about our current supply method of getting the gold and silver. He has a new idea and I think we ought to hear him out."

⁓

Unbeknown to any of the men inside the White House, they were soon to receive another visitor, and not one they expected. Outside, in a nearby lane, towards the rear of the house, Corporal of Horse William Thompson, had just tethered his horse to a tree.

He dismounted, removed his shako, unbuckled his sabre, stooped and removed his spurs. For a moment he toyed with the idea of keeping the sabre with him, but decided against it. If he had to move quickly, it could get in the away; in any case, he still had his revolver. Thompson placed the sabre alongside his spurs, under a nearby bush.

Climbing back onto his horse, he stood on the saddle, reached up and caught hold of an overhanging branch of an oak tree, and pulled himself up onto the garden wall, before climbing down the tree on the other side. He landed quietly, waited for a moment and then moved through the shrubbery by the edge of the lawn. Waiting in the shadows, he carefully studied the house.

Thompson froze as he heard the sound of a trotting horse on the driveway at the front of the house. A visitor at this hour of the night, could only mean another member of the Organisation, possibly the other partner. If so, then so be it.

Having inspected the house perimeter, he made his way to the only window which was lit. He could hear voices from inside, but, even with his ear pressed firmly against the glass, they were too indistinct, being muffled by the heavy curtains. The only way to find out what they were planning, was to get inside the house.

He was certain that, with the right sort of information, he would be able to make a good deal with the Royal Mint and the Bank of England. With a handsome reward, change of identity, and a pardon for all his own crimes, William Thompson would be set up for the rest of his life. For that, it was well worth taking the risk.

Cautiously he crept round the outside of the house, trying to find an insecure window or door. But, it was not his lucky night, until he came to the scullery window. Like all the others, it was closed and locked, but that was no obstacle to him. He soon discovered most of the putty was in a poor state, being loose or missing. Thompson took out his pocket knife and began working at the remaining pieces.

It did not take him long to remove it. By inserting his knife under the pane, he soon discovered most of the glass was also loose.

Gently he put pressure on the knife, and took out the glass which he carefully lowered and propped up against the outer wall of the house. He waited for a few seconds to see if anyone had heard him, and was not surprised to hear a low growl from Brutus, Cooper`s dog.

Quickly reaching into a bag around his waist, Thompson took out a piece of meat and threw it in the general direction of the animal. He was gratified to hear the growl turn into the sound of sniffing, quickly followed by a gulping sound which told him the dog had swallowed the meat.

Thompson threw in two more pieces of meat, which were quickly swallowed. Soon there came the unmistakable sound of the animal collapsing. He waited for another minute or so, just to make sure there were no other dogs around. When he was satisfied there had only been the one, he reached through the hole and released the window catch.

After opening the window, he began to climb into the scullery. The drop down inside was deeper than he thought. As he struggled to keep his balance, his other foot still outside, swung into the pane of glass and broke it. The sound seemed deafening to his ears.

Undecided what to do, he held his breath and waited in the window, still only half inside the house. His initial reaction was to run, but he decided to wait and see if there was any reaction. He had come this far and might never get another opportunity like it again. When he realised there was no reaction to the breaking glass, Thompson breathed a sigh of relief and dropped down into the scullery. Cautiously, he opened the door into the kitchen. By the light of the dying fire, he could see the door leading into the hallway. Quietly, he tiptoed across the kitchen floor and opened it. He was gratified to hear the sound of voices coming from the room just across the hallway, and could now hear what they were saying.

Thompson was so intent on the voices, he forgot to check the kitchen. Consequently, he failed to see the figure in the dark, who was watching him intently.

ভ৩

"Of course, Charles," said the new arrival, "If you can get rid of Thompson and his cronies, it will mean less expense and a far greater profit."

"It`s time we parted company," said Pearson. "Thompson is becoming far too greedy, and I think the time is fast approaching for him to meet with a little accident. You know, James, the sort you specialize in."

"NO! I absolutely forbid it," said the third man. "I have always been against violence. At the moment, even if we are caught, the worst we can expect is Australia, where I have no doubt we can find a reasonable life."

"It`s a bit late for that," came Cooper`s reply.

"What do you mean?" said the other man.

Before Cooper could answer, he saw the door start to open, and he turned towards it, angrily. "I specifically told you we were not to be disturbed......." His voice tailed off when he saw the reason for the door opening.

Suddenly Thompson had forgotten why he had broken into the house. He had just heard them planning his murder, and anger had taken over. Taking out his revolver, he pushed open the door and strode into the room.

"So, I`m going to meet with an accident, am I?" he smirked angrily. "I think you`ve just increased your payments to me. Or I go to the crushers. I`m sure there must be a big reward for your capture!"

Thompson was thinking rapidly, already regretting his outburst which might well now spoil his grand plan. The only alternative, was to get as much money from them now, and run. He reasoned Cooper must have plenty of money in a house like this, but was not so sure about Charles Pearson`s finances. Quickly looking at the other man, he did not recognise him, but guessed he was their mystery leader.

Thompson studied the three men. For once Cooper seemed devoid of his usual bullying manner and looked for guidance towards the other two, both of whom said nothing. The atmosphere in the room had become very tense. Only the fire hissing in the grate made any sound.

"Come on!" snapped Thompson. "I`m waiting. What`s it to be? I`m not going to wait all night!"

He was suddenly surprised and disconcerted to see a malicious grin spread over Cooper`s face, mixed with a look of relief. At the same time, he heard a slight noise behind him. Unsure of what action to take, he hesitated, then decided to ignore Cooper and the others, and turned to see what was behind him.

As he did so, he was vaguely aware of a dark form behind him, which suddenly moved, and seemed to be above him. Too late, Thompson realised what was happening and raised his hand for protection. A heavy object crashed down onto his unprotected head.

At first all he felt was a numbing sensation which quickly gave way to excruciating pain, accompanied by a roaring in his ears. This was soon followed by complete blackness. Thompson`s knees buckled and he fell onto the carpet.

For a moment none of the men in the room spoke. They looked

at Monk, who was standing in the doorway, clasping a now somewhat damaged and bloodstained brass candlestick in his hand.

The first man to move was their late night visitor. He knelt beside Thompson. Using his two fingers, he felt for a pulse in the man`s throat, but was unable to find any. Looking at Monk, he shook his head.

"He`s dead," he said. "You`ve killed him!"

CHAPTER SEVEN

A busy night

Monk remained unmoved. "Now you`ve had your little accident," he remarked drily.

"But, it didn`t have to happen here, damn you, in my house!" snarled Cooper. "Why did you have to kill him here?"

"Killing him hadn`t been my intention. He must have had a weak skull.  But, you were all in a load of trouble, and I had to do something. A little bit of gratitude wouldn`t go amiss."

"I`ll see you damned first! Fancy killing him here! In my house!"

"This arguing isn`t getting us anywhere," interrupted Pearson. "And for God`s sake, keep your voices down. We don`t want to waken any of the servants."

"They`re not important," retorted Cooper. "They know what goes on here, and will do as they`re told."

"Maybe so, but there`s no need to bring them into this and increase our risk."

"This arguing is pointless. We have a problem, so let`s think about how to resolve it, rather than blaming one another," interrupted the other man. "As you all know, I am totally opposed to any form of violence, and would never have agreed to killing him."

"You wouldn`t have had any option," sneered Cooper.

"That`s totally immaterial now. The man`s dead and we`ve got to do something about getting rid of his body. And, let me remind you, this is my operation  and its gone too far now to be spoiled.  So stop arguing and start thinking. We can`t keep his body here."

"The obvious place is in the river," said Monk. "With luck, Mayfield will believe its a suicide. And, with even more luck, Thompson might not even be found for some time and could even be well downstream when he is."

"That`s an excellent idea," said the other man. Pearson nodded his agreement.

"And just how are you going to get him there?" said Cooper sarcastically. "What are you going to do? Carry him through the town and hope nobody sees you? Anyway, the canal would be much nearer."

"No," replied Monk. "The canal`s too close to here, and he`d soon be found. No, it has to be the river and we`ll use your carriage."

"Like hell, you will!" exploded Cooper. "I`m not having that ...that.... thing in my carriage!" He pointed to Thompson`s body.

"Pull yourself together!" ordered Pearson. "After all, its not the first time you`ve arranged some clearing up after a death."

"But not in my house, or using my carriage."

"What other similar clearing ups, are you talking about?" queried the other man.

"I think its best you don`t know sir," advised Monk.

For the first time since this venture had started, the other man suddenly knew fear. True he had set up the whole operation, and now it ran very smoothly. On reflection, he thought, he should have seen the warning signs. He should have realised that not everyone, and especially not his partners, had the same benevolent feeling he had for his fellow men.

Robbing houses, setting up and operating, what was basically his own private mint, was one thing; but murder was something different. In the event of discovery, it also meant the difference between the rope or transportation. And he knew which of those two alternatives was more inviting.

He was now in the presence of three very dangerous men, who would not hesitate to remove, permanently, anyone who might interfere with their plans for extreme wealth. That, he realized, included himself. It was definitely time to move on. Although he would stay for the next minting session, but then he would go.

Undoubtedly it would mean leaving Warwick for a while, if not for ever. If that was to be, then so be it. In any case, he had enough money of his own and would never starve. But now, it was time to take charge again.

"Monk`s right, James," he said. "Both Charles and myself came on horseback. Charles doesn`t have a carriage. I know I do, but if I go back home now, and fetch it, I`m bound to disturb some of my servants. They would talk and it wouldn`t be too long before Mayfield got to hear of it."

Cooper opened his mouth to speak, but the man stopped him. "I know your feelings towards him, but believe me, the man`s no fool. He came highly recommended from London. Do not underestimate him. And remember, there`s not much that goes on in Warwick that his sergeant doesn`t know about. No, James, it has to be your carriage."

"Like it or not," said Monk. "We`re all in this together. And, don`t think just because I was the one who killed him, that you can peach on me. You go to Mayfield about me, and I`ll make sure he knows everything about you. We might not like him, but he`s no fool."

"He`s not a gentleman," commented Pearson.

"For God`s sake spare us that!" snapped the other man. He turned to Cooper. "What would you rather happen? Remove Thompson in your carriage, or have your servants find him here and get Mayfield involved?"

"O.K." sighed Cooper. "You win."

"Good," said the other man. "Charles and Monk can get rid of Thompson and I`ll help you clear up here. Then Monk can stay in town and Charles can bring the carriage back."

"Fine," said Monk. "I`m supposed to be on night duty, but that idiot Snow has stood in for me, but I must get back to my patrol, as close to midnight as possible."

"What did you tell Snow, to explain your absence?" asked Cooper.

"That I was visiting my dear old and very ill mother," chortled Monk. "The man`s a complete idiot. If you told him the moon had fallen on the Common, he`d believe you. He was a good choice to be a policeman, Mr Cooper. You chose well!"

All four men laughed, easing the tension between them.

❧

Half an hour later, Charles Pearson stopped the carriage on the Banbury Road Bridge. It had been an uneventful drive from the White

House, through the town, out by the Castle and on to the bridge. Both men waited for a few moments and listened. It was a still night, when sounds carried, but neither man heard any sound.

Swiftly, they opened the carriage door and pulled out William Thompson`s body. After taking a final look about them and having another listen, they heaved his body up onto the bridge parapet, where it lay on his stomach, with his head hanging over the river. They had discovered, how Thompson`s body was much heavier than expected, and took them all their strength to lift. With a final heave, they pushed it over the edge and into the blackness beyond.

"Pleasant dreams," mocked Monk.

Moments later, they heard a splash as it hit the dark waters of the Avon. A second, quieter splash was the candlestick, which had followed the body.

Thompson sank quickly and the waters closed over him. In a short while, the ripples on the river`s surface ceased, and it was if they had never been disturbed. They climbed back into the carriage and Pearson took the reins. Both men failed to notice Thompson had not been wearing his sabre and spurs.

"Will you drop me in the Butts, just up from Eastgate?" Monk asked.

Pearson nodded and shook the reins for the horse to walk on. The mare needed no second urging. She had not appreciated being woken up in the middle of the night and now wanted to go back home again. Minutes later, Pearson stopped the carriage in the Butts and Monk climbed out. Neither man said a word, but just nodded to each other. Monk watched as the carriage drove up the Butts, back towards Cooper`s house.

Suddenly, he heard the sound of breaking glass coming from Smith Street. Remembering he was, for the moment at least, a police constable, he ran to investigate.

❧

Silas Whiting was not a lucky man, but he was fortunate in only having one son. Having suffered quite a serious accident at Cooper`s foundry, he now found himself unemployable. Luckily, his wife Kate, as far as he knew, remained there in steady employment. She was a good looking woman, but had met with some sort of accident recently, which had given her two black eyes and a badly bruised face. When he asked what had happened, she had not elaborated, but talked about having fallen down some stairs, which was almost true.

In reality, she had been beaten up by Cooper and then pushed downstairs. At the same time as her accident, Silas discovered she seemed to have taken a cut in her wages. For several weeks, Kate had told him she was earning some special bonuses, although never explained exactly how they were earned. She always changed the subject, when he asked her. Nevertheless, the extra money was useful.

Silas would have been horrified to know she had earned her special bonuses, by visiting Cooper at home, and satisfying his sexual needs. With a young son and a husband out of work, she had to do something to keep the money coming in, but it had not been her idea. Cooper had suggested the arrangement and then insisted, coupled with the threat of her not being able to get work anywhere else in Warwick, if she refused.

He had beaten her up a few nights ago, when she had tried to finish the arrangement. In time Kate would discover Cooper had arranged for Silas to have his accident, just so he could get his hands on her. Previously she had always resisted his advances.

Conscious now of his own shortcomings, Silas had been spurred into action, and intended to surprise her when she came home, off the night shift. He would go out before she came home and bring in some meat and other food, just to show her he could. Not having any money was a problem, so his answer was to break into the butcher's shop in Smith Street, grab the first bits of meat from the window and run.

He found the job was not as easy as he had thought, and it took some time to force open the shutters without making too much noise. Once they were open, he was faced with the next problem: the shop window, which he had no option but to break. Silas picked up the large rock he had brought with him, and threw it at the glass.

The window shattered with a crash, which Silas thought was loud enough to waken the whole town. He hesitated only for a moment, before reaching through the broken glass and seizing three joints of meat, which was all he could carry. Already he could hear sounds coming from over the shop, as the family woke up.

Clutching the meat, he ran up Smith Street and through the old Eastgate arch and straight into Patrick Monk. Before Silas had time to react, Monk had already hit him hard in the stomach.

Silas sank to his knees, gasping for breath, letting the meat fall to the ground. Monk then hit him again and again, knocking Silas to the pavement. Although there was no fight left in Silas, in fact there never had been, Monk kicked him several times around the face and head as he lay screaming. It was Arthur Webb, the butcher who stopped Monk from hitting him any more.

"For pity`s sake, man!" he cried. "There`s no need to kill him."

His words seemed to bring Monk to his senses. He bent down and pulled Silas to his feet and half marched and half dragged him back to the police station.

$$\wp$$

John Mayfield had been some time falling asleep. His mind kept churning over every bit of conversation, he had enjoyed that evening, with Harriet. At last, he drifted off into a deep and fairly dreamless sleep. So it took his brain sometime to react to the sound of knocking.

He first heard the sound in the distance, but it became louder and much nearer. As he struggled to wakefulness, he could hear a voice calling his name as the knocking increased.

"Mr Mayfield! Mr Mayfield!" Slowly, John realized the knocking was coming from his own door, and it was his name being called.

"What is it?" he called, now wide awake.

"I`m sorry to disturb you, sir."

John recognised Mathew Harrison`s voice. "But, something has happened, which you ought to know about now. I feel it cannot be left until the morning."

"I`ll be with you in a few minutes," answered John, already getting out of bed.

Feeling around in the dark, his fingers found the tinderbox, and he quickly had a candle lit. Picking up his pocket watch, John saw the time was 2.30am, as he looked for his uniform. By now, he had enough confidence in his sergeant, to know Mathew would not have disturbed him, unless it was really necessary. There was no point trying to speculate about what had happened. It would soon be revealed.

After he had finished dressing, John left his room and made his way across the to the police station. Mathew jumped to attention and greeted John. "Good morning, sir. My apologies once again, for disturbing you."

"At ease, sergeant," replied John. "What has happened?"

"Firstly, Monk has made a very good arrest. He found a man breaking into Arthur Webb`s shop, in Smith Street, and arrested him."

"Monk? Monk did this?" asked John incredulously. He broke off when he saw the serious look on Mathew`s face. "But, there`s more, isn`t there? You didn`t get me up just to tell me this, did you?"

"No, sir," replied Mathew, unhappily. "Come with me, please," and led the way to the cells.

On entering the cell, John saw a thin man struggle to get to his feet. Even when he was standing, he had difficulty in remaining upright. At first, John thought the man was drunk, but as he got closer, the reason became obvious. The man had been subjected to a vicious and sustained beating.

"Let me introduce you," said Mathew. "This is Silas Whiting. He was caught burgling a butcher`s shop by Monk!"

"Who proceeded to do this?" John pointed at Whiting`s face.

"Yes. Tell Mr Mayfield what happened?"

"It`s like I said. I were doing the shop, when I had to run. And I bumped into your crusher coming down the Butts and under the Eastgate Arch. And he did this to me."

"Tell me again," instructed Mathew. "Which way did the police officer come from?"

"As I keep saying. Through the Eastgate, from the Butts, sir."

"What`s the significance in this?" queried John.

"Bear with me sir. Are you sure, Silas, that is where he came from?"

"I keep telling you, yes. I`d kept an eye open down the street. I remember a carriage going up the Butts, just before I ran."

"Then why did the officer report he had chased you up Smith Street? In other words, in the opposite direction to what you say?"

"I don`t know, sir. Why should I tell you lies?"

"Also," continued Mathew. "The officer says you attacked him first and he only acted in self defence. What do you have to say about that?"

"It ain`t true. I`ve never hit anyone in me life."

John led Mathew out of the cell. "Have you arranged for him to be seen by a doctor?"

"Yes sir. I`ve left a message for Doctor Waldren, to attend, just as soon as he gets back. He`s already out on a call."

"Why should Whiting lie, about the direction Monk came from? And about not hitting him?" asked John.

"Perhaps he is telling the truth. And I think he is. He doesn`t look capable of hitting anybody. If so, then Monk is the one who is lying, and the question is why?"

They were prevented from further speculation by the sound of Thomas Waldren`s voice from the front door. Mathew let him in and led the way to the cell. He watched dispassionately whilst Whiting was examined and his injuries treated. When he had finished, Thomas asked for some water and washed his hands, before being shown into John`s office. John stood up to receive his guest, who had a grim look on his face.

"Your prisoner has received a particularly savage beating. Had it gone on much longer, I have little doubt he would have been killed. Would I be right in thinking one of your men was responsible?"

John nodded his head slowly.

"I assume you know which one?"

"Oh yes. It`s Cooper`s man, Monk. He says he was acting in self defence."

"I know him. He`s a hard, vicious man, with a temper. He should never have been appointed."

"Along with that buffoon, Snow, who also should never have been considered, let alone appointed."

"Be careful, John. Cooper means to sabotage you any way he can. Be careful!"

"Thanks for the warning. But, will you also take a look at Monk for me? I`d be interested to see if he has any injuries to his hands, which he might have received defending himself from Whiting."

"I will, but I`m sure Sergeant Harrison will agree that Whiting`s a very mild inoffensive man. I cannot believe he attacked Monk first. Can you Sergeant?"

"I quite agree, sir."

"Where is Monk, now?" asked John

"I sent him back on patrol, as I thought it would be a good idea to have him out of the way, until after you had been told what was happening."

"If you don`t mind," interrupted Thomas. "I`m going to bed now. I`ll let you have my report, and bill, in due course. I`ll look at Monk later in the morning. Good night."

Mathew escorted Thomas out of the station and returned to John`s office, a few minutes later, armed with two mugs of tea.

"Have you spoken to Monk about this?" asked John.

"Yes. He maintains Whiting attacked him first."

"But you don`t believe him?"

"No. Then there`s the mystery of why he is adamant he came from Smith Street and not from the Butts. That just doesn`t make sense."

"I think we`ll see Monk when he comes in and.........."

The two policemen stopped as they heard the sound of running feet, coupled with the furious pounding on the police station door. Mathew stood up and walked across the office and went to the door. As he opened it, a partly dressed, heavily perspiring man staggered in.

"Come quickly!" he gasped. "The master`s house has been robbed."

Stopping just long enough to grab their hats and lanterns, John and Mathew followed the flustered servant to his master`s house. Although they did not know it just then, this was only the first of five such similar calls, they would receive. It was going to be a very long night.

Monk would have to wait.

CHAPTER EIGHT

A Busy Day

By midday, John and Mathew had been to five large houses, all of which had been burgled. In each case, only gold and silver had been stolen. Robert Andrew was given the task of collating details of the stolen property. From these he made up handbills, which were then printed and posted up around the town. Other copies were sent to surrounding police forces, by each departing stagecoach.

John had Samuel Perkins called out on duty, and he was given the task of visiting all the jewellers and pawnbrokers in Warwick, with lists of the stolen property. When these revealed nothing, he was sent into the neighbouring town of Leamington, to continue his enquiries. These also failed to provide any information. Elijah Snow was left to patrol Warwick on his own. John and Mathew decided not to involve Patrick Monk. Apart from anything else, somebody would have to work the night shift.

As St Mary`s Church clock struck half past three, John instructed Mathew to go home and get some sleep. The big sergeant did not object. John`s body also cried out for sleep, but he had enjoyed some before being called out. For a while he just sat in his office, thinking through the events of the past few hours.

At every house they had visited, John experienced some resistance to his questions, which was nothing unusual. Everybody seemed to know how a policeman should conduct his enquiries, and took great delight in telling him what to do. What business was it of his, to know what time the household had retired?

Time and time again he had heard such remarks. Each time he, and countless other police officers did so, they had to bite their tongues and maintain an air of patience and good humour. But, with very little sleep, that became harder as the morning progressed. And, as for those two elderly sisters, who lived somewhere off the Coventry Road, he could cheerfully have strangled them.

Firstly, they were annoyed he had used the front door, and not gone round to the servants entrance, and instructed him to do so. John refused and the conversation that followed, was carried out via the butler, as neither lady, and here he used the word advisedly, would lower herself to speak to a common policeman, regardless of his rank.

The butler saved the day when he produced lists of the stolen property and details of the staff, and confessed how he had served a few years in the police himself, until his sight began to fail and he needed spectacles. He also apologized for the behaviour of his mistresses. John thanked him and returned to the station with Mathew.

In all, it had not been a very auspicious beginning to his new police career. As he sat, looking at the lists of stolen property, John wondered how long it would be, before James Cooper came on the scene, and knew it would not be too long.

Two things however, struck John. Firstly only gold and silver had been taken. The other thing, was the distance between each of the houses. From the times the last member of the households had retired, to when the first ones arose, was not long enough for one person to do each job. Was it just co-incidence that these burglaries had all happened on the same night? But, John did not believe in co-incidences, and there were too many similarities, for each crime not to be connected. He listed them.

No house had been entered before all the lights were out. Each house had been entered by a kitchen window, mainly by a knife, or something similar, being used to force open the catches. In the two houses which had dogs, both animals had been drugged. Lastly was the fact that only gold and silver had been taken. There had been other treasures well worth stealing, but these appeared to have been left alone.

In all his experience, he had never investigated such a run of burglaries, which looked like they had been committed by the same person, but clearly were not. He had the feeling, it was almost as if these houses had been burgled to order. That meant it had to be a gang.

If it was a gang at work, they had to be travellers, as Mathew could not remember anything like it happening before in the area.

The more John thought about the stolen property, the more he thought about Daniel Roberts and his enquiry. Could they possibly be connected? He would have to write to Daniel, or better still, try and see him.

John picked up his pen and began making some notes for himself. Tomorrow, he would need to begin enquiries around the inns and taverns, to establish if there had been a group of strangers in town in the past few hours, apart from Major Pearson and his recruiting party. He hardly noticed Robert Andrew quietly walk in with a steaming mug of tea.

Robert put the tea down on John`s desk, and waited. John picked up the mug, took a mouthful gratefully, then looked at the officer, who waited patiently.

"Permission to speak, sir?" he asked.

"By all means," replied John. "But, in my station, you never have to ask permission to speak. I can`t abide all that nonsense. If you have something to say, then please say it. Especially if it is police work."

"It is, sir."

❧

Katherine Wilding, or Kate as she was more commonly known, seethed with frustration, anger and a sense of loss. All the pain and degradation, she had suffered at Cooper`s hands, had come to nothing. Why? Because her stupid husband, Silas, whom she loved dearly, in an attempt to help their finances, had gone out stealing. And, to make matters worse, he had been caught. As if that was not bad enough, he had also been severely beaten up by Police Constable Patrick Monk.

Ironically, that was the only thing she was glad about. Not his having been beaten up, but the fact Monk had done it. She had seen the new Police Superintendent, John Mayfield, going to be sworn in, and liked what she saw. He looked and gave the appearance of being an honest man. Added to which, already he was becoming recognised as a fair man, who was prepared to stand up to James Cooper, and that was a good thing.

Being completely honest with herself, Kate knew she was attracted to him, after having seen him that first time. She knew it could only ever be one way. Yet, she found herself going up into town, more often than before, just on the remote chance of seeing him although she doubted if he had even noticed her existence.

She was wrong; he had. John also felt immediately attracted to her. Kate was an attractive woman, and he had noticed her a few times since in town, but he had been out when she called to see Silas.

Kate was not stupid. Had she been able to enjoy the benefits of an education, her life would have been much different. She had been born in the workhouse, to a mother who had been a governess, and left to fend for herself on becoming pregnant. Her mother had taught her to read and write.

Nobody was interested in the identity of her father, other than he was a passing American businessman. Brains counted for nothing in the workhouse and Kate was put out to work as early as possible. Cooper`s foundry was the obvious choice of the workhouse master, for which he was paid accordingly.

Whilst she was there, Kate met, fell in love with and married Silas Whiting. It was a love match, and in many ways unusual. Their son, Edward, was a sickly child, and seemingly unlikely to live. Yet, he had confounded everyone and survived. For some time, she had resisted Cooper`s approaches, claiming she was happily married and not in need of other male company. After Silas had met with his accident, and was no longer able to work, Cooper approached her again.

After making his threats, Cooper gave her a few hours to think it over. The only alternative, was to seek shelter in the workhouse. Even if the workhouse accepted Silas and Edward, it would be unlikely to have her back. She knew Cooper`s spite would stop any chance of that happening. If matters ever got that far, Kate would have murdered Silas and Edward and then taken her own life, before going back there. Faced with no other alternative, she agreed to Cooper`s proposal.

As part of the deal, she kept her job in the foundry, but was allowed more working flexibility, and she quickly lost her reputation. Luckily, none of the other employees really knew Silas, and were fairly unlikely to meet him. Many of the workers sympathized with her, especially the women who had preceded her.

As the weeks progressed, Kate began to build up her savings, but never told Silas about them. Every day she prayed he would never find out about her and Cooper. She really loved Silas.

Then only last week, she had overheard some foundry women talking about her and referring to her relationship with Cooper. Kate was aghast to discover none of them thought Silas had really met with an accident, but had been deliberately injured on Cooper's orders. Later that day, she confronted Cooper, who made no attempt to deny her allegations, but only laughed unpleasantly. That was when Kate told him they were finished.

He laughed once more before punching her hard in the face. The beating which followed was both painful and humiliating. Kate had sworn she would get her revenge on him, and now a scheme was beginning to form in her mind.

Originally, she had been saving the money to buy a passage for the three of them, to emigrate to America. That idea was now over, as it seemed more than likely her stupid husband would be transported to Australia instead. She now reasoned, if that was the case, there was nothing to stop her and Edward going to join him. Kate knew the system could be manipulated for her to find herself in the same settlement as Silas. And, if she could manage it, Silas might be able to come and work for her.

Her main worry was if he would be able to survive the voyage? At least now, it only took some three months, about half the time it had at the beginning of the century. She hoped the ship's captain would take pity on him, as he would be unable to undertake strenuous manual work.

Even without sufficient money, Kate still had her body to sell for the sake of her husband's well being. She knew it was prostitution, but could think of no other way to save her family. One day, she knew, there would come a reckoning, when Silas discovered what had happened. But it was a risk she would have to take. She could see no other way. Damn James Cooper. It was all his fault.

As she mentally cursed her employer, Kate had another idea.

Cooper had caused all their misfortune. Monk was Cooper's man.

How satisfying it would be to make Cooper suffer. Once she got herself back into his bed, it should be possible to find a way. Along with many other people in Warwick, she was quite convinced he was involved in secret and probably criminal matters.

If that was so, how could she get the evidence and make Mr Mayfield believe her? This was something she needed to start on right away. Granted there were a few weeks before the Assizes and the next sailings to Australia, but she could not afford to waste any time.

The more Kate thought about getting her revenge, the more the idea appealed. She was very much aware Cooper`s friend, Major Charles Pearson, was also in town. He was a regular visitor, to the White House though not always with his soldiers. Whenever he was there, she knew there was always one of the special night`s work at the foundry.

Shifts were changed and only a handful of specially chosen employees worked on that night. There were all sorts of rumours about these shifts, but she had never been invited to partake in them. The general feeling was they were probably not legal, but nobody knew exactly what. If only she could find out.

"Hold on, Silas, my love," she murmured. "Have courage and strength. I`ll get you out of this mess yet!"

❦

Back in the police station, John waited for Robert Andrew to enlarge. "There are two things," Robert started. "Firstly, Whiting is due in court tomorrow. Had you forgotten?"

"Oh God!" John buried his head in his hands. "With all these burglaries, you`re quite right. I`d completely forgotten."

Robert handed him a sheaf of papers. "I thought you had, so I did the paperwork for you." John looked up in amazement.

"It might not be the way you Londoners do things," continued Robert. "But I didn`t think you`d object too much!"

"I just don`t know how to thank you," replied John. He took the papers and quickly glanced over them. "These seem to do the job admirably. I truly thank you! Now, what was the second matter?"

"I think you know my home is in Aylesbury. Well, my mother often sends me the local newspaper, especially if there have been any major crimes in the area. She likes to think she`s helping me. Or sometimes she just sends me the clippings. However, this time she sent the whole paper, although its a few weeks out of date." He handed a newspaper to John.

John controlled his impatience, desperately wishing the officer would get to the point. Yet, he could hardly complain, as Robert had just done the paperwork for Whiting`s appearance in court. How Cooper would have loved John to have made a mess of his first court case in Warwick. He took the newspaper, which was a few weeks old, from Robert, and saw an item had been ringed in pencil.

It referred to a spate of burglaries in and around Aylesbury and included a list of the stolen property. In all cases, bar one, only gold and silver had been stolen. The difference was in the last house, where a jet and jewelled snuffbox, and engraved *W T* had been stolen.

"That is interesting," mused John. "So Aylesbury seems to have been hit by the same gang." He looked at Robert and sensed there was more to come.

Robert took the newspaper back and turned a page and returned it it John. Another article had been ringed, this time in ink. It referred to the visit in Aylesbury of a recruiting party for the 87th Regiment of Dragoons under the leadership of a Major Charles Pearson. The article commented how the party had not been particularly active as no local men had joined the Regiment.

"Could it be a co-incidence, sir?"

"Possibly, but I don`t believe in co-incidences in police work. Do you?"

Robert shook his head." No sir."

"I`ve yet to find a policeman who does. This is worthy of much further investigation, although I fear you`ll be writing many more letters," continued John.

"I anticipated as much, and have already started."

John looked at Robert. This was a capable officer who would make a good sergeant in time and made up for Monk and Snow. And that reminded him: he still had to see Monk

Robert left the office and John returned to his list, but now with his mind buzzing about the possibility of a connection between Pearson and the burglaries. Might there also be one with Cooper? He stopped himself, knowing the problem had to be approached with an open mind.

It would be too easy to go for Cooper out of spite or even revenge. And what would happen if he was wrong? The answer did not bear thinking about. John knew he would have to deal with the man, sooner or later. But when he did, it would have to be right. He would only have the one chance.

John reached out and picked up his mug of tea and took a swallow, which he quickly spat out. It was cold. Putting the mug down he picked up the bell on his desk.

He was just about to ring it, when Robert Andrew knocked on the door and walked in.

"That was quick," smiled John. His voice tailed off as he saw the look on Robert's face.

"You'd better come, sir!" he announced. "A body's just been found, down by the river bridge. It looks like it's one of the recruiting soldiers."

John's heart sank. As if matters were not difficult enough. A body was the last thing he wanted. With a bit of luck, it might be a suicide or even an accident. But deep down, he knew it would never be that easy. Stopping only to collect his hat, and lantern, as the light was fading, John left the office.

Outside, Robert was talking to a cab driver. "He'll take you, sir," he said. "It'll look better than arriving after a brisk walk. Snow's already there."

"Thank you," said John as he climbed aboard.

"There's no charge, Guv'nor," said the cab driver. "Yon crusher's a friend of mine and I'm glad to assist."

Before John could reply, the cab set off at a swift trot. Short though the journey was, he was thankful as it gave him time to gather his thoughts and composure. When the cab stopped, John climbed out calmly, thanked the driver. Then he scrambled down the side of the bridge and headed to the riverbank.

CHAPTER NINE

The River

"Get back yer lot!" instructed Elijah Snow, as John made his way to the river bank. For once, Snow`s face had lost its amused look. Surprisingly, the crowd obeyed him.

Arriving at the water`s edge, John saw the sodden, uniformed body of a soldier, who by the chevrons on his tunic, had to be a Corporal of Horse, lying face downwards. He was clearly dead. Inwardly John cursed himself for not having instructed Robert to call out a doctor. John knew he was not thinking straight at the moment, and put it down to being tired.

"What have you got?" came a familiar voice behind him.

Turning, John was relieved to see Thomas Waldren standing behind him. "Your Constable Andrew had me called," he explained.

"He`s a good policeman. Thanks for coming. I`ve only just arrived myself. He looks fairly dead, but I was about to check for any signs of life."

As John spoke, Thomas knelt beside the body and felt for a pulse. Shaking his head, he looked up at John. "He`s dead, and, I think he has been for some time." Standing up, Thomas took out his pocket watch and opened the cover. In the gathering gloom, he peered at its dial. "I pronounce life extinct at ten minutes to five."

"Thank you doctor."

Together they turned the body over onto its back, and looked at the face of William Thompson, whom John recognised as being one of Major Pearson`s recruiting party. He was vaguely aware of Elijah Snow retching somewhere behind him.

"Do you think he drowned?" John asked.

"Too early to tell. I'll have him taken back to the surgery where I can examine him properly. On the face of it, I'd say probably yes....." He stopped as John pointed to the side of the dead man's face and head.

"That looks to me to be something of a fresh injury," said John, pointing at some marks.

Thomas had a closer look. "You could be right. However, get him back to my surgery and I'll take a closer look at him."

John looked up at the bridge above them, and recalled Mathew Harrison's words about it being a good place for a suicide. With a bit of luck, that's what it would be. "Will you carry out an autopsy on him?" queried John.

"Willingly, but I am afraid it won't be until tomorrow. Unfortunately, the needs of the living have to take precedence over the dead. Oh, by the way, have you made any progress with the unfortunate Silas Whiting affair?"

John shook his head. "No. I've been rather busy today," he chuckled ruefully.

"So I've heard. I wish you good fortune with those. I do just have a feeling you will need all the luck you can get. As you can well imagine, our mutual friend is enjoying himself at your expense. Take care, John."

Thomas picked up his bag and hat, and climbed up the river bank to his waiting carriage. John took another look at Thompson's body, and already the cosy idea of suicide was beginning to vanish. It felt wrong. Thompson's body was trying to tell him something, but he could not quite say, just at the moment, what it was.

It would come to him in due course. For several more minutes, John studied the scene in the fading light. He had to admit it looked like suicide, but how did the man come by the injuries to his head? As far as John could remember about the bridge, there were no protruding pieces of metal or anything else.

From what he had seen of the wound, albeit quickly, made him discount the possibility of the stonework causing such an injury. But if it had: if only it had, then it should be a clear case of suicide. The last thing John wanted now was a murder. Yet, that was what his instincts were telling him. Deep down he knew they were probably right, as they had been on more than one occasion.

He turned to Snow. "Have this body removed to Dr Waldren`s surgery," he ordered.

The man looked at John and nodded his agreement. Minutes later, John watched dispassionately as two men appeared with an old door, which they laid on the ground. Unceremoniously they lifted up the body and put it on the door. One of them produced an old sheet and covered the corpse. With assistance from some of the other spectators, they carried their load up the bank and on to the road, where they put it into a waiting cart and prepared to drive off.

"Do you want a lift, Mr Mayfield?" One of them called down to John.

"Thank you no. It`s a fine evening and I`ll enjoy the walk."

The man acknowledged John with his whip. "Walk on!" he commanded the horse.

John climbed up the bank and onto the road and started walking back towards the police station. On the way he mulled over the coincidence of the burglaries; the suspicions Robert Andrew had raised over the recruiting party, and now one of that party definitely dead, apparently drowned. To that he added his own feelings about the dead soldier. He did not believe in coincidences.

"There are too many coincidences. Just too many," he said aloud.

"I beg your pardon superintendent. Were you speaking to me?"

John shook himself and saw a grinning Harriet Foxton standing in front of him.

"My apologies, ma`am," he spluttered, acutely embarrassed. "I am afraid I was thinking aloud."

Harriet touched him lightly on his arm. "Don`t worry," she chuckled. "I promise not to tell anyone, especially Uncle Thomas."

For the first time that day, John laughed, and his tiredness left him. This woman had that effect on him.

"Rather than talk to yourself, would it help if you talked to me about it?"

"I don`t know," hesitated John. "It`s not really the thing I could talk to a woman about."

"Believe you me, there`s not much I haven`t seen on my travels. Especially in Australia. I know what Uncle Thomas told you, last night. It`s all true."

John saw her lips begin to quiver and her eyes glisten at the memory. Clearly she had loved her husband dearly. What chance do I stand? thought John, by now acutely aware how much he enjoyed her company. He desperately wanted to know her better and hopefully come to be part of her life.

"Actually," he said. "I might just do that, but not tonight. I must do a report for the coroner and that has be done right away."

"Any time you want, John. I`ll be happy to listen."

For a while they talked about other matters, until, all too soon, they reached the Waldrens` house in High Street. For a moment they stood on the step.

"I meant what I said about being happy to listen," said Harriet.

"I know and thank you."

John waited until Harriet had gone inside before making his way back to the police station, with quite a spring in his step. There would have been an even bigger one had he turned round, because he would have seen Harriet watching him from a window.

℘

At the same time as John was climbing into the cab, to go down to the River, Kate made her way home, having just come from seeing James Cooper at the foundry. She had very mixed feelings.

One part of her was unhappy at the thoughts of having to share his bed again. However, the other part was glad, as she had taken the first step towards getting her revenge. If it meant a few more sessions in his bed, so she could get the information she wanted, it would have been worth it. How she loathed that man!

As Kate had expected, Cooper needed very little persuasion to take her back again. He had always found her more interesting than the other women he bedded, but at the same time, he was under no illusions. It was not his body she wanted, but his money. Yet, already he was tiring of her. The only reason he had taken her back, was because he had no other woman in mind just at the moment. Soon, he would move on from her.

Now, as she tidied herself up and prepared for her visit to the White House, Kate was glad young Edward was out. She hated telling him lies about going off to work. Added to which, he was old enough to know she did not dress up to go and work in a foundry. Kate adjusted her hat and left the single room she shared with her husband and son.

It did not take her long to feel the disapproval, which radiated from the neighbours. She had to acknowledge they were right, even more so with her husband awaiting trial. However, Kate took comfort from the fact she knew the real reason for what she was doing. It was a big sacrifice, but one she had to make. But, as she walked up the drive to Cooper`s house, Kate felt her confidence evaporating, and was not sure she could go through with it.

Then she thought of Silas, and her resolve returned. She quickened her stride and going to the rear entrance by the kitchen, went inside. She met, as usual, the air of hostility coming from Cooper`s domestic staff. They did not approve of her, but could do nothing about it. Kate ignored them and went into the kitchen, where she sat and waited.

$$\text{❧}$$

John was almost halfway back to the the police station, with his mind firmly on Harriet Foxton, and not the unfortunate William Thompson. "Mr Mayfield, sir!" came a voice from behind him, interrupting his thoughts.

He turned and saw Redman hurrying towards him. "I`ve a message from the mistress," he continued. "Will you please return to the house with me?"

"Willingly. There`s nothing wrong, is there?"

"No sir," smiled Redman. "She knows you`ve been busy today, and won`t have eaten anything. So she`s laid on some food for you."

John walked with the butler, back to the High Street, without even pretending to argue. It would mean seeing Harriet again, and he was hungry. As Sarah had so rightly guessed, he had eaten nothing all day, but such was the nature of police work. He had not noticed any hunger pangs until now, when the subject of food was raised.

He was greeted by both women, taken into the dining room, and sat down to a plate of cold meat, cheese, fresh bread and butter accompanied by a large pot of tea. There was little conversation until he had finished eating, then they bombarded him with questions about the burglaries and the body. In spite of his training, John told them nearly all they wanted to know, but kept back some details. No doubt, the local newspaper, the *Chronicle* would fill in most of the gaps in its next edition.

At last, he was able to ask a question himself, and asked where Thomas was. Sarah replied he had been called out.

"That`s a pity," commented John. "I had hoped he might have made a start on the soldier`s body."

"If you want to take a look at him," said Sarah. "I`m sure he won`t mind. Though, please forgive us, for not coming with you."

"Thank you," said John rising to his feet.

"I don`t mind going with you," suggested Harriet.

"I absolutely forbid that!" replied Sarah, quite forcefully, as she rang the hanging bell by the fireplace.

Harriet made no attempt to argue. John was quite surprised at Sarah`s tone. It showed a totally different woman, to the one he had come to like. Further thoughts were interrupted when Redman arrived. Sarah quickly instructed him to take John to her husband`s laboratory, which was in a room in a small outbuilding near the house.

John followed him out into the hall, and through an inconspicuous door leading out to a small courtyard. Redman stopped for a moment whilst he lit a small oil lamp, before leading John across the yard, to the laboratory. He unlocked the door stood back and motioned for John to wait.

"If you don`t mind waiting here, a minute," he instructed John. "I`ll just go and light the gas lamps. It will be much safer."

Redman lit four gas lamps round the walls. Once their glow quickly lit up the laboratory, Redman invited John to enter. Although he had been in similar places, they never ceased to fascinate him. He looked around him, like a child in a sweet shop.

There were several shelves, crammed with bottles and jars, some containing pills, or coloured liquids and others holding what looked like anatomical specimens. In the middle of the laboratory, was a table, on which lay a sheet covered form, clearly that of a body, which was undoubtedly William Thompson. John was also aware how Redman was hanging back, clearly unhappy.

"Will you be alright, sir. Or do you want me to wait?" asked Redman, as if reading John`s mind.

"No, you carry on," he replied gently.

 Looking at death was not to everybody`s taste. If John was honest, he too would would prefer not to look at the body on the table. But, it was his job, and he knew bodies could not hurt or frighten him any more. Reaching out, he peeled back the sheet, and uncovered the naked body of William Thompson. For a moment, John wondered where the man`s clothes were, but then saw them on another smaller table.

The next thing he noticed about the body, was some of Thompson`s hair had been shaved back over the left ear, and on towards the temple. In so doing, it had uncovered the wound he had seen earlier. It was roughly in the shape of a **T.**

Over the years, John had seen numerous wounds, both in the army and the police. Where the upright met the cross bar of the **T** shape, he saw the wound was deeper. It indicated some sort of instrument with a point, as opposed to something flat. What could have caused it?

"Interesting, isn`t it?" came a voice behind him.

CHAPTER TEN

The Body

J ohn spun round guiltily. "I didn`t mean to intrude," he apologized
to Thomas Waldren. "But Sarah insisted I came on in."

Thomas laughed, clearly amused by the whole incident and John
relaxed. It was then he saw Thomas was accompanied by William
Slattery. The other man was also grinning, as he shook John`s hand.

"I could do with a drink," said Thomas. "Will you join me?....Sorry,
John, I`d forgotten you are still on duty. And Slattery only drinks tea.
We`ll have some later. Now, what do you make of this mark?"

The three men bent over the dead soldier. Thomas held a lamp over
the man`s head, and the strange mark John had seen before was now
clearly illuminated. "This is the puzzle," he said. "What`s caused it?"

"Off the bridge, surely?" suggested Slattery. "I hope you don`t
mind my being here?" he added.

"Of course not," said John. "After all, you are a magistrate and may
become involved further. But, my feeling is that this injury was not
caused by the bridge. What caused it, as yet, I don`t know. It may not
even be important, but somehow I think it is. Could it have caused this
man`s death?" he looked at Thomas.

"Possibly. I`ll know a lot more tomorrow, when I carry out the
autopsy."

Thomas made to to leave, but John stopped him. "Can I have a
quick look at his uniform and any possessions he has?" he asked.

Thomas nodded and John crossed over to the uniform. As he lifted
up the tunic, he saw a small snuffbox, bearing the initials **WT,** which
looked vaguely familiar to him. He held it up. "Where did you find
this?"

"Inside a small pocket sewn into his breeches."

John looked thoughtfully at the tunic once more. Picking it up, he ran his fingers over the buttons, before taking it to where there was a brighter light.

"I thought so," he said. "These metal buttons are scratched and badly so. I can`t see them being worn like this. This has happened since his death or just before it."

"What`s so important about that?" asked Slattery. "Forgive me being inquisitive, but this is the first time I`ve ever seen someone like you at work."

John smiled. "No soldier would be permitted to wear a tunic with buttons in this state." He showed the buttons to the others. "It almost certainly means he did not jump into the river. Normally, if he had taken his own life, I would have expected him to have jumped off the bridge. That`s what suicides tend to do. The chances of him having pulled himself across the parapet and rolling over the edge, are extremely remote."

Once more he looked at the uniform and realised what had been bothering him, ever since he`d first seen the body by the river. "Where are his shako, sabre and spurs?" he asked.

Thomas shook his head. "I don`t know. They weren`t on him when we first examined him down by the river."

"No," agreed John. "They weren`t. It`s possible his shako is somewhere in the river, but that doesn`t explain the missing sabre and spurs. They were not likely have come adrift when he fell. And I very much doubt he would have gone out without them. He would have been improperly dressed."

"Perhaps he didn`t want them to end up in the river?" suggested Slattery.

"Possibly, but I doubt it. I might have been convinced if they were missing and his buttons weren`t so badly scratched. I`m beginning to think he might well have been been pushed off the bridge, rather than jumped."

"This is rather destroying any theory of suicide, isn`t it?" asked Slattery.

John nodded. "I`m afraid so. I think I`ll have the river dragged tomorrow. You never know what we might find. Meanwhile, I`ll keep this snuffbox for a while. I`ll give you a receipt. Now Thomas, what about that tea you threatened us with?"

The three men adjourned into the house where Thomas poured himself a large brandy, whilst John and Slattery, joined by the women, drank tea. Finally, John found he could not stop yawning, so made his apologies and left.

St Mary`s clock was just striking eleven when he entered the police station. He was not surprised to find Mathew Harrison waiting for him. Quickly John told him all about the body and his plans for the morning with having the river dragged. Mathew offered to make all the arrangements and write the coroner`s report. John went to the *Woolpack*. Once he saw his bed, it required a great effort of will to undress before getting into it.

In spite of all the activities of the day, he fell asleep almost at the same time his head hit the pillow.

✑

Kate had been obliged to wait for some time before Cooper returned with Pearson. They had insisted she sat in the dining room, with them, whilst they ate, which only increased the hostile glares she received, from the other servants. Slowly, she realised they kept plying her with drink, most of which she managed to tip away. With a growing sense of horror, she listened as Cooper planned the rest of the evening. They both had intentions on her body, but were as yet undecided whether or not they should do so individually or together.

Respite came from an unexpected quarter when they all heard the sound of a horse trotting up the drive.

"Who the hell can that be?" snarled Cooper. He did not have long to wait.

There came a knock at the door and the butler entered and gave Cooper a card. Kate could not see the name on it. "He says it`s urgent, sir," said the butler.

"You, get out, now!" Cooper ordered Kate. "Wait in the bedroom." As she left the dining room, he turned to the butler and instructed him to admit the visitor.

Seconds later, the man who had been there, the night Thompson was killed, came into the room. He was clearly annoyed and worried.

Kate left the dining room and climbed upstairs to Cooper`s bedroom, knowing, only too well, where it was. She also knew, and suspected he did not, that there was a loose floorboard directly over the dining room. Swiftly she pulled it up, and lay down on the floor, and listened to the voices below her.

She did not recognise the voice of the visitor, but the others clearly knew him. And they even seemed to be in awe of him.

"I take it you already know," he said. "Thompson`s body has turned up already and Mayfield is involved."

"So what?" said Cooper. "They`ll think it`s suicide."

"In the old days, perhaps, but not now. Mayfield does not buy that idea. I think he already knows it`s a murder."

"Bah!" snorted Pearson. "If and when he comes to me, I`ll soon tell him Thompson had tried to do himself in before now. That`ll shut him up."

"And it won`t work," commented the visitor. "How did you and Monk put him in the river?"

"We just shoved him off the bridge. Heaved him onto the parapet and pushed him off. So what?" replied Pearson.

"So what? So what? You idiots. Doing it that way, you managed to scratch all his buttons. Why didn`t you just drop him?"

"Listen!" snarled Pearson. "You were so keen not to get your precious hands dirty that you left it all to us. If you had your way, Monk wouldn`t have killed him and we`d all be in the County Gaol right now. Apart from which, his body was too damned heavy for just the two of us."

Upstairs, Kate could not believe her luck. She did not know about the body, but clearly that monster, Monk, was involved. Mr Mayfield would appreciate that information. It would give her an excuse to see him and, who knows what might happen. Then realization hit her.

She was now in a house with at least three murderers: people who, on the face of it, were pillars of society. Whoever would believe her? Kate knew she would have to have more proof than just her word to stand any chance of being believed. She went back to her listening.

Unfortunately, they had moved away, and she could hear them leaving the room. Quickly she replaced the loose board, and lay back on the bed, but nobody came. After a while, Kate got off the bed and tiptoed to the door, quietly opened it and looked out.

She could see no signs of the men and wondered where they had gone. Carefully, she crept to the top of the stairs and looked down into the dim hallway. There was still no sign of them, but then she noticed a thin beam of light shining under the study door, and cursed to herself.

There was no way she could find out what they were planning, without going downstairs and listening at the door. Even for Silas, that was just too risky. If any of Cooper's staff saw her, they would enjoy telling their master what they had seen. No, she would have to find another way. Suddenly, the study door opened and the men came out.

Kate pulled back into the shadows. She could easily recognise Cooper and Pearson, but was unable to see the third man's face. He seemed vaguely familiar, but she could not see enough of him, especially his face, which remained in shadow. The more she thought, Kate was certain she saw him regularly in town.

Cooper was holding a sheaf of papers, and a small notebook, which was a good sign. She knew he recorded everything in that book, and it rarely left his study. If she could only get hold of that, who knows what information it might reveal? He was notoriously untidy, and with any degree of luck, the papers and book would remain on his desk. But how could she get in there?

"We must get this right," said the third man. "If it goes wrong, there'll be no second chances. We can make a fool of Mayfield and he will be finished. But, make no mistake, someone else will replace him. Whilst James and me may have some say in his appointment, it can't be guaranteed."

"And if this plan doesn't work?" queried Cooper.

"It will. I will see to that."

"Rest assured," said Pearson. "If it doesn't work, then I'll enjoy seeing to him."

"No violence!" instructed the third man.

"It's too late now. Perhaps if you'd been here earlier last night, this might not have happened," added Pearson.

"I told you. I had a guest who would not go."

"Mayfield has to go, one way or the other. I'm sure an accident can be arranged for him."

"Of course it can," chuckled Cooper. "After all, that's my speciality."

Kate felt her blood run cold. There could be no possible doubt now, about who had caused her husband`s accident. It had all been arranged by this loathsome man.

"A week tonight, it will be finished for a while, possibly for good. We just have to keep Mayfield out of the way till then. Permanently if necessary," continued Cooper. "Then we can have a meeting, weigh up our profits and decide where we go from there. It`s all in here." He patted his notebook.

"Is all arranged for next Saturday?" asked the third man.

"Of course," replied Cooper. "I`ve got the usual bunch to work an extra night shift." He was making notes, in his book, as they spoke

The three men walked down the hallway and out of Kate`s vision and hearing. So, they were planning something for Mr Mayfield, were they? Not if she could help it. And she must discover more about their plans for the following Saturday. She had to get into the study, and find that notebook, no matter what it cost her. Meanwhile, she returned to the bedroom and prayed for strength to endure Cooper`s onslaught.

She woke with a start and found herself lying, still fully clothed on the bed. It seemed her prayers had been answered, but then Cooper came in. He was clearly the worse for drink and scarcely able to stand up. For a moment he pawed at her dress and then collapsed in a stupor on the floor, by the bed. Kate breathed a sigh of relief, and was very tempted to kill him. However, common sense returned. As a gesture, she pulled the blankets off the bed and covered him up as he lay there. For the time being, at least, he was more use to her alive than dead.

Quietly she collected her cape and left the room. It was time to go home, but already she was beginning to have an idea. On reaching the hallway, Kate was about to try the study door.

"What are you doing here?" Kate spun round and saw one of Cooper`s servants behind her. He was carrying some logs and clearly making for the study.

"Just leaving," she replied acidly.

"Then use the back door, not the front. You know your place, whore."

She had not realized how late it was, and the first servants were stirring. Had she taken Cooper`s key, then she would have been found in his study, which just did not bear thinking about. Going to the back door, she let herself out and walked home.

John slept well, but was awake and dressed by the time Robert Andrew came on duty. "Where's that Aylesbury newspaper, you showed me yesterday?" he asked.

Robert produced it and watched whilst John turned to the page relating to the Aylesbury burglaries. He scanned down the page until he came to the description of the stolen snuffbox. John produced the snuff box he had taken from Thompson's possessions and showed it to Robert.

"What do you think of this?" he asked, trying to keep the excitement out of his voice.

Robert picked it up, studied it and looked again at the illustrated initials in the picture. "I'd say it was one and the same, Guv'nor. Can I ask where you found it?"

John noticed he had dropped the *sir,* and was using a more informal address of *Guv'nor.* He was quite happy with that and told Robert where he had found it. They both agreed it tended to indicate the late soldier had stolen it, possibly during the Aylesbury burglary. Both officers agreed more than one man would have been employed to carry out the burglaries in Aylesbury and Warwick. And Major Pearson's troopers had to be prime suspects.

"But, how involved is the major?" queried Robert.

John shrugged his shoulders. "We need to know. His Regiment has its headquarters in London. So get the next available coach, preferably tonight, and see what you can find out about Major Charles Pearson. I'll give you a letter of authority. Stop off in Aylesbury, call on your mother, but also get this snuffbox identified and glean any other information you can. And, get as much of it written down as possible, and signed. Then get back here as quickly as you can."

Robert's face lit up. "Yes Guv'nor!"

"A word of warning. Keep this between ourselves. I'll tell Sergeant Harrison, but nobody else is to know."

Later that morning, Samuel Perkins and Elijah Snow climbed down to the river, under the bridge. It was a cold morning and both men were glad of their greatcoats. A breeze blowing off the water added to the overall chill.

"I thought we was going in a boat?" grumbled Snow.

"Here it comes," replied Samuel, pointing in the direction of Warwick Castle, as a rowing boat made its way up from the weir.

"What are we looking for?" muttered Snow, starting to shiver.

"The Guv`nor told you. We don`t know. We drag the river with hooks and see what we can find.

CHAPTER ELEVEN

The Search

The boatman, George Kent, rowed across to the riverbank, where the two policemen climbed on board. Samuel was relieved to see some coiled ropes, tied onto grappling hooks, lying on the bottom of the boat. He uncoiled one of them and motioned to Snow to do the same with the other. Gently he lowered his rope into the water.

"Row across to the other side and then back again, please," he instructed the boatman.

"And just what do you think you`re going to find? This is a waste of my time. I`ll take you across and back the once and that`s it," Kent sneered.

He clearly had a low opinion of policemen and of all forms of authority. Working for the Earl of Warwick, he considered himself to be above such menial work, and was not all pleased with having been detailed for this particular task.

"No," replied Samuel. "We`ll go across this river as many times as I think fit. Then, if we`ve found nothing, we`ll do it again."

"Says who?" sneered the boatman, pulling his oars on board. "That`s it. Out you get! I`m not having a kid like you, wearing a fancy uniform, telling me what to do." As he spoke, Kent reached out and grabbed Samuel`s ear.

"I suggest you do as you`re told and let go of my ear!" instructed Samuel.

Kent laughed, unpleasantly. "Or what........aaaagh!" His words ended in a painful cry, as Samuel took hold of the man`s little finger, and bent it backwards. The boatman let go of Samuel`s ear and the constable released Kent`s finger.

"Now," said Samuel mildly. "Can we get on?"

Kent nursed his finger and glared at Samuel. "I`ll get you for that. Just you wait!"

"Any time you want," replied Samuel. "But now, can we get on?"

"Complete waste of time," muttered the boatman.

"You`re probably right,"agreed Samuel. "But you, like us, are being paid to do a job, and I don`t think the Castle steward will be pleased, if you don`t do as instructed."

The boatman had no answer to that particular observation. This young policeman seemed to know too much, and so he would have to search the river. But, he vowed to get his own back. A dark night, with a couple of friends, would settle him once and for all. Even his own mother won`t recognise him by the time they had finished. He took up the oars and began rowing again.

They stopped on the other side and Samuel began to reel in his grappling hook. Snow copied him. "It`s just like fishing," he chuckled. The other two men ignored him.

When both hooks broke the surface, they were empty. "Back to other side!" instructed Samuel.

So the morning passed. After a while, Samuel noticed a small crowd had gathered on the bridge to watch and offer advice.

"Your hook`s too big for the fish in this river!"

"What do you use for bait?"

And so the catcalls continued.

Late morning, Samuel decided to call a halt so they could stretch their legs and take some refreshment. As they landed, he was surprised to see Monk climbing down the river bank towards them. He was not in uniform and clearly off duty.

"What the hell are you doing?" he demanded truculently as Samuel and Snow climbed out of the boat.

Samuel took him on one side. "What does it look like?" he replied. "Because Mr Mayfield wants it done. Even you must realise it`s in connection with the dead soldier..." He broke off as he noticed the boatman`s sudden interest in their conversation.

Monk caught his eye and they both moved away. "Mr Mayfield feels we might be looking at a murder. And I agree. Too many things just don`t add up. So we`re dragging the river. Looking for clues."

"Mr Mayfield! Mr Mayfield!" mimicked Monk. "What does he know about it, eh? He`s only a foreigner from London. Obviously the soldier took his own life. So, what does he hope to find?"

"Who knows. It might be the murder weapon."

For a moment, Monk seemed lost for words, but not for long.

"What a waste of time," he sneered. "Obviously the man took his own life. If I was you, I`d finish now and go for a drink. Tell Mayfield you found nothing. He`ll never know!"

Samuel stiffened. "I don`t think you understand the need for thoroughness in police work."

"Bah! Who do you think you are? The Saviour of the World? A knight in shining armour, riding to everyone`s rescue? It`s only a job!"

"Not for me. I actually believe in what I`m doing. If you haven`t got that sort of belief, then what are you doing in the police? You should be working elsewhere."

Monk turned on his heel and walked away. However, after a few yards, he stopped and came back to Samuel.

"What makes you all think it`s a murder?" he asked as calmly as he could, but was hard pressed to conceal his agitation, and keep the tremor out of his voice.

Cooper had told Monk about Thompson being found, and instructed him to find out all he could about Mayfield`s investigation, and to sabotage it, if at all possible. If only Snow had been on his own, that would have been easy, but Perkins was a different matter.

He had made some enquiries about him, and quickly discovered the young man was no fool. Once he realised Samuel would not be deterred from searching the river properly, Monk knew there was always a chance of the candlestick being found. But, even if so, they might not associate it with the dead man. His hopes were short lived.

Samuel looked squarely at Monk. "Firstly, the man has a head injury that does not seem compatible with his having jumped in the river. Secondly, although wearing his dragoon`s uniform, the man`s improperly dressed. His spurs and sabre are missing."

"What`s the problem with the man`s head?" asked Monk, aghast.

"It seems he received a hard blow to the side of the head," replied Samuel. He pointed up at the bridge. "And there`s nothing there to have caused it."

Monk stood still for a moment. Samuel thought the man seemed shaken by the information he had just given him. From being totally disinterested, he was now very interested. Aware Samuel was studying him, Monk turned on his heel and walked back up to the bridge. Samuel watched him thoughtfully.

Unlike Sergeant Harrison, Robert Andrew and the Guv`nor, this was his first attempt at being a policeman. The idea had grown on him in recent weeks, and it had been a logical move to join the new Warwick Force, which was where he had been born. Only too aware of his youthful appearance, he had been pleasantly surprised to be appointed. Yet, he had noticed the smirk on Cooper`s face on having his appointment confirmed.

It seemed this member of the Watch Committee found his appointment particularly amusing, an attitude which surprised him. Why should a man, in Cooper`s position, be so opposed to the new Police Force? How could he have arranged the appointment of people like Snow and Monk? Why was he trying so hard to sabotage them? What did he have to hide?

"Have we finished?" Kent`s whining voice brought him back to the present.

"No. Let`s go back upstream and start again."

The boatman sighed and picked up his oars as the two policemen climbed back on board.

"What are we looking for?" moaned Snow. "There can`t be anything left in this damned river."

He indicated the riverbank where a collection of broken lamps, an old suitcase, a gate, a boat, a tin trunk and a dead dog now resided. All the metal objects were thick with rust and had clearly been in the water a long time.

Samuel sighed heavily. "I keep telling you, I don`t know. We have to see what we can find."

Even as he said the words, Samuel wondered how Snow had ever been appointed. To say the man was slow witted, was an understatement. He treated everything as a joke. True, he had been quite shaken by the discovery of the soldier`s body, but he was another of James Cooper`s appointments and Samuel wondered why.

On the other hand, he trusted Sergeant Harrison and the Guv`nor.

As yet, he did not really know Robert Andrew, but the man had a confident air about him, knew his job and did not mind sharing information and gave good advice. His thoughts were interrupted when his grappling hook broke the surface of the river. In its prongs was a large brass candlestick.

He reached over the side of the boat and pulled the candlestick on board. The first thing he noticed was it was too clean to have been in the river for very long. Apart from being slightly bent, there seemed to be no obvious reason for it to have been thrown away. Possibly it had been because of the damage, but it could still have been used.

Looking back to the bridge, Samuel saw it was easily within throwing range to where the boat was. Also, with the weir so close, it was unlikely to have fallen off a passing boat. The more he thought, Samuel knew there had to be a reason for it being in the river. Perhaps this was what they had been looking for?

They continued dragging the river for another hour, but found nothing else. Samuel decided to call it a day, and was well aware of a small crowd gathered on the bridge, which had been there for a while. The boat landed them on the bank by one of the piles of debris dragged out of the river.

"What are we going to do with this lot?" asked Snow, pointing at the pile.

"Leave it. Someone else can have a chance to pick it over."

"Remember," snarled the boatman at Samuel. "You and me have some unfinished business to attend to."

"Any time you like," smiled Samuel, picking up the candlestick and making for the bridge.

"Oi! Crusher!" called a voice from one of the crowd. "What`s the candlestick for? You frightened of the dark?"

The crowd howled with laughter and Samuel sensed Snow stiffen. "Easy, man!" he whispered.

Changing tactic, Samuel grinned back at the crowd. "Yes. Have you got a candle?" he called back.

The crowd howled with delight and more good natured banter passed between them as they followed the constables up Castle Hill.

John Mayfield sat in his office, studying the lists of the stolen property. It made no difference how many times he studied them. They always showed only gold and silver had been taken: no jewellery or paintings. More and more he kept coming back to his recent meeting with Daniel Roberts. Any further thoughts were quickly interrupted.

"MAYFIELD! MAYFIELD!"

The shouts came from the front of the police station and he did not have to be told the identity of their owner. Any lingering doubts he might have had, were quickly dispelled as his office door was flung open, without any knocking.

In stormed an angry James Cooper, holding out his arm in an attempt to try and stop the door bouncing back onto him. It did not work, and the door swung back hard, making him even angrier. "MAYFIELD! Didn`t you hear me call you?"

John ignored him, stifling a grin as the door hit his visitor, and spoke to a clearly flustered Constable Snow, who had followed in behind Cooper.

"It`s all right, Snow. I`ll deal with it."

Snow withdrew thankfully.

John waited until the door had closed before turning to Cooper, who shouted: "How dare you ignore me! I said didn`t you hear me?"

When Cooper stopped to draw breath, John spoke. "Yes, I heard you," came his quiet reply.

"Then why the devil didn`t you come when I summoned you?"

John remained seated and folded his arms. He looked at Cooper`s red perspiring face and answered, still in a quiet voice. "Whilst you may be the secretary of the Watch Committee, I am not one of your hired lackeys, who has to jump at your every command."

"You damned insolent dog!" shouted. "I`ve a good mind to give you the thrashing of your life." At the same time, he raised his riding crop over his right shoulder.

Slowly John stood up. Standing very still, he leaned forwards on the balls of his feet, and his eyes never left Cooper`s face. "You would be ill-advised to try that." John`s voice was very quiet.

Cooper faltered. For a moment it seemed as if he would still go ahead with his threat. But there was an ice-cold menace in the policeman`s voice, and he was clearly not in the least bit intimidated.

It was a situation Cooper had never experienced before, except with this man. Perhaps this was not the time for a reckoning, although there would have to be one some day.

Cooper now realized a direct frontal attack would never work. No, he would have to be more devious than that. Now, more than ever, he wanted to ensure Mayfield lost his job and be totally ruined in the process. Yes, a little accident would have to be arranged. He would find a way to really hurt him, but not kill him. Find a way of giving him a fate worse than death. Slowly, he lowered his crop.

"Now, Mr Cooper," said John still in a very calm and icily polite voice. "What do you want?"

Cooper slowly drew breath before replying. "Perhaps I was a bit hasty, Mayfield."

John could see what an effort it was for the other man to force himself to be calm, but made no attempt to help him. He did not trust him. Everything Cooper did, seemed to be for a reason, usually one that suited him and nobody else.

"But," continued Cooper. "I cannot possibly see how you can justify using two men to go sailing on the river, when you have all these burglaries to investigate." Although Cooper`s voice struggled to appear calm, John noticed it lacked its usual note of confidence.

"For your information, Mr Cooper," he replied. "It is my belief that there has been a greater felony committed, which concerns the death of a soldier. Nobody has reported him missing and Major Pearson seems to have vanished. So we don`t as yet have a name for him."

He paused, but there was no reaction from the other man. How he would like to be a fly on the wall when the two of them met and discussed Cooper`s meeting with John.

"What do you mean?" queried Cooper. "I agree the man has taken his own life and that is the greater felony. Yet, you`re hardly going to take him to court, are you?" he chuckled.

John remained impassive. "If that was really the case, then I would agree with you. But, it is my belief this was not a suicide nor an accident." He paused. "I believe he was murdered!"

Cooper erupted into a fit of raucous but nervous laughter. "You can`t possibly be serious?"

His laughter died away when when he saw the look on John`s face.

"My God! You are serious, aren`t you?"

Cooper`s heart began to pound away as he realised the implications of what John had just said. It confirmed the worries of their leader from the night before. If the police really thought, so soon, that Thompson had been murdered, then how long would it be before they discovered other things as well?

This man, Mayfield, was not so stupid after all. He ran his finger round the inside of his sweaty collar, as if already feeling the hangman`s noose there. He decided to try a different, softer approach. "Look, Mayfield, I know we don`t exactly see eye to eye, and you are supposed to have some ability, but it`s obvious the man took his own life, or possibly he fell."

"And what makes you so sure, Mr Cooper?" queried John. "Have you seen the body? Were you there when he died, or do you know something I don`t?"

"Er! Well, no. Of course not!" Cooper was clearly shaken by John`s last questions.

"Well I have, and the marks on his body do not appear to have been self inflicted."

"Absolute nonsense. How on earth do you expect anyone to believe such rubbish. Do a nice report for the coroner and that will be the end of it."

"No Mr Cooper. That will not be end of it. I will not prepare any nice report for the coroner or anyone else until I am completely satisfied as to how this man met his death."

"I`m telling you the case is closed. Understand?"

Cooper fought hard to keep his temper, and control his rising fear. "Anyway, what are the marks you are so concerned about?" he continued.

"I could say this is a police matter and nothing to do with you. However, in view of your position on the Watch Committee, I will tell you. There is a mark, a large dent if you like, which is a strange shape. And whatever caused it, almost certainly fractured the man`s skull and probably caused his death."

"I can assure you, you`ll get nothing from dragging the river bed, so don`t waste any more time doing it. In fact, I forbid you to spend any more time there. You will stop it immediately!"

"In matters of police investigation, Mr Cooper, you will forbid me nothing. My duties and responsibilities are laid down by statute and not by you. Whilst you may be the Secretary of the Watch Committee, I doubt you have investigated many murders, if any at all. On the other hand, I do have some experience in such matters."

It was a cheap jibe and John knew it.

"I forbid you to do anything else in this matter. Do you hear me, Mayfield?"

"I hear you," snapped John. "And I repeat, you will forbid me nothing. You do not have that authority."

"Now look here......"

"No! You look here!" John`s voice had a strong, icy tone. "If you continue in this manner, then I will consider you to be obstructing me in the execution of my duty. And that might mean your appearing before the magistrates."

For a moment, Cooper was lost for words. Then he pointed his crop at John.

"Very well, Mayfield," he snapped. "Have it your own way. You won`t listen to advice, but I`ll give you some all the same."

John continued looking stonily at Cooper, and had a good idea what was coming next. He was not mistaken.

"You`re only here on sufferance and, your career to date has not exactly been spectacular. Unless you very soon discover the felons responsible for all these burglaries, then your days here will be numbered!"

By now Cooper`s face was purple with rage. John saw flecks of spittle around the man`s mouth and became genuinely concerned for Cooper`s well being. He decided to terminate the meeting.

Crossing over to the door, he opened it. "I bid you good day, Mr Cooper."

Turning his back on John, Cooper stormed out of the office, and nearly collided with Samuel Perkins. He saw the candlestick the officer was carrying and the blood drained from his face.

"What`s that?" he asked, almost in a whisper.

"A candlestick, sir." He was about to say some more, but looked first at John for guidance. John shook his head.

"I can see it`s a damned candlestick! Don`t get funny with me," snapped Cooper. "Where did you find it?"

Samuel looked at John, who nodded his head. "In the river, sir."

Cooper stretched out his hand. "Give it to me," he instructed. "I`ll get rid of it for you."

Samuel did not need to look to John for guidance. "I can`t do that, sir!"

"I`ve told you to give it to me. Do as you are damn well told!"

"Good day, Mr Cooper!" interrupted John. "Constable Perkins will not give you that candlestick. So will you please leave the police station now."

Cooper spun round. "Now see here, Mayfield!" he begun but was unable to finish.

"No!" commanded John. "You see here. Please leave now. If you do not, I will arrest you for acting in a disorderly fashion in a police station and you will end up in court."

For a moment Cooper hesitated. Then he turned back to John and raised his crop again.

But John spoke first. "I would remind you there is now a witness to any more threats you happen to make to me." He nodded to Samuel who was standing expectantly with his fists clenched, having already put down the candlestick. "I advise you to leave now!"

Cooper turned and left John`s office without another word. For a few moments, neither policeman spoke, as they watched Cooper storm out of the police station.

"What did you find?" John broke the silence.

"Only this candlestick, which rather excited Mr Cooper."

He handed it to John.

CHAPTER TWELVE

Another Crime

John took the candlestick, stood it on his desk, and saw immediately that it had been damaged and leaned noticeably to one side. "Have you dropped it or damaged it at all?" he asked.

Samuel shook his head. "No Guv`nor." He had also adopted the term as opposed to the more formal *sir.* "That`s how it was when I took it out of the water. And, it`s still clean, so it can`t have been in there very long."

"I wonder! I wonder!" mused John. Picking up the candlestick, he carefully tested its weight. It was a solid piece of brass. "This could do someone a lot of damage."

"My thoughts too, Guv`nor." Samuel paused. "May I ask why Mr Cooper was so concerned about it and where it had come from?"

For a moment John looked at the younger man. Samuel might not have a police background, but he was shaping up well in the few days John had known him. He had the makings of being a good policeman. Quite clearly he was no fool.

"In a word, I don`t know. But he was most unhappy to see you with it, and I wonder why?" He paused for a moment, then stood up. "Come on, let`s go and take another look at our body. And bring the candlestick with you."

&

Thomas Waldren lit another cheroot and bent over the body of William Thompson. The man was beginning to smell, but the tobacco smoke went a long way to disguising the fact. If he was honest with himself, Thomas could think of other things he would prefer to be doing at this moment. He had been up most of the night for one reason or another, including a difficult birth.

Now that mother and baby were both gaining strength, he had decided to do this autopsy before going to bed, and get it out of the way. With a bit of luck he would be able to tell John something about this dead man. He just hoped John would not come too soon.

Selecting a large scalpel, he made a deep incision into Thompson`s chest and exposed the rib cage. He was even more grateful now for the cheroot. Just as he picked up a saw to cut through the ribs, there came a gentle knocking at the door leading into the back garden. For a moment he was tempted to ignore it, but knew he could not do so. Looking up, he could see a vague silhouette the other side of the glass panel in the door.

Putting down his scalpel, he quickly pulled a sheet over William Thompson, and washed his hands. "Just a minute," he called. Wiping his hands dry, he crossed to the door and to open. As he did so, he heard the front door bell ring.

"Damn," he swore, knowing that at this time of day, it would have to be for him. The last thing he wanted right now was any interruption. For a moment he was undecided what to do.

❧

Harriet was crossing the hallway of her uncle`s house when she heard the doorbell ring. "I`ll get it," she called to Redman, who was carrying some plates into the dining room.

"Thank you, Mrs Foxton." Whilst not approving of her opening the door, he was too polite to show it.

Outside, John was both delighted and surprised to see the door opened by Harriet. "Good evening, Mrs Foxton," he said, experiencing a rush of pleasure in seeing her again.

"Good evening, Mr Mayfield," she smiled. "And constable....?"

"Perkins, miss," Samuel introduced himself, at the same time touching the rim of his hat in a salute. John was quick to follow his example.

"Is the doctor at home?" asked John.

"Of course. Please come in. He`s in his laboratory but I`ll take you there."

John smiled to himself. Harriet knew full well he knew where it was. Clearly she wanted an excuse to get in there herself. Anyway, he was more than happy just to be in her company. Samuel followed behind them and looked admiringly at Harriet`s trim figure. But he kept his thoughts to himself. Harriet led the way to the laboratory and knocked on the door.

"Uncle Thomas," she called. "It`s John Mayfield to see you."

John liked the way his name rolled off her tongue.

There was no reply to Harriet`s knocking, although they could hear movements coming from the other side of the door. Harriet knocked and called again. As if in reply, they heard the sound of breaking glass from the laboratory.

"Uncle Thomas? Are you alright?" she called urgently. There was still no reply.

John pushed her firmly to one side and tried the door handle. It was not locked, and he pushed the door open. Behind him, Samuel had drawn his staff from his belt. The two men entered closely followed by Harriet.

At first glance, it seemed the laboratory was deserted, apart from a pile of broken glass jars on the floor. They saw the back door, into the garden, was open.

"Look Guv`nor!" pointed Samuel. A dark shape was climbing over the garden wall.

At the same moment, they heard Harriet cry. "Uncle Thomas? Oh God, what`s happened?"

Meanwhile, Samuel had run out into the garden after the shape. "STOP!" he shouted, but it was too late.

The shape vanished over the wall into Castle Lane. Seconds later, Samuel heard a whip crack, followed by the sound of hooves on the road, accompanied by the rumble of carriage wheels.

Barely checking his speed, he jumped up at the wall. His hands found the top and he hauled himself up, just in time to see the dark shape of a carriage vanishing down the Lane towards Stratford.

Samuel quickly lowered himself off the wall and ran in pursuit. As he began to close the gap between himself and the carriage, he was vaguely aware of two urchins studying his approach. He had almost drawn level with them, when they both pulled hard on a rope which

Samuel had not seen lying in the road, with one end firmly attached to a tree.

The rope caught him just below the knees, making him lose his balance and fall heavily on the road. He slid several feet before coming to a stop against a garden wall. The fall totally winded him, and he was only vaguely aware of the laughing urchins running away. They did not spare him another look. It had been easy money.

A strange, well dressed man, had paid them to pull up the rope if another man came running down the Lane. They were surprised and well pleased when they saw their victim was one of the new policemen. But they did not hang around, trusting in the darkness to hide their identities.

"Are you alright?" came a voice from somewhere over Samuel`s shoulder. "You took quite a fall. Here let me help you up."

Samuel looked up and recognizing William Slattery, was grateful for his assistance Briefly he explained what had happened and William nodded sympathetically. When he offered to help Samuel back to the doctor`s surgery, the policeman did not object. His hands and knees hurt and so did his head from hitting the wall.

❧

On hearing Harriet`s cry, John turned back into the laboratory, where she was on her knees, cradling Thomas`s head in her arms. Thomas was lying amongst another pile of broken glass. "He`s breathing, thank God. Go and get some water," she instructed.

John looked round, found a bowl and took it over to the pump. He quickly filled the bowl with water and took it back to Harriet, stopping to pick up some cloths on the way. By the time he had returned to Harriet, he was relieved to find his friend stirring.

Taking one of the cloths, Harriet soaked it in water and gently wiped her uncle`s face. A few moments later, they were glad to see Thomas open his eyes. Harriet made her uncle lie still for a few moments before allowing him to sit up.

"She makes a fearsome nurse," he joked with John as they helped him to stand, a short while later.

Thomas stood for a moment looking at the mess in his laboratory.

Then he stopped.

"Well damn me! The body's gone!"

They all looked where the soldier's body had been. The slab was empty. There was only a bloodstained sheet lying nearby.

"Suppose you tell us what happened?" asked John.

Thomas told them briefly how he had been examining the body, when he heard a knock at the back door. He had opened it, only to find nobody there.

"Then, the next thing I can remember is lying on the floor with Harriet leaning over me." As he finished speaking, they heard the front door bell ring. "It's a busy night," he quipped.

They made their way to the front of the house, just as Redman opened the door and admitted a dishevelled Samuel leaning heavily on William Slattery.

"Come into the surgery," invited Thomas.

"But you're in no state to do anything," objected John. "You both need some attention."

"Then allow me," instructed Harriet. "Redman, please tell my aunt that we will be a little late for supper tonight. Also, I expect we have a few extra guests." She led the way into the surgery.

Sarah soon joined them. Like Harriet, she was quite adept at attending to men's injuries although neither man was badly hurt. Thomas had a graze to his head and seemed to be rather shaken as a result of his fall. Samuel was well bruised and had several grazes to his knees, hands and chin. He was far more concerned about his trousers, which were badly torn.

"Don't worry about those," said Slattery. "I know where there are some spares and I'll see Cooper doesn't make too much fuss."

Harriet tended to Samuel, and the young policeman enjoyed being the centre of her attention. He related what had happened as she continued bathing his injuries.

Thomas winced as Sarah dressed the cut on his forehead.

"Luckily it's not very deep," she said. "But I think you'll have a headache for a while."

"I already have," replied her husband. "In fact we all have. How can the inquest proceed tomorrow without a body. Somehow I don't think the coroner will be very impressed."

Everybody nodded in agreement.

"I must apologize, John," he continued. "I should have inspected the body sooner."

John shrugged. Inwardly he was disappointed Thomas had delayed so long, but was now far more concerned, as to why somebody should go to such extremes, as to actually steal the body. It was a new experience for him. He could only think someone, almost certainly the murderer, was worried about what secrets the body might reveal. He was now totally convinced the soldier had been murdered.

"What`s done, is done," he replied philosophically. "The more pressing problem is what am I going to tell the coroner tomorrow?  I haven`t met him yet, and this is not a promising start."

"And, I`m sorry to have to tell you, John," interrupted Sarah. "But Julius Hopper is a big friend of Mr Cooper, as well as being his doctor."

"Will it affect his judgement?" asked John.

Thomas held his hands up. "I just don`t know. He has very high standards and makes all of his judgements on the facts available, having little time for opinions unless they are backed up with hard facts."

"Without a body," added John. "I cannot get a positive identification, which means there doesn`t seem to be much more I can do about pursuing a murder enquiry, which this undoubtedly is."

Thomas stood up and went across to his desk and opened a drawer. From it he took a piece of paper, with a mark drawn on it. He spread it out on top of his desk. John recognized the mark as being very similar to the one he had seen on the soldier`s head the previous night.

Picking up the candlestick, he handed it to Thomas, and watched him line its base up with the mark. John was very conscious of Harriet gripping his hand in excitement.

"I`d say that was almost a perfect match," breathed Thomas. "Without doubt, I would say this candlestick was used to kill the soldier. If that is so, then the man was certainly murdered."

"I`m sorry to put a damper on this," said Slattery. "But, speaking as a magistrate, that evidence will never be acceptable in court."

CHAPTER THIRTEEN

Other Enquiries

Robert Andrew enjoyed his journey to Aylesbury. He had not been home for a few weeks and was always happy at the thought of seeing his mother and sister again. It would be quite a surprise for them. At the same time, he was also conscious it was a working visit, and not just for pleasure. Yet, he had to stay the night somewhere, as it would be pointless arriving at the barracks until later tomorrow morning.

As he had thought, his mother was overjoyed to see him, although concern masked her face as she clearly thought something was wrong. Quickly he re-assured both her and his younger sister, and explained he was here on official police business. His mother was delighted that it was her newspaper, which had become so important in her son`s life. After a while, he went off to make his enquiries before returning to the family cottage.

From common courtesy he first went to see the local ward constable and explained what he was doing. Although a product of the old policing system, Toby Jackson was highly respected, and over the years, he had more or less become the official policeman for the town. He was a successful thief-taker and there was not much that happened in Aylesbury, which the constable did not know about.

Robert knew the man from way back, having been chased by him in his younger days. Without revealing too much detail, he explained why he was in Aylesbury. Toby Jackson listened to him in silence.

"Did you have the military in town, by some chance, when this happened? The 87th Dragoons?" Toby asked abruptly, interrupting Robert.

"Why do you ask?" hedged Robert. The Guv`nor had specifically told him to play down that side of the enquiry.

"I`ll take that as a yes. You never were a good liar. Remember the apples?" chuckled Toby.

"Remember the apples? How could I ever forget? I couldn`t sit down for a week!"

Some years ago, Toby had caught him with some stolen apples. Robert tried to convince Toby they had been given to him, as visions of being transported to Australia suddenly appeared before his eyes.

Toby was no fool. He knew the apples had been stolen, but he also knew Robert`s mother was ill and that the boy had only taken them for her sake. Deep down he knew Robert was a good lad, and trying desperately hard to stand in for his recently dead father.

Toby could not let the matter go unpunished, but decided against taking him before the court. That would only cause even more misery to Mrs Andrew, and wouldn`t really help her son. Instead, he had thrashed Robert with his staff and sent him on his way, still with the apples. It was a salutary lesson for Robert. He never stole again.

On becoming a police officer himself, he always administered the law justly and fairly. Toby had a liking for Robert and was actually quite proud of him when he joined the police. For a while they talked about old times and, for the first time, Robert really appreciated just how much he owed Toby.

"You got this snuff box on you?" asked Toby.

Robert took it out of his pocket. The other man took it and studied it from different angles. At last he stopped and handed it back.

"There`s little doubt it belongs to Walter Taylor." Toby took out his watch. "He should be back from church by now, so I suggest a little stroll up to his house. I`d better come with you as he is now very wary of strangers and is likely to think you took it from him in the first place."

Side by side the two law officers walked up to Walter Taylor`s house. As Toby had predicted, the old man was now quite nervous and very unsure about Robert. Acting on his instructions, Robert let Toby do all the talking. After a while, the old man relaxed and invited his visitors into the study. Robert saw the shutters were well fastened. Walter`s house would not be burgled so easily again. Sadly, thought Robert, it`s yet another case of shutting the stable door after the horse has bolted.

Slowly, Toby brought the subject round to the burglary. For a moment Robert thought the old man would refuse to discuss it, but, with a little coaxing from Toby, he soon relaxed again.

"We think," said Toby. "We may be on to the culprits. It seems they have struck again in Warwick, which is where Constable Andrew comes from." He stopped and looked meaningfully at Robert.

"That`s correct. Mr Jackson`s right. And, we think, this may be yours." Robert paused and took out the snuff box and handed it to Walter.

The old man took it with a shaking hand. Toby and Robert were embarrassed to see his eyes water as he held it. Walter nodded, and a single tear ran down each cheek. "Yes, its mine. Actually it was my grandfather`s and has been in the family ever since. I don`t care about all the other items, but this is so precious to me."

"Bastards!" muttered Toby, under his breath. He had witnessed this type of scene so often, as had Robert. It was always heartbreaking when sentimental treasures were stolen. Their monetary worth could not be valued against what they really meant to the owners.

"Agreed," muttered Robert.

Then began the difficult task of persuading Walter to return the snuff box to Robert, as it was vital evidence and would be needed in Court, assuming the case got that far. Toby added his support and reluctantly Walter handed back the snuff box to Robert. They could see the old man was tiring, but Robert had one more task to complete.

Producing a pen and paper from the small case he carried, Robert asked if he could use Walter`s desk. The old man agreed.

Robert quickly wrote out a short statement, in which Walter gave the date of the burglary, plus the details of what had been stolen, and then identified the snuff box. After Robert had written it, he read it through to Walter and got him to sign it. Bidding the old man goodnight, the two law officers left the house.

"What`s that all written stuff about?" Toby could barely contain his curiosity until they were out of the house.

"It`s his evidence, in a written form. This way, if he dies before we get to Court, then at least his evidence will still stand. It`s a trick I`ve learned from my Guv`nor. I don`t doubt everyone will have to do it in due course."

"God save us," replied Toby. "As if we haven`t got enough to do without putting it all down on paper. Now, have you got time for a quick noggin before you go back to your ma?"

"I thought you`d never ask."

Laughing, they made their way to a nearby inn, completely at ease in each other`s company.

✂

Meanwhile, back in Warwick and, as yet, unaware of the incident at Dr Waldren`s house, Mathew Harrison had come on duty early. His first call was to the *Green Dragon*, where Major Pearson`s troops were billeted. On entering the inn, all conversation stopped, with the exception of the soldiers who jeered and gave him catcalls. Mathew took the landlord on one side.

Mickey Cassidy did not like any form of uniform, especially if worn by police, or soldiers. He blamed it all on his Irish background, in spite of his never having set foot outside the Midlands, let alone crossed the Irish Sea. Yet, he was sufficiently worldly-wise not to go out of his way to annoy the new police. Granted there were not that many in Warwick, but ultimately, he knew, their numbers would grow, just like weeds, all over the place.

He had no intention of remaining in Warwick all his life. The advent of the railways was killing off the coaching trade, which provided him with a reasonable income. Mickey had set his sights on Birmingham, where there was a strong Irish contingent, and that was where he knew, he could make a difference. Not only was Mickey a big strong man, he was also something of a thinker and planner. He wanted to stay as an innkeeper, but also knew a bad reference from the Warwick police could make that difficult.

Taking Mathew into his own parlour, Mickey offered him a drink. Mathew politely declined, but could read nothing in the man`s round face. He did not know Mickey that well as the *Green Dragon* was not somewhere he visited socially. There was something about the large Irishman that bothered him, although he could not say exactly what.

Mathew had never known of any trouble happening there, but occasionally, he had seen some of the inn`s regular customers sporting

114

bruised faces, and being obliged to drink elsewhere. Mickey had a reputation for sorting out his own troubles, which Mathew could believe, and he had no wish to discover for himself at first hand. He began asking the landlord about the soldiers he had billeted at the inn.

Inwardly, Mickey heaved a sigh of relief. Causing trouble for the soldiers would be an unexpected bonus and do his reputation with the police some good. But, it would have to be done carefully. The big sergeant would not be an easy pushover. His refusal to accept a drink had shown that very forcefully.

"Surprisingly," he said reluctantly. "They're not a lot of trouble, mainly because they're so often out, till quite late." He scratched his head. "In fact, they didn't come in at all the other night."

With further careful questions, Mathew discovered the night they hadn't returned, was the night when the burglaries had happened. He kept an air of nonchalance, with difficulty, as he asked if any of them had left the inn permanently and unexpectedly.

"Funny you should ask that," replied Mickey. "One of them, their Corporal of Horse, I think he's called Thompson, has done just that."

Careful questions revealed Thompson went missing the night before the body was found. Mickey was quick to follow the line of Mathew's questions. "Is he the one who was fished out of the river?"

"Is Major Pearson here?" Mathew, totally ignored Mickey's question.

"Not at the moment. He spends much of his time with Mr James bloody Cooper. He often comes in late, and occasionally not at all."

Thanking him, Mathew moved back into the bar and approached the soldiers.

"Where's Corporal of Horse Thompson?" he asked.

The soldiers fell silent and looked away.

"Who?" demanded one of them.

"Stop messing me about!" snapped Mathew. "Your party is one member short. Where is he?"

"Oh him!" replied the same soldier. "He's gone back to barracks, doing a job for the major."

Mathew had to be content with this answer. He knew the man was lying, but was not in a position to prove it. Perhaps tomorrow, if the Guv'nor agreed, he would take these men to look at the body. If nothing else he would be able to judge their re-actions.

His good humour soon evaporated when he discovered what had happened at Dr Waldren's house.

❧

Next morning found Robert in London at the barracks of the 87th Regiment of Dragoons. As he expected, the Colonel was otherwise engaged and far too busy to see him, so he was directed to the adjutant, Major Hinde. With ill-concealed resentment at being interrupted in his work, Hinde went through the motions of listening to Robert, whilst he continued reading a report. Then, suddenly his ears picked up.

"What do you mean by a recruiting party in Warwick?" he asked, now very much alert.

Patiently Robert explained again, very much aware how the Major had not really been listening before.

"But we don't have any recruiting parties out, anywhere, at the moment. Are you sure they're from this Regiment?"

"Absolutely. They're under the command of a Major Pearson."

"Who did you say?" Hinde asked very quietly.

Robert repeated his answer. Hinde stood up and instructed Robert to follow him. In a few moments they had arrived at a door, which was partly open. Hinde knocked on it and entered with Robert. Colonel Bennett looked up.

"I think you had better hear this, Colonel," announced Hinde and instructed Robert to repeat his story.

Colonel Bennett listened intently then rang a bell on his desk. An orderly quickly appeared.

"Find Major Pearson!" he instructed. "Give him my compliments and bid him stop whatever he's doing and come here right away."

The orderly disappeared. Bennett asked Robert all manner of questions about the recruiting party, with special attention to their uniforms. Robert described them in detail whilst Bennett and Hinde nodded. Then came a knock at the door and another officer entered.

"This is Major Pearson," announced Bennett. "So if he's supposed to be in Warwick, what the hell is he doing here?"

Robert looked at Major Pearson briefly.

"Because, Colonel, the Major Pearson in Warwick is not this

gentleman here, although there does seem to be a slight resemblance. One of them has to be an impostor and I suspect it is the one in Warwick."

"I suspect the other Major Pearson is my brother Charles, who was cashiered from this Regiment some years ago, for larceny, fraud and cheating at cards," replied Major Pearson.

It was an hour and a half later before Robert was able to leave, only to find he had missed his coach. It had taken some effort, on his part, to get the Major to agree to make a written statement, about his brother, but he had, and it was worth its weight in gold. The Guv`nor would be delighted and, hopefully, excuse Robert`s lateness.

He had no idea about the problems the Guv`nor was experiencing back home at this moment.

CHAPTER FOURTEEN

A Long Afternoon

The morning had gone smoothly enough.
Silas Whiting had appeared briefly in court. The nature of his offence meant he would have to be tried at either the Assizes or Quarter Sessions, neither of which was scheduled for several weeks. As bail was out of the question, he was remanded in custody, in the County Gaol, to await his trial.

When Silas returned to the police station, prior to going to the Gaol, Kate Whiting was waiting to see him. John had only seen her briefly before, but was taken by how attractive she looked, although clearly upset about Silas. He had seen her around the town, but now she had a name, and, ruefully he thought, a husband. Her visit, albeit to her husband, was to be the highlight of John`s day and it was going to be a long afternoon.

During the morning, Thomas had sought out the coroner, Dr Julius Hopper, and explained what had happened. Hopper had not been impressed, and made it quite clear he would not postpone the inquest, set for that afternoon. Now John and Thomas sat in the Court House, waiting for the inquest to begin.

John was very conscious of a smug looking James Cooper and Charles Pearson amongst the spectators. All too soon the usher entered.

"ALL STAND!" he commanded, banging his staff down onto the wooden floor.

When the scraping of chairs had finished, Dr Hopper made his entrance. He was a medium sized man, dressed in black, with a glistening bald head, and wearing a pair of spectacles on the end of his nose. Such hair as he had was grey. At first glance he seemed a tidy man, but a closer inspection showed that was not the case; as highlighted by food stains on his waistcoat and specks of dandruff on his shoulders.

Everybody stood respectfully, as he took his place in the middle magistrate`s chair and settled himself comfortably in it. Next he shuffled some of the papers around and re-arranged the pens on the desk. Only when he was completely satisfied, did he nod to the the usher.

On receiving the signal, the usher turned to face the spectators, banged again with his staff, and commanded everyone to sit. Before the inquest could begin, he took a Bible and swore in the jurymen.

Only then did the coroner speak, after clearing his throat. "Gentlemen of the Jury," he intoned, peering over the top of his spectacles. "This is a most unusual case. Never have I come across anything like it, in all my life. I have to conduct an inquest, for which there is no body."

Hopper paused, and looked around the room, for effect, and was rewarded by the sudden buzz of interest. Milking the moment, he waited until everyone was quiet before resuming. "It appears it has been stolen!"

A new outbreak of voices greeted his remarks. John could see a young man feverishly writing in a notebook, and guessed, rightly, he was a reporter for the local newspaper. The printers would be working late tonight.

It took the usher several attempts to restore order, banging his staff and calling for silence several times. He only succeeded when the coroner raised his hand. "I will clear this court if there are any more such unseemly interruptions," he said.

Whilst everybody knew he enjoyed the attention, and it was, probably, an idle threat, they took no chances and the talking ceased. When silence resumed, Hopper continued: "Back to business. The inquest will continue."

The first witness was a boatman who had found the body. All too soon it was John`s turn to testify. As he took the oath, his stomach was churning, knowing, he was in for an unpleasant time. To make matters worse, he saw both Sarah and Harriet sitting at the back of the court. They gave him smiles of encouragement.

In answer to the coroner's questions, he described being in the police station when he heard about the body and making his way to the river. He described examining the body and finding the mark on its head.

"So, you examined the body?" asked Hopper.

"Yes sir."

"And what medical qualifications have you?"

"None, sir."

"None? None?" queried Hopper, in an amazed voice. "Then, pray explain, sir: Why did you examine the body?"

"I may not have any medical qualifications, but I am no stranger to dead bodies, and have dealt with several over the years in London."

"I couldn't care less what you did in London!" Hopper's retort was sharp. "This is Warwick. Now, will you please answer my question. Why did you examine this body?"

"To see if there were any obvious, specific causes of death."

"And were there?"

"Not immediately so. But on closer inspection, I saw a strange mark on his head."

"And what had caused that?"

For a moment John was tempted to testify about the candlestick, but on quick reflection, knew there would be no point. He would keep that information to himself, for the time being. It often paid not to broadcast all of one's evidence too soon. Regardless of what Hopper might think, John was investigating a murder. And it was conceivable the murderer might be in the Court House at this very moment.

"I don't know, sir," he replied.

"Was it the cause of his death?"

"I don't know, sir."

"Is there anything you do know, about this man's death?" came Hopper's next, sarcastic question. A ripple of laughter accompanied this comment. It was quickly silenced by Hopper peering over the top of his spectacles.

"With my lack of medical qualifications, I had no alternative but to leave that side of the enquiry to Dr Waldren."

There was a ripple of muffled laughter in the Court. John knew he should not have risked antagonizing the coroner, but could not help himself.

Hopper glowered at the spectators, and the laughter stopped. He turned again to John: "And just what, if anything, can you tell us about this....this missing body?"

"It was a male, aged about 35 and wearing a military uniform. That uniform!" he emphasized, pointing at Pearson.

There was a quick, stifled gasp from the spectators.

"Major Pearson," asked Hopper. "Do you have any of your soldiers missing?"

"No, sir. They are all accounted for, at least, they were this morning." Another chuckle came from the spectators. "I fear the superintendent is mistaken."

"Mr Mayfield," continued Hopper. "I don`t doubt this body was wearing a uniform. I assume you are capable of recognizing a military uniform when you see one?"

"Yes sir. It was the same uniform Major Pearson is wearing. The only difference being, the major`s is an officer`s uniform. The one on the body belonged to a corporal of horse, as denoted by the chevrons on his sleeves."

"May I make a suggestion, sir?" suggested Pearson. "If the superintendent can show me the uniform, then I can definitely tell whether it belongs to my Regiment or not."

"A good idea," said Hopper. Turning to John, he asked "Where is the uniform? I assume its here in Court or nearby?"

"I don`t know where it is. It was stolen along with the body."

This time, total uproar broke out in the court. John felt his ears go red. He was even more upset when he saw Cooper look at Pearson, and grin smugly. Just what were those two up to? He had the distinct feeling of being outsmarted by them. Something told him they knew about the missing uniform. But how could they?

John was fairly sure he could rely on Redman`s integrity, and he knew Thomas had not mentioned it to the coroner. So, if the word had been put about, it must have been done so by those who stole Thompson`s body. Pearson maintained none of his men was missing, and was clearly lying: but why?

John had recognised Thompson`s body from his first encounter with Pearson, in the Market Place. The only reason for denying his disappearance had to be because Pearson knew he was dead, and probably who killed him. And, he probably knew about the missing body last night. Just whose carriage had been used?

He was suddenly aware of Hopper addressing him.

"Let me ask you again, superintendent. That is if you are able to give me some attention. Why was the body stolen?"

"I believe the man was murdered and his murderers stole the body."

"Preposterous!" snorted Hopper. "Its more likely to have been stolen by resurrection men. No doubt it`s in London by now, being cut up by some doctor."

For a moment John contemplated arguing with Hopper, reminding him that recent legislation had done away with the need for grave robbers, as corpses for medical use were now much easier to acquire. But he decided it would probably only make matters worse. Gratefully he was allowed to sit down, but was obliged to watch Thomas having his reputation torn to shreds. The inquest was finally adjourned indefinitely, but Hopper still had to make his final comments. John was his first target.

"Such total incompetence defies belief. In all my days, I have never seen worse. Why, even the inmates of a lunatic asylum could have done better."

A great guffaw of laughter greeted his remarks, and John saw Cooper and Pearson grinning widely at one another.

Then the coroner turned his attention to Thomas. "I`ve heard of doctors losing patients before, but, in all my experience, I have never heard of them losing a corpse......until today."

With that he stood and left the court.

"All stand," smirked the usher.

As they left the court, Cooper and Pearson collapsed with laughter. The sound of their laughter lingered in John`s ears for a long time. He just hoped Robert Andrew had returned with good news.

John returned to the station and found Monk in the charge office, who made no attempt to hide his smirks. Then he saw the look of pure venom on John`s face and left very quickly.

Several minutes later, John had changed out of his uniform and joined Thomas in the *Woolpack* For a while, both men sat quietly, brooding over their drinks, deep in their own misery.

Thomas suddenly broke into John's thoughts with a passable impersonation of Julius Hopper. "Such total incompetence defies belief."

John rose to the challenge with his own impersonation, which was slightly better. "I've heard of doctors losing patients before..."

It did the trick and they both fell about laughing. After two more glasses of mulled wine, Thomas went home and John went back to the station. He was relieved to find Robert Andrew waiting for him, and offered the young officer a chair.

"I hope, by the cheerful look on your face, that you've got some good news for me. After this afternoon I could do with some. I suppose you've heard about the inquest?"

Robert nodded. "It's all over town."

He reported all he had discovered both in Aylesbury and London. As he finished, Mathew returned to the station and Robert repeated his story. When he finished, Mathew made his report.

"Well done, both of you," said John. "We now have a definite link between the Aylesbury burglary and Pearson's men. Plus, we know Pearson's a fake. I think there can be little doubt he knows who murdered the soldier, and stole his body. But, without that, we will be hard pressed to make any charge stick in court."

For a while they discussed the case and made plans. Robert had already sent off letters to all the existing police forces, in the country. He had asked for details of burglaries where only gold and silver had been stolen, when a military recruiting party had been the area.

His next task was to make enquiries with all the Warwick carriers and establish if Cooper had received consignments from those areas. It was still too early to specify any particular area, so Robert would have to get details of all consignments the man had received. It was a tedious, but necessary job. How John wished he had some more men, or at least other officers on whom he could rely and trust.

After Robert had left, Mathew looked at John.

"Before you ask," he commented. "I've heard all about the inquest. I should think all the town has, by now. And, to make matters worse," he shook his head. "The *Chronicle's* printed tonight. I think they'll be working late."

"So be it. I don't suppose it will be the only bad press we ever get. Now, what are we going to do about Monk?"

124

Before Mathew could answer, they were interrupted by the arrival of one of Thomas's servants, with a message for John. "Can you come to the house right away, sir?" he said.

John quickly made his way to High Street. The door was opened even before he reached the step. Redman took his coat and hat and showed John into the drawing room. Two men sat by the fire, each holding a glass of wine.

"Come in John," said Thomas. "I believe you know my guest."

John stared in amazement as the other man stood up, with a sheepish look on his face.

It was Dr Julius Hopper.

❧

Leaving the police station, Mathew, made his way towards the Butts. He had knocked on most of the doors to see if anyone had seen the unfortunate Silas Whiting being arrested by Monk; so far nobody had. But he left Agnes Jenkins till last.

Nobody knew how old she was, but there was not much Agnes missed, especially since her husband had died several years ago. She slept very little and spent much of the time just looking out of her window. As a youngster, Mathew had spent many happy hours with the couple. In so many ways they had been more like grandparents to him, and he had been devastated when the old man died. He always kept an eye on Agnes, and, if he was honest with himself, this visit was a mixture of business and pleasure.

Agnes welcomed him as usual and several minutes later he was sat in her parlour with a large mug of tea. He started to ask how she was, but Agnes stopped him.

"I'm glad you've called, Mathew. There's something funny going on."

"Tell me more," he prompted, feeling a sudden surge of excitement.

He listened as Agnes told him about the carriage she had seen go down the Butts and into Castle Hill. She had been surprised when it returned a few minutes later and stopped almost outside her house. "Then one of your new policemen got out of it, and made his way back to Eastgate," she ended her tale.

Mathew sat upright, now very interested. The policeman could only have been Monk. What was he doing in the carriage? Where had he picked it up? Whose carriage was it? It certainly verified Whiting`s tale about Monk having come at him from the Eastgate direction and definitely not the other way about. So, why was Monk lying?

"Agnes," he asked. "Just one last question and this is very important. How long was the carriage out of your sight? And was it the same one you saw earlier?"

"That`s two questions," she chuckled. "It was gone for about ten minutes, so it can`t have gone much further than the bridge." Agnes stopped as she saw the look on his face. "Oh my God! You don`t think it could have something to do with that poor man, who was found in the river, do you?"

The same thought had also just occurred to Mathew. "I don`t know, but it`s certainly a thought. But, was it the same carriage?"

"I think so."

They talked for a while, then Mathew stood up to leave. On the step, he gave her a big hug and made his way back to the police station. It had been a worthwhile visit.

❧

John was lost for words. After all that had happened that afternoon, here was the coroner, drinking with Thomas, as if nothing had happened. Hopper came towards John, holding out his right hand.

"No hard feelings, Mayfield?"

John took the proffered hand. It was a firm grip, which totally belied the impression he had formed about the man.

" No, sir," he relaxed. "All in a day`s work."

"Sit down, John!" Thomas instructed, handing him a glass of wine. "Julius wants to discuss the case some more, and I think you should be frank with him and then hear what he has to say."

John sat down and outlined his thoughts, including the candlestick. Hopper said nothing, but merely nodded his head from time to time. At last John finished.

"From what you say," said Hopper after a few moments. "I`m inclined to agree with you. I think your man was probably murdered.

But, you`ll have to provide more proof than that. I also think Major Pearson knows much more than he is letting on, especially now we know he`s a fraud. That means we could have him for unlawfully impersonating an army officer, but........" he paused. "Let me be frank. I think it would be worth while keeping this information to ourselves for the moment and go for something more serious, such as the murder or these burglaries. Don`t you agree?"

He noticed John hesitate.

"I know what you`re thinking," resumed Hopper. "Just where do I fit into all this? Am I right?"

"Yes," John replied. "I had you down for being Cooper`s man."

"Quite right. It`s what he likes to think and I encourage him in that thought. Look, Cooper runs this town. There`s not much going on that he doesn`t influence, one way or another."

He looked hard at John.

"You`re the only person ever to have stood up to him, and he doesn`t like it. It`s never happened to him before, at least not in this town."

John said nothing, but waited for Hopper to continue.

"Furthermore, I think you are the only one, who has the ability to break up his empire. Once it begins to crumble, you`ll find all the support you need. But, to make it crumble, we must be in a position of real strength. We`ll only get one chance."

John still said nothing, his mind in a whirl. Just how far could he trust this man? Was he really as honest as he would appear?

"You should know," added Hopper. "Cooper has already tried to influence my verdict, by agreeing to it being suicide. The fact I have not done so, might help you decide to trust me."

"O.K," John agreed, at last. "But do you think Cooper was involved in the murder?"

"Probably, but not directly. He`s far too clever for that."

"I believe he`s not locally born?"

"Correct. But before you ask, no one knows where he originated. He keeps that a very close secret. So don`t waste time trying to discover more about his background."

For a while the three men discussed the case and possible courses of action. Hopper was the first to move and bid his farewell. Thomas went to show him out. Before doing so, he instructed John to go into the dining room and see Sarah and Harriet. He needed no urging.

Both women made a fuss of him, and soon established he had not eaten. Bread, cold meat and cheese were summoned from the kitchen. Just as John sat down to eat, Thomas came in, followed by William Slattery and Mathew Harrison.

"My apologies, Guv`nor," started Mathew. "But I think you should hear what I`ve discovered."

Briefly he related his meeting with Agnes Jenkins. They all agreed it was interesting. Then Thomas reminded them how James Cooper owned a carriage, quite similar to the one Agnes had described. None of them needed reminding how it was a carriage which had taken Thompson`s body away.

"I think," said John. "It`s time we paid a visit to Mr James Cooper. And I think we`ll need to pay special attention to his carriage."

Sarah said nothing, but Harriet protested. "Do you think that`s wise?"

"Possibly not, but I`m tired of being on the defensive all the while. It`s time to go on the offensive. However, to be on the safe side, I think we ought to have a search warrant. Can you oblige Thomas?"

Slattery spoke first. "I think it`ll be better if I authorize the warrant. It`ll seem less like you and Thomas trying to get your own back. Come home with me now, and I`ll do it right away."

Mathew resumed his duty, whilst John made his farewells and followed Slattery home. He took the proffered Bible and swore out the information and several minutes later, the search warrant, duly signed, was in his possession. On leaving Slattery`s house, John realised he had left his hat at the other house and called to collect it.

Sarah had gone to bed and Thomas had gone out on a call. So he was delighted to find Harriet still up. It was nearly an hour later when he left the house.

CHAPTER FIFTEEN

Sabre and Spurs

Whilst John was having his meeting with Thomas and Dr Hopper, Kate Whiting got ready to go out, making herself look as attractive as she could. Kate hated what she was doing, but felt it was the only way to ruin Cooper and, hopefully, get out of this mess. Her main thoughts were for Silas and her young son, Edward.

"Must you go out tonight, ma?" called young Edward.

He was a sickly child, who was barely able to do any work. Aged 10, by now he should have been bringing in money, but instead had to rely on his wits, most of the time, just to survive. She hated leaving him alone, especially at night. However, she was also conscious there was no food in their solitary room, in Friars Street, and the boy was hungry. It would not have been so bad had that bastard Cooper paid her, but he had not yet done so.

The good news was he hadn`t used her either, but her genuine salary, from the foundry, had been delayed, and she knew it was all part of his bringing her to heel. At the same time, it was not easy for Kate to get at the money she made from selling her body, as she secretly banked it after being paid.

It was this shortage of money which had led her stupid, but loving husband to get himself arrested. Unlike poor Edward, he would at least be getting some sort of food in gaol. Cooper must be made to pay.

"I shouldn`t be too long, my love," she lied. "Just you go to sleep and I`ll be back by the time you wake. And I`ll bring us in something for breakfast."

She promised herself she would, even if it meant stealing it from Mr bloody James Cooper. Adjusting her bonnet, she gave Edward a small kiss, and left the room. Going down the stairs, Kate was very much aware of the hostility towards her from the other women, gathered in the hallway.

"Whore!"

"Slut!"

These were some of the words hurled at her, by them.

As she passed, Phoebe Morris spat at her. Kate turned, ready to fight if she had to, but the other woman just sneered.

"You wouldn`t dare," she scorned. "I`d make such a mess of your face, your fancy man wouldn`t even recognise you. How could you, go with that creature? And, with your man in gaol and your boy upstairs?"

Phoebe spat at Kate again, then stopped. She had seen the small crucifix at the other woman`s neck. Before Kate realised what had happened, Phoebe had grabbed it. Cackling with laughter, the older woman pulled hard and broke the chain. Still cackling, she triumphantly waved the crucifix in front of Kate.

"Oh no!" wailed Kate. "Not that, please. It`s the only thing I have to remember my mother. Please give it me back."

"I`ll tell you what," Phoebe cackled. "I`ll give it you back when you`ve earned its return." With that she ran off, cackling and holding the crucifix tauntingly over her head.

For a moment Kate was tempted to run after her, but she knew it would be no use. One day, she vowed, she would get her crucifix back. Holding back her tears, she left the lodging house, still with the catcalls of the other women ringing in her ears, and made her way to the Birmingham Road and never once looked back.

Had she done so, she would have seen young Edward following her.

He was surprised to see her heading out of town, instead of going to the foundry. She crossed the bridge over the canal and went through the gates of large house set back from the road, which he knew was the White House, home of James Cooper. Here his nerve failed for a moment, but then he too passed through the gates. Keeping off the gravel driveway, he followed his mother, and saw her go towards the rear of the house.

By now, Edward was even more unsure of what to do. As luck would have it, the decision was taken out of his hands. At that moment he heard a horse trotting up the drive, and he quickly hid behind a bush, and waited until the rider had passed. When he looked out again, there was no sign of his mother. She had disappeared.

☙

On hearing the horse approach, Kate had stood back into the shadows and waited, then watched as the man dismounted and knocked on the front door. He was admitted almost at once. Although he stepped into the light, she could only see his back. There was no doubt, in her mind, he was the same visitor as before, and his back view was vaguely familiar. But, who was he?

With mixed feelings, she realised if the visitor was there, it was unlikely Cooper would have need of her tonight. He had not been expecting her in any case. Apart from not getting her money, she was glad. She would draw out some of her precious savings tomorrow, so Edward could eat. Yet, if the strange man was here again, it must be important, and so she decided to wait. And she had another plan.

Soon after his arrival, she saw a light appear in the study. From experience she knew it was unlikely many words could be heard from there. Nevertheless, Kate decided to take a chance and try to hear what was being said. But, as she expected, it was no use. The windows were closed and the heavy curtains were drawn. All she could hear was the murmur of voices. Then her luck changed.

"I tell you," shouted a voice, she recognised as Cooper`s. "It has to be this Saturday night. I`ve got the men arranged for then. I can`t bring it forward. I don`t care................" His voice tailed off.

Soon afterwards the meeting broke up. She saw the army major leave, accompanied by the other man, but his face was still in the shadows. The two men mounted their horses and trotted off down the drive together. Their foggy breath mingled with that of the horses, in the cold night air.

Kate waited for a while until she saw Cooper go up to his room, and at last the house was still and dark. She was very cold, and scared, but determined to burgle Cooper`s study, as was her plan.

She was amazed and not a little frightened when she discovered how easy it was to put the knife, she had brought with her, in between the sash windows, and slide back the catch. Gently she pushed the lower window up. Hopefully, if she disturbed Brutus, Cooper`s dog, he would know her and not worry.

The window travelled up about twelve inches, then stopped. Try as she might, Kate could not get it any higher. And there was no way she could get through the gap. It would have to be someone much smaller. If only Edward was here!

She began to walk away, then stopped. Turning she went back and closed the window, hopefully nobody would worry about the catch not being fastened. Already an idea was forming in her mind. Could she persuade Edward to come and help her? If he was caught, then she would be as well. The whole family would appear in court and all be transported. It might just be worth the risk.

❧

When Edward lost sight of his mother, he panicked, not knowing what to do. Something told him he would be in trouble if she found him here. But, curiosity finally got the better of him and he started to explore.

Common sense told him not to go near the house, but that did not deter him from looking around the coach house and other outbuildings. Then joy of joys, he found some bread and a little cheese. Both were a bit stale, but still tasted good. He sat down for a while, and without realizing it, fell asleep.

When he awoke, it was still dark, but already servants were moving about the yard. It was time he left. Waiting until there was nobody in the yard, he left the coach house and went towards the gates. Edward was nearly there, when he heard horses coming down the drive.

Without hesitating, he ran through the gate and turned right, away from the road. Finding a convenient bush, he sank down behind it and waited for the riders to go. It had been a wise choice to avoid the road.

After several minutes, he stood up and was about to follow after the horses, but decided to relieve himself first. Whilst pulling up some grass, his fingers felt something cold, which, for a moment he thought might be a mantrap or snare of some kind, and waited for it to snap.

But nothing happened.

132

After carefully pulling back the grass, he slowly felt for the object. A few seconds later, after some gentle feeling, he relaxed and pulled the object towards him.

It was a cavalry sabre.

Smiling, Edward examined it as best as he could in the dark. The weapon was in its scabbard and came out easily enough. There did not appear to be any rust on it, so it could not have been there long. His eyes lit up, and he knew just the man to take it to, and who would give him a good price for it, which would all help his ma. Tucking the weapon under his arm, he made his way back to town.

❧

St Mary`s Church Clock was just striking 6.0 am when John entered the police station. He had been out in the town already.

"All correct, Guv`nor!" called Robert Andrew, leaping to attention as John entered.

"Carry on please," replied John.

He entered his office, took off his hat and coat, after removing the two pies from its pocket. They had been freshly cooked and he enjoyed the smell. Putting them inside his desk drawer for a moment, John sat down and then saw the *Warwick Chronicle* lying there.

The door opened after a soft knock. and Robert entered bearing a steaming mug of tea. He knew what was in the *Chronicle*, having read it before putting it on the desk. Quietly he withdrew, hiding a smile with difficulty.

Robert was smiling, not because of what was in the *Chronicle*, but at his Guv`nor trying to keep his fresh pies a secret. He had smelt them the moment John came into the station, and was correct in thinking he had paid for them.

Samuel had introduced Robert to the butcher and they both got their pies for free. Perhaps someone should tell the Guv`nor? Then, on second thoughts, he reasoned, it might be best not to.

Back in the office, John sipped his tea and turned to the middle pages of the *Chronicle*. In common with newspapers of the time, the first pages were filled with advertisements, followed by national and international news. Local news would be somewhere in the middle.

He found what he was seeking, and read, with a growing anger.

NEW POLICE FARCE

Readers will no doubt recall our earlier support for requests to police our town. Against advice, a London man was employed to take charge, and has been in post less than a week. Let us examine his successes to date.

True, a man has been reported for allowing his horse to deposit manure in West Street. But, during the same period, five houses have been burglariously entered and much gold and silver stolen. A man has drowned in the Avon and his body stolen! Finally, our notable Dr Waldren has been grievously assaulted and now lies in a precarious state in his own home. Pray, what has our new Chief of Police done?

His men spent a day fishing on the river, just to find a candlestick!

All persons in our town deserve better than this. If Superintendent Mayfield cannot police Warwick properly----then he should go.

John threw the paper down in disgust. There was no mention of the arrest of Silas Whiting, though on second thoughts, that might just be as well. True, Thomas had been assaulted, but he was not in any danger. It was a very biased unfair piece of reporting. His thoughts were interrupted by a knock at the door.

"Come in!" he snapped, immediately regretting his short temper.

Robert Andrew came in, pushing Edward Whiting in front of him.

"What is it?" queried John. He saw Robert was holding something behind his back, but could not see what it was.

Robert noticed it was a much more friendly tone.

"This is Edward Whiting, son of Silas Whiting," he paused. As he spoke, Robert brought his hand from his back, and placed the object he held on John's desk. John saw it was a cavalry sabre. "Young Edward had it with him when I stopped him."

Slowly John picked up the sabre and examined it closely. It was a typical military issue, complete with its scabbard. It was not the thing any soldier would dare to lose or have stolen, particularly by a small boy. With a thudding heart, John looked at Edward.

"And where did you get this?" he asked.

Edward looked at John defiantly and said nothing.

Robert caught John`s eye and indicated if he should give the boy a slap on his ear. John shook his head slightly, much to Robert`s relief. Neither man approved of gratuitous violence.

John repeated his question, but still received the same defiant silent look. Then he had an idea. Opening his desk drawer, he brought out six one penny pieces. Very slowly he put them into two equal piles on his desk, saying nothing. He was aware of Edward watching his every move.

"Now Edward," he continued. "Here`s the deal. One pile of pennies for you, when you tell us where you found the sabre. The other pile is when you take us to where you found it. Do you understand?"

Still Edward said nothing, but John could sense his resolve weakening. For a few more moments he studied the boy`s pinched face before opening his drawer again. This time, he took out the two pies he had purchased on his way across the Market Place. Very slowly he selected one of them, and took out his clasp knife. With slow, deliberate movements, he cut the pie in half and then into quarters. Edward`s eyes never left the pies.

"Are you hungry, Edward?" John asked.

The boy nodded.

"Would you like some pie?"

Again Edward nodded and reached out to the desk.

John moved the pie out of the boy`s reach.

"Here`s the new deal, Edward. One pie and three pennies, when you tell us where you found the sabre. The remaining pennies and a proper meal when you show us where you found them. Is it a deal?"

"Yeah," came Edward`s reply and he stretched his hand out for the pie, which John moved out of his reach.

"Information first, Edward."

"I found it down the Birdgignanamum Road."

"Where?" queried John.

"He means the Birmingham Road," translated Robert, grinning.

John pushed the pie and three of the coins to Edward. The boy took the pie and ate it greedily. He was clearly starving. Seconds later, he pocketed the coins, and John gave him the second pie, which vanished just as quickly as the first.

Minutes later, the three of them walked down the Rock, onto the Saltisford, and into the Birmingham Road. Edward led them over the canal bridge, before stopping at the gates to the White House, which John knew belonged to James Cooper.

Then he led them away from the gates and into a lane running by the side of the garden wall, and seconds later, pointed out the spot where the sabre had been found.

John dropped to his knees and began carefully pulling back the undergrowth and feeling around. It was still dark and his search was hampered by having to use the light from their lanterns. As it happened the lantern light was more than useful. By their light, John saw something glinting up at him. He pulled back some of the grass and found a pair of cavalry spurs.

"They could have been stolen, along with the sabre," said Robert, looking meaningfully at Edward.

"Yes, they could," agreed John. "But I am sure we would have heard about their loss by now."

Proving they were Thompson`s spurs and his sabre, would be almost impossible. But, it would be interesting, though, to see Pearson`s reaction when he was shown them.

John spent a few minutes studying the surrounding undergrowth, before looking studiously at the garden wall. He saw a tree growing the other side, with overhanging branches, none of which were within reach.

"Could you climb that wall?" asked John.

"Yes, if I had something to stand on."

"Such as a horse?"

"Such as a horse," agreed Robert.

"But, could you climb that wall wearing spurs and a sabre?"

"If I had to, but preferably not from choice."

"So, if these and the sabre were Thompson`s," continued John, pointing at the spurs. "He probably took them off to make his entry easier, and quieter, intending to collect them on his return."

"Only he never returned," emphasized the other officer.

"Only he never returned," repeated John.

Soon the three of them returned to the police station.

Several minutes after their return, a furious and worried Kate

Whiting forced her way into John's office. She had gone home only to find Edward was not there. Phoebe Morris had enjoyed telling how Edward had been seen being taken to the police station.

"You bastards!" she screamed. "I suppose you're beating him up like you did my poor Silas! If he's been thieving, I'll be the one to punish him, not you!"

Kate flew at John punching him on his chest. All kind thoughts about him had gone. He caught her wrists, actually enjoying the touch of this woman. She drew back her head to spit at him, and then bite his face, when she stopped, all her anger suddenly gone. The fight went out of her as she saw Edward.

Her son was sat at John's desk, eating a huge plateful of bread and meat. By his side was a mug of steaming tea. The boy was clearly unharmed, enjoying his breakfast and utterly amazed by his mother's outburst.

John let go of her wrists, almost reluctantly, and let her hug Edward. By now she was quietly weeping. Looking up at Robert, who still stood in the office doorway, but now clearly relaxing, John lifted his hand and shook it, indicating the need for a mug of tea for his sudden visitor. Robert nodded and quickly left the office.

When it arrived, John took her gently by the shoulders and led her to a chair. Suddenly she clung to him sobbing.

"I'm so sorry," she sobbed. "Please forgive me. I was so worried, I....." Her words were lost as she sobbed.

For a while John held her, again enjoying the experience, but shocked to feel how thin her body was. Yet, it felt like an electrical charge had run through his body as he held her. And, from the look on her face, it was clear she had experienced it as well. Robert gave a small smile and left the office. His Guv'nor certainly knew how to find attractive women.

When she finished sobbing and he had, reluctantly, released her, John explained what had happened, stressing Edward was not in any trouble. John looked at Edward, over her shoulder, and carefully winked at him as he explained how the boy was on his way to hand in the sabre at the police station.

As yet, she had not asked where the sabre had been found and Edward hoped his mother would forget about that. He did not want her to know the true circumstances behind his finding the weapon.

CHAPTER SIXTEEN

The Warrant

Once Kate and Edward Whiting had left the station, John settled down to some paperwork, although his thoughts lingered on her, and wondered how she came to be married to Silas. They seemed such an unlikely couple.

Finally, putting thoughts of Kate Whiting aside, he began to plan his visit to the White House, with Mathew Harrison, later that afternoon. He was unaware of the time, until Robert appeared with some post and Thomas Waldren.

"I can`t stop, John," said Thomas. "But I thought it only right to let you know Cooper has called for an emergency meeting of the Watch Committee for this afternoon. He`s almost certainly going to demand your services are dispensed with."

"Is he likely to get his own way?"

"Probably yes. You have some friends, but too many people are frightened of him, and will follow his lead."

John`s earlier optimism at the finding of the sabre and spurs began to dwindle. He was becoming more and more convinced Cooper was behind all his problems. It was not just the antagonism of the man, but John now felt he was heavily involved in the burglaries, and probably Thompson`s murder. But how could he prove it? Thomas left him mulling over these problems, and he began to open his post.

For the most part they were notices from other Forces, giving details of recent crimes, something Robert was very good at collating. However, the last envelope was handwritten, and addressed to him, in a fairly uneducated scrawl. He opened it up, and was not surprised it had no address or signature. on it.

For a moment he was tempted to throw it away, but then saw it was headed *The Missing Body*. The note was clearly made up of words cut from the Chronicle and pasted onto paper. He read on.

THE MISSING BODY
you will find it buried in James Cooper`s coach
house underneath his coach

Normally, John would ignore such letters, but this one might just provide the answer, he was hoping to find, and it tied in with the information Mathew had discovered. In any case, they would soon be at the White House and now had something else to look for. It might be a blessing Cooper would be at the Watch Committee meeting and not at home. His mood became buoyant again.

℃

St Mary`s Church clock was striking 2.0pm, when John and Mathew left the police station and started walking to James Cooper`s house. Secure in the knowledge, that Cooper would be at the Watch Committee meeting for a fair part of the afternoon, should give them time to execute their search warrant, before he returned. Both men were so engrossed in their thoughts, they failed to see the horse and gig slowly following them.

On arrival at the White House, they went to the front door and rang the bell. The door was opened by a liveried footman, who made no effort to disguise his contempt for the police officers.

"Tradesmen use the back," he snarled, beginning to close the door.

John had anticipated such a move and already had his foot in the doorway, stopping it from closing. "We are police officers, not tradesmen," he said. "We have come to see Mr Cooper."

Although John`s voice was cool and restrained, the footman was taken aback by the cold hard eyes staring back at him. His defiance collapsed.

"It`s no good forcing your way in here," he whined. "The master`s in town."

"That's not a problem. We'll speak to whoever is in charge. Would that be his butler? Please tell him we would like a word with him." John's voice was icily polite.

"No, it wouldn't be the butler!" came a new, but familiar voice.

"It's me." Charles Pearson appeared in the hallway. "What do you want?"

"I'm glad you're here," replied John. "I wonder, do you recognise these?"

Opening the case he was carrying, John took out the spurs he had found earlier that morning, and gave them to Pearson. Mathew watched Pearson's reaction intently. For a moment, it seemed as if he would refuse to look at them. His hands almost recoiled, as if they had been burned. Reluctantly he took them from John.

"Do you recognise these?" he asked mildly.

"No."

"Would you say they are military issue?"

"Probably."

"From your Regiment?"

"How the hell should I know?" snapped Pearson, starting to lose his temper. "And if you knew anything about the army, you'd know I couldn't possibly identify them."

"Even though you are wearing an identical pair?" John paused, and looked pointedly at Pearson's spurs.

The man said nothing.

"Thank you, major," he continued. "That will be all for now."

"How dare you dismiss me!" shouted Pearson, raising his fist. "You'll regret that remark."

John stood still, and looked the other man squarely in the eye. He was aware of Mathew stepping back a pace and reaching for his staff. For a moment Pearson stood undecided. Like Cooper, he too found there was something about this policeman that bothered him. The man was not afraid, and was probably quite experienced at looking after himself in a brawl. He lowered his fist and smiled. Not for him a street brawl. No, he had other ideas.

"Before I leave this town, I will teach you to respect your betters."

"You're welcome to try. Any time you wish."

"Ha! You think I mean a fight with our fists. I don't. I mean with

141

swords. I know they`re gentleman`s weapons, so I don`t suppose you will have the first idea of how to use one. It will be a pleasure to teach you."

"As you wish."

John watched Pearson walk away. "And now," he said to the footman. "The butler please."

The footman scurried off, leaving the two policemen in the hallway. Suddenly Mathew nudged John and pointed to the dresser in the hall. John saw there was a single brass candlestick on it. However, on the other end, nearest the window, there was a slightly darker shape, on the wooden surface, but with no candlestick on it. It clearly marked where another object had stood recently, and protected the wood from the sun.

The shape seemed to match the base of the candlestick which was back in John`s office. Also, the candlestick on the dresser, seemed identical to the one, now locked up in the police station. Yet another pointer towards Cooper`s guilt. Their thoughts were interrupted by the arrival of the butler, who was clearly not pleased to see them.

"We want to search the coach house," John announced without any preamble.

"Alright," came the grudging reply. "I hear you`ve got a warrant."

"By the way," John indicated the dresser. "Have you lost a candlestick?"

The butler shrugged. "I wouldn`t know. The master hasn`t told me anything. Anyway, what`s it got to do with you?"

"Just curious."

"Reid!" the butler called out into the yard and a groom appeared. "Take these men, to the coach house," he instructed.

John and Mathew followed him towards the coach house. On the way, Mathew asked, "Where`s Brutus, the dog today?"

"Around," came the non-committal answer.

"Funny," continued Mathew. "He`s normally not far away."

The groom would not be drawn into further conversation, but led them to the coach house, opened the doors and stood back. The building was on two levels: the lower one housed the carriage, which was not there, whilst the upper floor, was used for spare harness etc. The only windows were small and somewhere halfway up the walls. Straw and hay littered the floor.

The groom went to leave.

"No, you stay with us," commanded John.

"Alright. But I must just go and put the horse away and arrange for its feed."

"Be quick," commented John.

The groom left them, quietly closing the door behind him, darkening down the area. The only light now came from the windows.

"This is too easy, Guv`nor," said Mathew. "And isn`t it a mess in here. I wonder why Cooper doesn`t have it cleaned up?"

"I agree. Why the comments about Brutus?"

"He`s a nasty piece of work. I just hope he`s not lying in wait for us somewhere."

"There`s the where the carriage would stand and the brickwork underneath it looks freshly disturbed. Let`s have a look."

As they made their way to the coach, there came the sound of breaking glass. They spun round just in time to see a lit oil lamp falling from one of the now broken windows.

Mathew saw the answer to his earlier question. The lamp hit the floor and shattered, spreading oil onto the straw laden floor, which quickly caught light.

They began to stamp out the flames, but the lamp was followed by others. In a matter of seconds, the floor was ablaze and the flames were licking up the wooden walls, by now too intense to be stamped out. John and Mathew ran back to the doors and pushed, but they refused to open. They were trapped.

The windows were a possible means of escape, but without a ladder, it was impossible to climb up to them. Looking around, they saw no signs of a ladder or anything else they could climb. Likewise, there was nothing they could use for a battering ram on the doors. Already they were coughing and their eyes were smarting, from the smoke.

They were caught in a carefully planned trap.

"Mathew, a last try, together at the door."

The sergeant coughed a grunted reply. Both men knew it would be useless, and John cursed himself for having been so stupid. As Mathew had said, it had all been too easy, and now they knew why. He should have suspected a trap, not that it made any difference now, but it galled him to realise how Cooper and Pearson had tricked them so easily, and now they would win.

And, what hurt him more, was he would never really get to know Harriet. What a stupid, useless waste.

Both men hurled themselves at the doors, which surprisingly opened, and they fell through the gap and lay panting on the ground outside.

"For God`s sake move!" came a familiar, lovely female voice, with a slight colonial accent.

John thought he was dreaming as he saw Harriet through his streaming eyes.

"Move it! Damn you!" she ordered. "We`re all in danger here."

Mathew reacted first by picking up the now semi-conscious John and bundling him into Harriet`s gig, then he threw in the case containing the spurs, before climbing up alongside her.

"Drive!" she instructed, and gave him the reins.

Mathew obeyed and flicked the reins to make the horse move. He was not a moment too soon, as several of Cooper`s workers suddenly appeared. Patrick Monk was amongst them, brandishing a pitchfork. He grabbed the horse`s bridle.

"Not so fast, " he snarled. "You`re going nowh........OW!"

Monk recoiled as Mathew lashed out with the whip, which curled round Monk`s shoulders. "Let go!" he shouted.

For a moment, Monk hesitated, then made another grab for the horse, but pulled up short. A revolver had suddenly appeared in Harriet`s hand and was pointing, unwaveringly at his face.

"Get back," she snarled. "Or I shoot. And, believe me, I know how to use this."

Monk laughed loudly and raised the pitchfork like a spear.

"You`re all going nowhere, except back into that fire. But, we`ll have some fun with you first, missy." He leered at Harriet.

She fired and the pitchfork was split in two by the bullet. The other men stood back. Reid the groom, now grabbed the bridle. Harriet fired again and he fell back screaming, nursing a shattered hand. Another man lunged at Mathew and started to climb onto the carriage. The big sergeant kicked him hard in the face.

"There`s only three of them!" shouted Monk.

"But she`s got a gun," came a shouted reply.

"And soon be out of ammunition," called another man. At the same time, he jumped onto the carriage and grabbed at Harriet.

She lowered her pistol and fired. He fell back screaming, holding his shattered knee. The other men hesitated.

Harriet's pistol was a five shot weapon and she only had two bullets left. Monk lunged forward again towards the horse. Mathew lashed out hard with the whip. It was a good aim and the thong cut deeply into Monk's face, splitting his nose, cheeks and ears. He would be scarred for life. Monk screamed and fell back, clutching at his heavily bleeding face.

Seeing Monk fall backwards took most of the fight out of the others. As they fell back, Mathew flicked the reins, cracked the whip and the horse moved off, straight into a brisk trot. One man made a half-hearted attempt to stop the animal, but changed his mind when he saw Mathew raise the whip again.

Just as the horse broke into a canter down the drive, another man appeared in front of them, armed with a scythe which he waved about violently, without giving ground. Mathew felt the horse falter slightly and knew if it suddenly veered away from the scythe, it could well upset the gig. He was too far in front from him to reach with the whip.

"Don't stop," called Harriet and took careful aim.

She fired and the man stared in disbelief as the scythe blade parted from the shaft and flew harmlessly onto the lawn. Seizing the moment, Mathew urged the horse into a gallop, knocking the scythe man over as he tried to get out of the way. Then they were down the drive and out into the road. Looking behind them, Mathew could see no signs of any pursuit, so he slowed the animal to a trot.

"I don't think they will follow us into town," he said. "How's the Guv'nor?"

Harriet looked onto the floor of the carriage, and was relieved to John starting to stir.

"He's starting to wake up," she chuckled. "Now that all the hard work's been done."

&

Ten minutes later, Mathew pulled up outside Thomas Waldren's house, at almost the same time he arrived with William Slattery. They had both come from the Watch Committee meeting. Several passers-by stopped and stared, as they saw John being helped into the doctor`s house They also noticed Mathew`s scorched uniform, singed hair and sooty face. It would soon be all round the town.

Once inside the house, Redman quickly appeared and organised bowls of hot water and a large pot of tea. Harriet refused to leave the two policemen. Mathew explained to Thomas and Slattery what had happened. By now John had regained consciousness, but was still in a state of shock, as he realised how close to death they had been.

Harriet admitted to having followed them to the White House, really out of nosiness, or so she said. What she would not admit to was an inner fear John might have made a mistake, underestimated Cooper and just might be glad of her help.

"If it hadn`t been for Mrs Foxton," Mathew took up the story. "We`d be dead by now. I just don`t know how to thank you enough, ma`am."

"Mathew," she chided. "After fighting together, we`re comrades--in-arms and can dispense with formalities." She touched him gently on the arm. "Don`t you ever dare call me Mrs Foxton or ma`am again. I shall always be Harriet to you from now on. Agreed?"

"Certainly, Harriet. But, rest assured, I will be your devoted servant for life."

For a fleeting second, John felt a pang of jealousy, but quickly dismissed it. Harriet was that sort of person. They left Thomas`s surgery and were standing in the hall, when there came a furious knocking on the front door, with a continuous ringing of the bell.

CHAPTER SEVENTEEN

Later

"I wonder who that can be?" mused Thomas. "As if we don`t know. He can just wait a while. Take your time Redman, you know what to do with this sort of visitor. Let us get into my study first."

When Redman finally opened the door, he was met by a furious James Cooper and Major Pearson. "Can I help you gentlemen?" he asked, keeping the bulk of his body behind the door.

"Get out the damned way!" shouted Cooper. "I know Mayfield and your master are here."

As Cooper pushed, Redman stepped to one side suddenly, and the door flew open. Cooper stumbled inside, fighting hard to keep his balance. Finally, he steadied himself and stopped short. Even Pearson stopped.

Inside the hall stood several of Thomas and Sarah`s servants, each armed with a club, poker or heavy saucepan. Both men saw the hard, stern look on their faces.

They looked at each other knowing, technically, they were intruders and the servants would be entirely in their rights to use whatever force was necessary to eject them. Thomas appeared from his study.

"What`s problem, gentlemen?" he asked, but made no move to dismiss the servants. "I would remind you that you are guests in my house, albeit I didn`t invite you in. Now, how can I help you?"

For a moment Cooper said nothing then his face went red.

"It`s Mayfield I want!" he shouted.

"Please don`t raise your voice, in my house, or I`ll have my servants throw you out. Also, as a doctor, I should advise you to calm down or you`ll have an apoplexy."

Pearson stretched his hand out and took hold of Cooper's wrist. "Easy, James," he cautioned. "Perhaps we could have a few words with Mayfield?" he continued, now looking at Thomas.

"Gentlemen," wheezed John, appearing from the study, still suffering from the effects of inhaling smoke. He was followed by Mathew, Slattery and Harriet.

"What the devil do you mean by burning down my coach house and attacking my workers?" hissed Cooper, struggling to keep himself in control.

"I think you will find, it was the other way round. We were locked in the coach house, which was deliberately set alight by your men. Luckily we were rescued by Mrs Foxton. Otherwise someone would be facing a charge of murder."

He paused and stared straight at Cooper and Pearson.

Cooper faltered. "Even if that were true, which I dispute, why did you shoot my men when they tried to help you? I demand an answer."

"That's just it," replied John. "They wanted to put us back in the blaze. Your man, Monk, particularly. I shall enjoy interviewing him very soon. I'm sure a chance for him to turn Queen's Evidence will enable us to get to the bottom of the mystery."

"And that wasn't all they wanted to do to me, before I joined these policemen in the blaze," added Harriet very quietly.

Cooper tried to ignore her, but was clearly bothered by her sincerity and what Monk might say. He knew she would make a very credible witness in court, and that was the last thing he wanted.

"I demand compensation for the damage and my men's injuries, And, if I don't get it, we'll come into town and take it ourselves." Cooper wagged his right index finger at John, emphasizing his threats.

"Please do, Mr Cooper," smiled John. "I would like nothing better than for you to do that. It would be considered an armed rising, against the forces of law and order. Then I could call out the Yeomanry and also go to the barracks for regular troops, and put the town under martial law. The people of Warwick would never forgive you for that."

"He can't do that, can he?" Cooper turned to Pearson, suddenly no longer so sure of himself.

"No, er no," came the uncertain reply.

"I`m afraid you`re out of touch, if you think that, major. I have a special authority to do so, if necessary, signed by the Home Secretary. Surely you know about these regulations? Your own Regiment would have been involved in a similar arrangement. Have you been away from your depot for so long? I really do find it hard to believe you are not aware of these arrangements."

John was enjoying himself. Pearson was faltering and clearly very uncomfortable, which made Cooper hesitant at not getting the support he needed. It made a change to have the opposition wrong-footed.

"Good day, gentlemen," announced Thomas. "I`ve got work to do, even if you haven`t. Show them out, please Redman."

"With pleasure, sir. This way, gentlemen, if you please."

After Cooper and Pearson left, Harriet began to tremble as reaction to the afternoon`s adventures set in. John and Thomas helped her into the drawing room and sat her near the fire. Mathew draped a blanket round her. Whilst this was going on, Slattery bade his farewells and left the house.

"Before you go, John," said Thomas. "A quiet word."

With a sinking heart, John knew it would not be good news. He suspected it was about the Watch Committee meeting, and he was right.

"Cooper and his cronies wanted you gone today. But, he met with some opposition: more than he bargained for. However, the Committee will meet again on Monday, and they will want results. If not, then I think the vote will go against you. Are you having any luck?"

"Not as much as I would like. But it will be interesting to hear what Monk has to say after this afternoon."

John and Mathew left soon afterwards. In his case, along with the spurs, John now had a warrant for the arrest of Patrick Monk.

꙳

On arriving back at the police station, John found Robert Andrew who had just come on duty. Elijah Snow was there as well, hoping to go off duty. He was not at all keen to carry on working for a while longer, and started to complain,

One look at both John and Mathew`s stern, burned faces, quickly made him change his mind. John handed over the warrant to Robert, and instructed the two officers to go to the *Bull`s Head*, in West Street, where Monk lodged, and arrest him.

Whilst John did not approve of police officers having lodgings in public houses, he could do nothing about it, whilst still lodging at the *Woolpack* himself. It was about time his quarters were finished, although, he mused silently, it will probably not matter soon. He took Mathew into his office to discuss the afternoon`s events.

"Before we start, Guv`nor," said Mathew. "We have a problem. Cooper seems to know every move we make."

"I know. They were waiting for us this afternoon. I didn`t mention any warrant and neither did you. Yet the butler knew we had one. So who knew we were going to pay Cooper a visit?"

"Us two, no other constables. Possibly Andrew might have realized after you found the spurs, and were sent that message, but I doubt it. Also, Pearson was clearly caught unawares when you showed him the spurs. No, I can`t see Andrew being the one."

"What about Perkins and Snow?"

"Snow hasn`t got the wit to understand what`s happening. Perkins? I don`t know. He seems a good enough lad to me. And, it was thanks to him, the candlestick was recovered. No, I can`t see it being him."

"That leaves Monk."

"A possibility, but where would he get the information? Your office is locked when you`re not here. I`ve got the only spare key." Mathew paused. "But, I suppose, as Cooper`s men are carrying out the building work, they could have had other spare keys cut. I`ll look into that in the morning."

"If it isn`t Monk, then who? I suppose there`s always Thomas Waldren`s servants or even Slattery`s come to that. After all, it was Slattery who gave me the warrant."

"Could it be either of them?"

"I don`t think so." But the thought disturbed John. "Anyway, after this afternoon`s battle, which apparently I missed, I think we can dismiss Harriet, your comrade-in-arms, from our list of suspects, can`t we?" teased John, raising his eyebrows quizzically.

Mathew blushed.

"But, nevertheless," continued John, "I refrained from talking too much about the case to Dr Waldren, this afternoon, although he was keen to know what was happening."

"There's also the anonymous letter," said Mathew, changing the subject. "That was just too convenient, and had to come from someone who knew what we were planning."

"I'm afraid that someone at Cooper's house wants me dead. That means we're getting close and bothering them. I think you can rest assured, it's not you, but me they want. You just happened to be with me at the wrong time."

"Forgive me for asking, Guv'nor, but do you really have a signed authority from the Home Secretary to call out the military?"

"What do you think?" grinned John, which he quickly regretted as it made his burnt face hurt.

Mathew looked at him with fresh respect. There was a lot to this Londoner. He hoped the Watch Committee would see sense and keep him. They would struggle to find a replacement anything like him.

"Didn't it rattle Pearson?" he chuckled.

Both men laughed, in spite of the pain it caused them.

❧

Meanwhile, in his lodgings at the *Bull's Head,* Patrick Monk was in extreme discomfort. He knew it could only be a matter of time before Mayfield came looking for him. If it hadn't been for that red-headed bitch coming on the scene, Mayfield would be dead. Harrison would have been a bonus and his appointment as the next superintendent would have been assured.

Instead of which, he had fallen greatly out of favour with his real employer, and had a painfully split face to endure. And, where was the money Cooper had promised him? His face would not stop bleeding and he knew he had to find a doctor of sorts, or just anyone who could fix it for him.

He realized any such treatment would cause him a lot of pain and money, plus he would be marked for life. Nobody in Warwick would dare to touch him and he had the feeling Cooper's empire was collapsing. So, it was a good time to be leaving Warwick, but one day, he would return.

When he did, then Mathew Harrison would wish he had never been born. And as for that red-headed bitch, he would really enjoy sorting her out, when she didn`t have a pistol or whip to hand. His thoughts were interrupted, when he heard a gentle sound outside his door.

Quickly picking up his pistol from the table, he pulled the cover round on his lamp, putting the room into total darkness. The door was already bolted, so he sat still and waited.

"Monk? Monk? Are you in there?" came a welcome and familiar voice. "Open up. I`ve got some money for you, and a horse round the back of the inn."

Relief flooded through Monk. It was like the answer to a prayer. Gladly, he opened the door.

❦

Snow and Robert were walking down West Street to the *Bull`s Head.* "Why we`ve got to arrest him?" Snow queried in a loud voice. "Ain`t he one of us?"

"Shush. Lower your voice, man," hissed Robert. "We don`t want him to hear us."

A few minutes later they arrived at the inn. Being unsure of where the landlord`s loyalties lay, Robert decided not to run any risk of him alerting Monk.

"Why ain`t we going to the landlord first?" queried Snow, loudly.

Patiently Robert explained, as they crept by the door to the taproom, and went quietly up the stairs. At the top, Robert tried the handle, of Monk`s door, gently, but it remained closed. Clearly it had been locked and probably bolted.

"Why don`t we just knock?" queried Snow, banging loudly on the door. "Patrick, are you in there?" he shouted.

Robert Andrew shook his head in disbelief. Was this man really so stupid, or was it an act? Either way, forcing the door open would be a waste of time. Monk would have long gone, assuming he had been there in the first place. Grabbing Snow by the arm he led him downstairs and out into the street.

Jerry Carter, the landlord, watched them go, with a smirk on his face. Did they really think he hadn`t heard them, especially after the noise Snow made.

It was an angry Robert Andrew who returned to the police station. He had left Snow to go off duty and went to see John. Briefly he explained what had happened. John sighed, both in exasperation and tiredness.

"Go and get some rest, Guv`nor," insisted Mathew. "We`ll get the inn watched and have Monk the moment he returns."

"I suspect our bird will have flown," said John unhappily.

"Guv`nor," insisted Mathew. "Leave it to us. If there`s no sign of him by the morning, I`ll arrange for his room to be searched."

Gratefully, John left the station and walked across to the *Woolpack,* hoping to be able to access his room without being seen, but he was out of luck. They must have been waiting for him to cross the Market Place.

As he entered the *Woolpack,* he found a large reception party waiting for him. The story of the *Battle of the White House*, as it was now being called, had spread everywhere. John, Mathew and Harriet were the toast and talk of the town. The reception party all burst into a round of cheering and clapping when they saw him. Protesting, he was bundled into the tap room and supplied with several glasses of mulled wine.

When he finally escaped to his room, John collapsed in an exhausted and partly inebriated state on his bed, and fell into a dreamless sleep. Sometime during the night, he woke, undressed and climbed into bed, and fell asleep again.

℘

When he crossed the Market Place, John had not noticed Kate Whiting watching from the shadows. Like everybody else, she had heard about the *Battle* and was relieved, for more than one reason, that John had escaped relatively unharmed.

If she was honest with herself, that was her main reason for hanging about by the *Woolpack*. She needed to see for herself, that he was well. To be fair, she considered him vital to her plan, if tonight was to be successful. Had he been killed or seriously hurt, she would not have known where to go.

Kate hardly knew John, yet she trusted him. Her instincts had been greatly reinforced when Edward told her the full story of what had happened that morning. When she saw her son eating a hearty meal,

153

Kate regretted having attacked John.

On the other hand, though, she had enjoyed the comfort of his strong embrace and the concern he had shown her. When she heard the great roar of cheering which greeted his arrival, in the *Woolpack*, Kate would have given anything to have shared it with him.

Yet, she knew it could never be, and he was rumoured to be sweet on Dr Waldren`s niece, who had apparently saved his life that afternoon. Kate knew she stood no chance. If only she had been the one to have saved John`s life. One day, perhaps she might be in with a chance? But it would all be in the lap of the Gods. Secure in the knowledge John was safe, Kate returned home, where Edward awaited her.

Persuading him to help her burgle Cooper`s house, had been easier than she had anticipated. She had convinced him, the book she wanted from Cooper`s house, would help his father, and Edward was only too happy to be doing something with his ma, even if it was illegal. After all, it would not be the first time he had done something similar, not that she knew anything about that.

It was long past midnight, as the two of them crept up the drive to the White House. There was still a smell of smoke lingering from the smouldering ruins of the coach house, and for a few moments Kate imagined what it had been like during the *Battle*.

Quietly she led the way across the lawn, to the study window, and listened for several minutes before accepting the house was all quiet. Taking a knife out of her pocket, she quietly opened the window again, and pulled the curtains back

Next Kate gave Edward the small lantern she carried. "You know what you`re looking for?" she whispered. "It`s a small notebook, with a dark cover."

"Yes ma. We`ve been over it a thousand times."

Edward was impatient. Unlike most children from his background, he could read and write, as Kate had taught him. Seconds later, he was through the window and into Cooper`s study.

Kate had told him the book would probably be on the desk, or if not, in one of the drawers. The desk top was littered with papers. James Cooper was not a tidy man, added to which, servants were only allowed into the room to light and clear out the fire. Sometimes, he did not go into the room for days at a time. Hopefully this would be the case.

Edward tried to take care, as he had been told, and to make as little mess as possible, but in his haste, he knocked some papers off the desk. Bending to pick them up, he noticed a small notebook amongst them, which he quickly picked it up and took back to his ma. Kate thumbed through it quickly. It was what she wanted.

She knew the notebook contained all the latest details of the special deliveries Cooper had received, from all over the country. These always came to his house, often late at night, and were always bulky. Whenever they were expected, Kate was instructed to wait upstairs, or go home.

But it had not stopped her watching what was happening. Whilst unsure of why they were delivered at such late times, she could only assume Cooper was involved in some form of criminal activity.

Cooper was a foundry man, so why was he accepting all these deliveries, which were clearly not connected to his trade? She had heard him talk about them being gold and silver, and wondered what he was doing with them. Sometime after several such deliveries, they vanished, usually round about the time he ran a special night shift at the foundry.

Once she recognized Ezra Crane, the carrier, making a delivery, late one night. Instead of going straight home, as instructed, she had watched from behind some trees as three travelling trunks had been unloaded and taken into the house. Nobody had goods delivered so late, without a very good reason. Her time with Cooper had been spent wisely, if not pleasantly.

She waited for Edward to put the papers back on the desk. When he returned to the window, she had a sudden idea and instructed him to carry out one more little task. Puzzled he returned to the desk and took a single piece of writing paper and an envelope from it. As he did so, they both heard a key turn in the study door.

Kate froze with fright. To have got this far and now be caught was so unfair. If only she hadn`t asked Edward to go back for the writing paper, this wouldn`t have happened. All she could do was wait and see, knowing she was too far away, and on the other side of the window to physically help her son. She felt sick.

Edward reacted first, and slid down behind the back of an armchair. Kate began to mentally praise him for his quick thinking, but stopped in horror as she saw he had left the still lit lantern on the desk. Whoever came in, could not fail to see it. Just as the door started to open, Edward remembered it. Creeping quietly out to the desk, he took the lantern and slipped back behind the chair. He was only just in time.

Cooper`s butler entered the study, holding a candle. They watched him cross to the table alongside the bookcase, put his candle down, and take a glass from his pocket, which he placed next to it. Selecting a decanter of port from the table, he poured himself a generous measure, before replacing the stopper, and putting it back.

The butler turned to the desk and raised the glass in a mock toast.

"Your very best health, Mr bloody Cooper," he said quietly. "After today, I think your days here are numbered. And I shall be gone in the morning."

He put the glass down and started to systematically search all through Cooper`s desk. Kate heard the occasional chink of coins and smiled quietly to herself. But, her smile stopped as he went across to the armchair. For a moment she thought he had seen Edward, but instead, the butler sat in the chair.

"Yes, Mr Cooper!" he muttered. "No, Mr Cooper! Certainly, Mr Cooper! with pleasure, Mr Cooper!"

The man was clearly drunk.

After what seemed an eternity, the butler finished his drink, and returned to the table. For a moment he clearly toyed with the idea of having another.

"Please don`t," Kate prayed silently. She followed it with a "thank you," as he left the study, locking the door behind him. When his footsteps faded, she whispered "Edward!"

He needed no second urging and returned to the window, and gave her the paper and envelope. Seconds later she had helped him back through, into the garden. After drawing the curtains, she closed the window. Then taking Edward`s hand, they both ran lightly across the lawn, onto the drive and back home.

Having seen Edward safely in bed, Kate penned a small note on the paper and put it in the envelope, which she addressed, in her best handwriting, to Superintendent Mayfield. She argued, to herself, if the letter was on quality paper, he would be more likely to heed its contents. If it went on cheap paper, he would probably ignore it. It was imperative he was given the notebook, but she had to give it to him and him alone.

Satisfied her son was finally asleep, she crept out of their room and went into the town centre. Very few people were about as she tiptoed to the police station, pushed the letter underneath the door, and was gone.

It would be a long day of nervous waiting.

CHAPTER EIGHTEEN

At The Bull`s Head

A crisp frosty morning greeted John as he staggered out of bed, dressed and made his way to the police station. Unlike the previous day, the thoughts of any food just did not appeal. His head and face throbbed, not only from the burns, and his stomach did not feel too good.

Samuel Perkins jumped to attention as John entered. He had heard about the party for the Guv`nor last night, and one look at his superintendent`s face, confirmed all he needed to know. John clearly had a large hangover.

"All correct, guv`nor," he said in a quiet voice.

"Thank you," said John, grinning ruefully.

"I heard. Tea?"

A few minutes later, having drunk a large mug of Samuel`s tea, John began to feel better and his mouth felt less like a sandpit. He looked idly at his paperwork and saw there was quite an expensive envelope, addressed to him, in fine handwriting. Clearly it had been sent to him by a female. Curious, he was about to open it, when Samuel appeared.

"Snow`s come on duty, now," he said. "I was instructed by Sergeant Harrison to try Monk`s lodgings again, and make an entry this time."

"I suspect he`s long since gone, but it`s worth a try."

Together with Snow, Samuel went down to the *Bull`s Head*. Jerry Carter, was sweeping the front doorstep, and looked up as the two constables approached.

"He`s gone," Jerry said, looking back at his sweeping and grinning.

"Who's gone?" asked Samuel, apparently innocently.

"Why your man, Monk, that's who." Carter sneered at the young officer. Clearly he was not much more than a child. They'd have no trouble with him.

"When was that?"

"Sometime before 'im," he indicated Snow. "And the other crusher came last night."

"Why didn't you tell us then?" asked Snow.

"You didn't ask. And even if you 'ad, I wouldn't have told you."

"Tell me," asked Samuel. "Am I right in thinking this establishment is actually owned by James Cooper?"

"Well, so what? I pays 'im my rent on time. So I do what 'e tells me. Minds me own business. Does you ma know you're out?" he sniggered. "Now you can bugger off!"

"I don't think so," snapped Samuel. "I've got a warrant, so we will have a look in Monk's room."

"I don't give a stuff for your warrant. Now bugger off!" Carter's voice rose and two men came out of the inn to see what was happening.

"Having trouble Jerry?" asked one. "Well, if it ain't Mr Crusher who told me what to do in me own boat."

Samuel recognised George Kent, the Castle boatman from their day on the river. The boatman now moved towards him with his right hand gripped round a cudgel. Another man followed him, with a similar weapon. Jerry Carter joined them waving his brush.

"I said bugger off," he repeated.

"I'm going to enjoy this," smirked Kent. "After the trouble he gave me the other day. Let me have him first."

Carter and the other man grinned and bowed mockingly and indicated Kent to come forward. He obliged grinning maliciously and smacking his left hand with the cudgel. "I'm going to enjoy this, crusher. I'll teach you a lesson you'll never forget."

Snow backed away and Samuel was not surprised to find he was on his own, as he waited for Kent to reach him. By now a few people had gathered to watch the fun. But, when they came to talk about it later, none of them could be absolutely sure what happened: it had all been so quick.

The boatman ran at Samuel with his cudgel raised, and brought it down heavily towards the officer's head. But it never landed, and

Kent found his arm parried by Samuel. Before he knew what happened, his arm was twisted round, far up his back until it was nearly dislocated from his shoulder. Even as Kent screamed in pain, he felt his legs kicked away from under him, and he fell heavily on the ground, and offered no further resistance. Snow gave him a hefty kick in the ribs.

The second man was nearly upon Samuel, when he saw what had happened. He faltered, for a moment, which gave Samuel the chance he needed. Ducking under the swinging cudgel he brought his knee up hard into his attacker`s testicles. The man screamed and sank towards the ground. Before he got there, Samuel kneed him hard in the face, breaking his nose and splitting his lips. He fell to the ground, unconscious, beside the now quietly moaning boatman.

"No!" instructed Samuel, as he saw Snow going to kick the injured man. Then he turned his attention to Jerry Carter. "Come on. What are you waiting for? It`s different now, without your mates, isn`t it?" Samuel invited Carter to approach with his right hand.

The landlord turned very pale and dropped the broom. He had seen this baby-faced boy around for some time, and laughed when Samuel joined the police. So did many other people. After what had just happened, they would never laugh at him again.

"You`d better come in," he said, in a subdued voice.

Carter led the way upstairs and stopped outside Monk`s room.

"Open it!" commanded Samuel. Any chance for a surprise entry, had long since vanished after the brawl downstairs.

Carter tried the handle. "It`s locked."

"I can see that. Don`t you have a key?"

"Yes." Carter produced a key, which he put in the lock and turned.

At the same time Samuel turned the handle and pushed. The door did not open. "It`s clearly bolted from the inside," he said. "We`ll have to force it."

"No," pleaded Carter, thinking of the damage it would cause. "I`ve got a ladder. You can get in through the window. The catch is easily opened."

A few minutes later, Samuel climbed up the ladder to the window outside Monk`s room. Peering through the glass, he nearly fell off the ladder in shock, as Monk`s bloated and lifeless face, stared back at him.

Samuel prised open the window and climbed inside. Carefully, avoiding Monk`s hanging body, he pulled back the bolt and opened the door.

"Send someone, to the police station," he instructed Carter. "Get Mr Mayfield here now. Tell him there`s a body."

As he spoke, Carter and Snow peered over his shoulder, into the room. Samuel heard Carter gasp in horror.

"Oh God," cried Snow, and promptly vomited over the stairs.

❧

Back in the police station, John had put the letter on one side, having decided to open it, once he heard how the search for Monk had progressed. He knew there was little chance of the man still being in town, which was a pity. Monk could have told them a lot, especially with the threat of the gallows hanging over him It was amazing how such a threat tended to loosen people`s tongues.

Whilst he waited, John began to write up his notes for the past day, including the anonymous letter. It would be nice to know who had sent it, but he knew the chances of discovering the identity of the writer were remote.

His writing was interrupted by a furious knocking on the charge office counter. For a moment, he wondered where Samuel was, and then remembered. Putting down his pen, he went to investigate. On entering the charge office, he saw a thin man, perspiring heavily.

"You`re wanted by your men at the *Bull`s Head,* right away. There`s a body."

Inwardly John groaned. That was all he wanted. Who had Monk killed now? he thought. Stopping only long enough to collect his hat and lock up the station, he followed after the messenger, who had now vanished and went towards the *Bull`s Head.* He soon became aware of other people hurrying in the same direction.

When he arrived, he found a large crowd had already gathered outside the inn. They parted on his arrival, and he saw two men lying on the pavement, being assisted to their feet, although nobody seemed too bothered about them. When he saw Snow in the doorway of the inn, the man was beckoning him towards the inn. John went across. "What`s happened?" he asked, pointing to the two men.

"They attacked Sam and me, but I sorted them out."

John stared at him in amazement. Somehow, what Snow had just said, did not ring true. His nose detected the smell of vomit and he was not surprised to see stains on Snow's uniform.

"What's going on?" he asked again.

"Can you come up, Guv'nor?" called Samuel, from upstairs. "But it ain't pleasant."

John quickly climbed up the stairs, carefully stepping over a pile of vomit, which he rightly assumed had come from Snow. Samuel stood outside the closed door.

"Before you go in Guv'nor," he said. "I was responsible for those two outside. They, and Carter here, went for me," he pointed at the ashen faced and subdued landlord. "So I had to defend myself."

"Snow's just told me he hit them, and I must admit I found it hard to believe."

Samuel told him quickly what had happened, and Carter nodded in agreement. "But that wasn't why I called you. That's in there." He indicated Monk's room.

"Is it Monk?"

"Yes," nodded Samuel. "It looks like he's topped himself, but, yet....it doesn't feel right."

"Let's take a look," said John, pushing open the door and entering the room.

Monk now lay on his back, facing the ceiling. Hanging from the beam was a piece of rope, which John saw was attached to the door handle. The other part of the rope, which had been tied around Monk's throat, had been cut, and the noose, such as it was, loosened from the body's throat, now lay around the Monk's shoulders. He was clearly dead. John looked at the body and then at Samuel, pointing at the noose.

"I loosened it, after I cut him down," confirmed Samuel. "Just in case there was any chance he was still alive." He shook his head. "But he was well dead. I've sent for Dr Waldren to confirm it."

John nodded. "What's the problem?" he asked, not so much to confirm his own views, which agreed with Samuel's, but to test what was worrying the young officer.

"On the face of it," replied Samuel, chewing his bottom lip. "It looks like he's topped himself. The door was locked and bolted from the inside. When I looked through the window, the body was hanging. Yet, when I opened the door, it`s feet touched the floor."

He had not liked Monk, and even now was not prepared to give the body a name.

"Then there`s this," he pointed to a stool, lying on the floor. "I get the impression he had stood on it and then jumped, pushing the stool over as he did so."

John said nothing, and just listened to Samuel, having the same doubts. The whole scenario was not quite right. It was too simple and convenient. He waited as Samuel continued.

"I`m not convinced he stood on it. Looking at the body as I found it, the stool just didn`t seem high enough. The rope`s just too short." He paused. "And there`s another thing."

"Go on."

"We had a hanging in the stables where I worked, only a few months ago. The man had clawed at the rope, whilst he was dying, as if trying to pull it away from his throat. There`s no such signs of Monk having done that."

"I think you`re right. Let`s put it to the test."

John took the noose off Monk`s throat and pulled the other part over the beam, and on to the floor. Going to the door, he opened it and instructed Jerry Carter to find him some string. Snow was instructed to go with the landlord.

Minutes later, Snow and Carter returned and handed the string to John, who took it and ordered Carter to wait outside. Snow went to leave with him.

"Not you!" instructed John. "You stay here!"

Snow came reluctantly back into the room, carefully avoiding looking at Monk. John took the string and used it to tie the two pieces of rope together. The join would not have taken any weight, but it served to join the pieces of rope together without altering its original length.

Next he stood the stool upright. Standing on it, Samuel looped the rope over the beam, so that it dangled on the far side of the supporting beam, where he had seen it originally.

"Stand on the stool and put the noose over your head," John instructed Snow.

"You can`t do this to me…………" cried Snow and he began to shake.

"You stupid sod!" hissed Samuel. "Mr Mayfield`s not going to hang you. Not that it wouldn`t be a good idea. You`re the same height as Monk and we want to see where the noose comes."

"In any case," added John. "Because of the damage, the rope wouldn`t bear your weight."

"More`s the pity," both he and Samuel muttered silently.

Still trembling, Snow climbed carefully onto the stool. The noose hung about six inches above his head. There was no way Monk could have stood on that stool in order to hang himself.

John crossed to the door. "Get off the stool and stand by it," he ordered.

Once Snow had done so, John opened the door. The noose fell nearly well down to Snow`s shoulders.

"You`re right, Samuel," said John. "There`s no way he could have hanged himself. This is a murder! The rope was too short. It had to have been tied to the door, before it was closed. When it was, the rope pulled Monk up off the floor and killed him. And the stool was placed to make us think he had jumped off it."

Suddenly the realization hit him.

Another murder! Two within the week and this time, one of his own men! This must certainly mean the end of his policing career. He wondered if the Metropolitan Police would have him back. Possibly, but he would have to start all over again as a constable. Nobody else would want to employ a failed superintendent. Surely, his appointment would have been for the shortest time on record.

"But Guv`nor," Samuel interrupted his thoughts. "How was he in a bolted room, which was closed from the inside?"

John snapped back into life. Suddenly he was back in London, at a murder scene he had attended several months ago, in an almost identical situation. He went across to the door and examined the bolt, which was a wooden one, complete with a knob enabling it to slide across into a socket.

Next he examined the way the door sat in its frame.

The *Bull`s Head* was an old building, and the door had long since dried out, and shrunk over time. This left a gap between the way the door fitted into its frame.

"Watch!" he instructed.

Taking some of the string he had not used on the rope, John looped it round the knob on the bolt, and carefully threaded the two loose ends through the door. Keeping the string tight, he went outside, taking it with him and carefully closing the door behind him.

Samuel and Snow watched, in amazement, as the bolt was slid home, by the string, which John was pulling from the other side of the door. When it was closed, John released one end and pulled it back through the gap in the door frame. Moments later, Samuel pulled back the bolt and opened the door.

"That`s how it was done," announced John triumphantly. "Now to find out who did it."

"I think Mr Carter can probably help us there," stated Samuel.

"He said he saw Monk leave his room, sometime before Snow got here last night. If he saw someone, it can`t have been Monk. It was more likely to be his murderer. I think he has some explaining to do."

John waited for the arrival of Dr Waldren, whilst Samuel and Snow took Carter off to the police station.

CHAPTER NINETEEN

Later

Thomas had been late arriving at the Bull's Head, and could not stay too long. He confirmed Monk was dead, but agreed the body needed a much closer examination, which he would carry out later that morning. John escorted the body back to Thomas's laboratory and went through its clothing. He was not surprised to find all the pockets were empty. Thomas arrived soon after noon, and together they examined Monk's body.

Unlike most bodies he had seen, and dealt with, John had no feelings at all for Monk. Once before he had been obliged to deal with a dead colleague, which had upset him, because he knew the man. But, it was not so with Monk. If he felt anything at all, it was a mixture of anger and despair, because the dead man had known what was happening, and might just have been persuaded to talk, or even turn Queen's Evidence.

He had, in fact, been John's only hope of succeeding and keeping his job, both of which, now seemed further away than ever. Time was running out for him, and he desperately needed some of the luck which was currently avoiding him. Surely his luck must change soon.

From examining Monk, Thomas confirmed he had died from strangulation, which was undoubtedly caused by the hanging. He, too, was concerned by the lack of any finger marks around the throat, caused by a last minute trying to remove the rope. The inference was Monk had been unconscious when he had been pulled up on the rope.

With the state of Monk's face and head, caused by the whipping given him by Mathew, it was impossible to see if there were any other later injuries. Possibly the man had been drugged, but he would need time to examine and analyse the contents of Monk`s stomach.

John shared a pie and a mug of tea with Thomas and returned to duty. He was glad, yet also sorry to discover Harriet was out with Sarah, knowing he was not good company just at the moment. Harriet was out helping with one of her aunt`s charitable works.

It was early afternoon before John was able to return to the station. He groaned on seeing the pile of paper, waiting for him on his desk. Before he could even look at it, Snow barged into his office, demanding to see him He did not even bother to knock.

"I don`t want anymore," he said, without any preamble.

"Any more what?"

"This job. Nobody told me it were dangerous and I`d `ave to deal with stiffs."

John looked at him hard. The man should never have been appointed in the first place.

"Me missus wants me to finish it now. She`s scared I could be killed next. So, I`m finishing. Now."

"Then go!" snapped John, letting his temper get the better of him. "You`re no use to man nor beast and should never have been appointed. You`ll get paid for what you`ve done, but not a penny more. And, I want your uniform back here within the hour."

Snow was amazed by John`s vehement response: it was not what he had expected. He had hoped John would have pleaded with him to stay. If so, Snow would have agreed, but not immediately. His instructions from Cooper had been specific....just keep undermining Mayfield`s confidence. Suddenly, he realised he was now without a job.

"Perhaps I might have been a bit hasty."

"There`s no way I`m having you back. I`ll leave you to explain to Mr Cooper why you have let him down."

Snow gulped. He had not thought about Cooper`s reaction. "Can`t you....." he began.

"NO!" interrupted John. "Just get out and remember to bring your uniform back. If I see you in it after the next hour, you will be arrested and taken before the court. Now get out!"

His eyes bored into Snow`s face, who now realized he had seriously underestimated the man from London. Cooper had said he would be a push over.

"Just unsettle him by making out you want to leave," he had said. "He`ll be desperate to have you back."

But Snow left John`s office, a broken man, knowing Cooper had no mercy on anyone who failed him. As he left, Samuel came in.

"I`m sorry, Guv`nor, I couldn`t help but overhear that. We`re better off without him. If it`ll help, I`m quite prepared to work extra until we can get some replacements, and I happen to know a couple of lads who were passed over when the rest of us were selected."

"Thanks, Samuel. Any luck with Carter?"

"That`s why I came to see you. I think you`d better come and listen to this."

John followed him to the cells. In one of them was a very unhappy Jerry Carter, sitting with his head in his hands.

"He`s convinced he could be facing an appointment with the hangman as an accessory to Monk`s murder," explained Samuel, for Carter`s benefit.

He unlocked the door and led the way into the cell, and Carter looked up. His dirty face was streaked and John saw he had been crying. They sat on either side of him.

"Now Jerry," said Samuel, gently. "I want you to repeat to the Guv`nor, everything you told me. Right?"

"It will help me, won`t it?" pleaded Carter.

Samuel nodded.

"It were like this," began Carter. "I saw Monk come back, late afternoon, with `is face all bleeding. `e didn`t say what had happened, but I `eard later. `e went up to his room, having told me to expect a visit from you lot. If that happened, I was to tell you `e were out. But the crushers never asked when they came."

"But somebody else came first, didn`t he?" prompted Samuel.

"Yes."

John`s hopes began to rise, only to be deflated yet again, as Carter continued.

"But I couldn`t see who it were. From where I was sitting, I couldn`t see `is face, only `is bottom half." He paused.

"Go on," came Samuel`s gentle request. "Tell us now what you actually saw."

"I suppose I heard `im go up, rather than saw `im. But `e came down about fifteen minutes later. I could see `e were wearing black trousers, with a golden coloured stripe down the side, all fancy at the knee."

"Like a soldier wears?" asked John.

Carter nodded. "And, `e walked downstairs sideways, like `e were wearing spurs. Sometime later you crushers came."

"Had you seen Monk at all after the first visitor left?" asked John.

"No. When `e didn`t answer the door, I assumed `e had heard the loud voiced crusher and just kept quiet. I swear I don`t know any more than that."

"Would you recognise the trousers again, if you saw them?" said Samuel, an idea beginning to form in his mind.

"I think so."

"Thank you."

They left Carter, locked the cell door and returned to John`s office. On the way, Samuel made some tea. He took one mug to Carter and the other to John.

"Bring yours in," commanded John. "And take a seat."

When Samuel reappeared, he sat down as instructed.

"Thanks Samuel, that was excellent work. I`ll get you to take his story down in writing, and have him sign it. Then I think we`ll keep him locked up for a night or two. It`s probably for his own safety."

"No doubt the trousers belonged to one of Major Pearson`s men."

"I suspect the phantom major himself."

"The phantom major?" queried Samuel.

John told him what Robert Andrew had discovered. Now all his reliable men knew the truth. "What we need are a pair of those trousers," he added.

"I`ll see what can be done," mused Samuel, who had been thinking along the same lines already.

They discussed the case for a while, and Samuel went away to start writing Carter`s statement, whilst John returned to his paperwork.

He was interrupted by Mathew coming on duty, holding a pile of discarded police uniform in his hands. John told him about Snow and the other events of the day.

Mathew tried to persuade John to go off duty, but he declined. Instead, he went across to the *Woolpack*, for some supper and debated whether or not to call it a day. He had completely forgotten about the letter. In the end, his conscience won.

The way things were going, he would soon have plenty of spare time, so he might just as well return to duty and do his paperwork. He needed some luck. Like many policemen, he believed you could get lucky sometimes, although you needed to work to make the luck. What more could he do?

It had just gone 9.20pm when he finished his last letter and tidied up his desk, and saw the envelope which had been there since early morning. He toyed with waiting until the following morning, but decided to open it.

The letter was written on quality paper and was in a feminine hand. There was no address at the top and, going to the bottom of the paper, he saw there was no signature. Another anonymous letter. He threw it to one side, but then had second thoughts, retrieved it and read.

Dear Mr Mayfield
Meet me tonight, at 10 o'clock, in the herdsman's hut by the racecourse.
I have some information which you will find of great importance in your dealings with James Cooper. Please come alone. I will only make myself known to you if you are alone. Believe me, this is not a trick.

A friend and well-wisher.

"Mathew!" he shouted.

His sergeant came, with a worried look on his face, but relaxed when he saw John's expectant face holding out a letter.

"What do you think of this?" he said.

Taking the letter from John's outstretched hand, Mathew read it quickly.

"What do think?" repeated John. "Is it worth the risk, bearing in mind what happened yesterday?"

Mathew hesitated. "You can't go there alone."

"Don't worry. I'd already worked that one out. I feel I've nothing to lose. But, I'd like you to be with me as well. It's voluntary. I can't order you to come."

"I'd still come, even if you told me not to."

"Thank you. Now can you get to the racecourse before I do and find somewhere to watch the hut?"

"I know just the place. And I think it will be a good idea, if both of us covered up our uniforms."

John nodded his agreement, stood up and crossed to his office safe. Selecting a key from his watch fob, he inserted it in the lock and turned. He opened the door, reached in, and brought out a wooden box. Putting it on his desk, he opened the lid.

Inside was a matched pair of revolvers. Taking one out, he handed it to Mathew, who took the weapon and admired it.

"This time we're taking no chances. Are you familiar with one of these?"

"Oh yes," grinned Mathew. "It's a nice piece. From Birmingham, I suspect and a rather new design?"

John nodded and handed him five cartridges. "God knows why we didn't take these yesterday. I just never thought it would have been so dangerous."

They quickly loaded the weapons and Mathew left the office. Moments later, John heard him leaving the police station. Looking at his watch, he saw it had only just gone 9.30pm, so there was no point in leaving for another fifteen minutes.

It was a long wait, but at last he heard St Mary's clock strike quarter to the hour. Rising, he put on his civilian coat and placed the revolver in its right-hand pocket. Putting on his hat, John locked his office, passed the time of day with Robert Andrew and left the station.

It was a short walk down to Friars Street and then on to the racecourse. He could see no signs of Mathew, but had every faith in the man. Going on to the course, he saw the dim outline of the herdsman's hut. Gripping the revolver in his pocket, he went towards it.

"Good evening Mr Mayfield," came a now familiar female voice from the shadows.

"Good evening, Mrs Whiting."

"Please, no names. If I'm discovered here with what I've got for you, my life will not be worth a farthing."

Intrigued he moved into the shadows, and accepted Kate's invitation to sit alongside her.

"I didn't think you'd come," she said.

"I nearly didn't. I couldn't be sure if it was another trap or not."

"I promise you're safe with me."

"Who else knows you're here?"

"Just you and me. And, before you ask, I wrote the letter. My mother had been a governess and she taught me to read and write. She was educated, but fell for my father and became pregnant. Her family couldn't accept the shame and we ended up in the workhouse."

"And your father?"

"I don't believe anybody ever told him. He returned to America. I love learning, but have no chance to do any more now." There was a wistfulness to her voice.

"One day, perhaps?"

"Who knows?"

They were silent for a while. Suddenly the clouds rolled back and bright moonlight shone on them both. Kate gasped as she saw the state of his burned face.

Gently she put her fingers to some of the burns. "You poor love. You poor, poor love," she whispered gently.

He made no move to remove her cool fingers.

"Why do you want to see me, down here?" He finally broke the silence.

"I have some information for you which should help put that bastard Cooper away for a long time."

"I have to ask. What is the price?"

"Nothing," she whispered. "Just say its my contribution to society." He did not believe her. Kate handed him the note book. "You'll find most of his dealings recorded in here. I know he doesn't trust anyone and so keeps a record of everything he does."

John took the note book. It was far too dark to read it now, so he put it in his pocket. He was reluctant to leave her, enjoying the quiet moment. Although John hardly knew her, somehow he felt comfortable in this woman's company.

"I won't ask you how you came by this. But, if it's what I think it might be, you might just have saved my career."

Kate put out her hand and took hold of his. Her hand was cold. "I hope so. But, stay. There's more. This Saturday night, he plans another ot his secret operations at the foundry. He handpicks his men and pays them well. They are a right evil bunch too. I don`t know what he does but it has to be something illegal and not ordinary foundry work."

"Sounds well worth a visit."

She tightened her grip. "No, John. Not without a lot of help. You wouldn`t stand a chance. He has armed guards. And, it wouldn`t be the first time someone has been found in the canal after one of these sessions. Promise me you`ll take care. I couldn`t......" her voice faded.

"I promise." He made to leave, albeit reluctantly.

"Stay a minute. I`ve something else." John needed no second urging. "I don`t quite know how to put this, but I think one of your close associates is betraying you."

"Who?" John was now very alert. After his discussion with Mathew, she was confirming his worst suspicions.

"That`s the problem. I don`t know. I`ve only seen him in shadows late at night. His figure is familiar. I don`t think he`s one of your men, and certainly not Monk." Kate shuddered as she mentioned his name.

"I get the feeling he`s someone important in town, a magistrate or something."

John went cold as Kate told him about the figure she had seen, especially the time he had talked about a dinner guest who would not go. Although he did not want to accept it, deep down his worst fears were beginning to surface. They were now much more than suspicions. All Kate had done was to confirm what he and Mathew suspected.

"Why have you told me all this?" he asked gently.

"Because I trust you. You have been good to Silas. I know you didn`t hurt him. And, I couldn`t believe it yesterday when I found Edward in your office having a good feed."

He sensed there was something else as her hand tightened in his. Then he was aware Kate was crying softly. He held her close, feeling her arms go around him, as she began the sorry tale of her relationship with Cooper and why she had done it.

John listened, saying nothing, but feeling a growing anger, which made him all the more determined to put a stop to the man`s activities. At last she finished, having told him everything, but made no move to leave the protection and security of his arms. Both could feel the charged atmosphere flowing between them. Clearly she felt the same as he did.

He wanted to take her, then and there, and sensed, correctly, if he had, she would not have resisted, as she wanted him just as much. The temptation was there, but deep down, he knew it would be wrong. Hopefully there would be another occasion. In the distance, they heard St Mary`s strike 11.0pm. Kate reluctantly broke away from him.

"I must go. Remember, my love. Please, please take the greatest care. Cooper is evil. And will stop at nothing, especially where you are concerned." She kissed him tenderly on his lips.

"One moment, Kate. I mustn`t build your hopes up too much, but with Monk now dead, there is no real evidence to connect Silas to the burglary. There`s a very good chance the case against him will collapse. Be strong. And, keep away from the foundry on Saturday night."

She kissed him once more , tenderly on the lips, and then was gone.

John sat still for several minutes, wondering if it had all really happened. He could still taste her salty tears on his lips. And, had she really called him "My love?" and "John"? What was he getting into? She was not just a married woman: her husband was in custody for burglary!

"Guv`nor? Is everything alright?" came Mathew`s worried voice. He had seen a figure leave the hut, but no sign of life from John.

"Yes fine. Let`s get back to the station. I think we`ve got some work to do."

Together they walked quickly back to the station. On arrival, Mathew made some tea whilst John began to read Cooper`s notebook. It was all there. Details of the Warwick burglaries, the ones in Aylesbury and many others elsewhere.

It even mentioned Thompson`s demise, with the blame put fairly and squarely on to Monk. If ever John`s prayers had been heard, it was tonight. He reasoned also, if Kate was correct about this information, then she would be about everything else. John handed the notebook to Mathew, who became just as excited as his superintendent when he read it.

John told him about the planned work on Saturday night, but refrained from adding Kate`s comments about who was betraying them. He had his own ideas and plans for dealing with that problem. Mathew did not ask who had given John this information and was not told. He had seen the slight figure, obviously female, leave the hut, but it had been too dark to identify her.

"What a stroke of luck, Guv`nor."

"Don`t forget, Mathew, you have to work to make luck work for you."

"Very true. But, bad luck can`t last for ever. It has to change some time."

"Now, I`m not going to be around tomorrow. You can tell everyone I`ve gone to London. If they really press, you can suggest I`ve gone to try and get my old job back. In fact, you`ll know where I am. Also, I want you to go and get an arrest warrant from William Slattery for Major Pearson. Then get a similar one from Dr Waldren. Let it drop, in conversation, that one will be executed on Friday morning and the other on Saturday. But, whatever you do, make sure they and only they know the dates. There must be no servants within hearing. Do this one first." John mentioned the name.

"Rely on me, Guv`nor," grinned Mathew. "I can see what you`re planning."

John went on to discuss his plans in more detail. Finally, he left the station, went to *Woolpack* and woke a sleepy ostler, explaining how he needed a horse to take him to Coventry, to catch the next train to London. Going up to his room, John quickly changed out of his uniform into more comfortable clothes, and returned to the stables. After collecting his horse, he rode to Coventry.

When he arrived at Coventry railway station, he left his horse in nearby stables. After purchasing a ticket, he waited a few minutes on the platform until the train arrived, and climbed aboard into a deserted carriage. A few minutes later, he relaxed as the train pulled out of the station.

Had there been anyone watching the train, he would have seen it was going to Birmingham, not London.

CHAPTER TWENTY

A Quiet Day

Samuel Perkins waited patiently, outside the *Green Dragon*, in the shadow of the Market Hall. Technically he was off duty, so his time was his own. He had seen his Guv`nor ride off and was a little puzzled at first, but then thought no more of it. At last the *Green Dragon*, subsided into silence and darkness, but all the same, he waited a few more minutes, before making his way to the back of the building, in New Street.

It did not take him long to climb up onto the inn`s boundary wall, which he quickly moved along, until it joined the rear wall of the building, by a small window leading onto the landing inside. Not too long ago, he had courted Meg, one of the serving girls from here, and knew the window catch was faulty. He quickly opened it and climbed inside.

Earlier that evening, he had gone into the inn, ostensibly for a drink, and to talk to Meg for old times sake. They had parted friends and had always remained so. By asking her the right questions, he soon discovered where Major Pearson was sleeping. Now he made his way along the landing to the man`s room.

Avoiding all the creaking boards, whose location he knew by heart, Samuel arrived at Pearson`s bedroom door. Holding his breath, he put his ear to the door and listened. At first it was difficult to hear anything over the noise of his rapidly beating heart. Once the pounding had quietened, Samuel could hear the sound of Pearson snoring steadily. Satisfied the man was asleep, Samuel tried the door, but as he suspected, it was locked.

He just hoped the key was not still in the lock on the other side.

Taking a pick-lock out of his pocket, he carefully inserted it into the keyhole. His luck was in: there was no key in the lock. Samuel turned the pick-lock quietly and unlocked the door. Still erring on the side of caution, he waited a few more minutes, but Pearson`s snoring kept its rhythm. Only when he was completely satisfied, did Samuel turn the handle and open the door.

Now came the difficult part. If he was recognised or captured, nothing could save him from going to Court, if he was lucky. After seeing what had happened to Monk, that morning, Samuel knew his actual chances of survival would be slight. He mouthed a silent prayer, as Pearson continued snoring loudly.

By now his eyes had become quite accustomed to the dark, and he had no difficulty in seeing Pearson`s uniform hanging up, on a cupboard door. Quietly, he crossed the room and gathered up the trousers. Just as he moved away, back towards the door, a floorboard gave a loud creak. Pearson`s snoring stopped and Samuel froze.

"What`s that? Who`s there?" mumbled Pearson, in a sleep befuddled voice.

Samuel held his breath and prepared to hit the man if necessary. He had taken the precaution of wearing a mask, but if any of the other soldiers were roused, his chances of escape would not be good. The bed creaked as Pearson sat up, and Samuel slipped a hand into his pocket and gripped the cudgel he had there. He would have no compunction about hitting him if necessary.

The bed creaked again as Pearson swung his legs over the side. Samuel took out the cudgel and prepared to use it. Seconds later there came the sound of trickling water as Pearson used the chamber pot. Samuel relaxed slightly.

Only when Pearson`s snores had resumed, did he dare move back to the door. Quickly he opened it, went through and relocked it behind him with his pick-lock. Moments later he was through the window, scurrying along the wall and back down into New Street.

Samuel was about to cross the Market Place, when he saw Robert Andrew quietly walking on his beat. Whilst Samuel was fairly certain Robert would approve of what he had done, there was no point chancing his luck too much. Waiting until Robert had gone, Samuel rolled up the trousers and hid them under his coat, before going in the opposite direction. He would take them home tonight, and show them to Carter, later in the morning when he was officially on duty.

Tomorrow morning would be interesting when Pearson found his trousers missing. He just hoped Meg wouldn`t tell anyone about their conversation.

Four hours later, Samuel arrived on duty before Robert had returned to the station. Going into the uniform room, he hid Pearson`s trousers under Snow`s discarded tunic. Once Robert had gone off duty, he went to see Carter, in the cells. He took a mug of tea with him and the trousers. Carter accepted the tea gratefully and gazed at the trousers.

Looking at Samuel, he nodded. "That`s them," he said, without any prompting. "Where did you get them?"

"Never you mind. You`re sure?"

"Yes." He pointed to the fancy braiding on the knee. "That`s why I remembered them. They`re not like any other army trousers I`ve seen."

Samuel heaved a silent sigh of relief, as his hunch had payed off. When Carter had first mentioned the fancy braiding, he remembered having seen some on Pearson`s trousers, and not on the other soldiers. Clearly it was for officers only. The main problem was, he had not obtained the trousers legally, so what would the Guv`nor say. Which reminded him. Where was the Guv`nor? He was normally on duty by now.

It did not take long for him to add to Carter`s statement about the trousers, and he returned to the charge office, where Mathew Harrison was waiting for him.

"What are those?" asked Mathew, pointing at the trousers.

For a moment, Samuel thought about saying he had found them on his way to the station, but decided on telling the truth, or at least part of it. He thought discretion was the better part of valour, when it came to confessing his criminal activities.

"Can I just say, sergeant, I..er....came across them."

"Whose are they?"

"Major Pearson`s."

Mathew burst out laughing. "What will he say when you take them back? He`ll not thank you."

"That`s the problem. They can`t go back to him. At least, not yet. I need to speak to the Guv`nor first."

"Perhaps you`d like to tell me the full story?"

Although phrased as a request, Samuel knew it was an order.

For the next few minutes he told Mathew about Monk`s hanging and what Carter had seen, and how he had now identified the trousers. Mathew listened intently. Samuel impressed him, especially as such a newcomer to this kind of work. He agreed the trousers should be kept until John returned, although he knew that would not be for several hours yet.

It was another way to unsettle Pearson, and the more chances of doing that, the better. Yet, it could only be a matter of time before the aggrieved major came to report their loss. Or would he?

❦

John enjoyed a profitable morning, for a change. He had made careful plans for the Saturday evening, and went straight from Curzon Street railway station, in Birmingham, and met up with Daniel Roberts. Although Daniel had not been on duty, he managed to persuade the duty sergeant to take him to where his friend lived.

"JOHN!"cried Emma Roberts as she answered to his knock. "How lovely to see you."

Once they were indoors, and out of sight of her neighbours, she flung her arms around his neck and kissed him. "Daniel! Benjamin! Come and see who`s here."

Benjamin was first to arrive. His little face broke into a huge grin when he recognized John, and ran across the room to him. John was shocked to see how frail the child looked. Both Daniel and Emma would be devastated if anything happened to him. He scooped the giggling little boy up into his arms and swung him round and round.

"Don`t you make him sick!" cautioned Emma.

When he stopped, John produced a small tin whistle from his pocket, and gave it to Benjamin. The boy stuttered his thanks and ran off, cheerfully blowing it.

"Thanks, friend," said Daniel, smiling, who had just appeared, in his nightgown, rubbing his eyes and yawning. "That`ll really help me sleep. Would I be right in thinking you haven`t had any breakfast yet?"

"What? And miss the chance of sampling Emma`s legendary cooking?" John looked at his friend, who had clearly only just woken up. "I`m sorry for waking you, but at least you`ve had some sleep. I haven`t even been to bed yet."

Over breakfast the three friends spoke about old times, including John`s non-existent love life. Although, when pressed on that particular subject, they found he was strangely quiet. After breakfast, Emma took Benjamin and left the two men to talk business. She was astute enough to realise John had not come just on a social call.

Once John had brought Daniel up to date, he began to outline his plans. Daniel left him for a few minutes whilst he shaved and dressed. Meanwhile John told Emma about Harriet, and his hopes, but said nothing about Kate. Neither of his friends would have criticized him, if he had, but he knew that could never develop into anything, much as he felt both of them would like it to.

He played with Benjamin and taught him a few notes on the whistle. The boy was a quick learner. All too soon Daniel appeared again, and it was time to say goodbye to this happy domestic scene Emma sensed his loneliness and gave him an extra big hug.

"I like the sounds of Harriet, keep at it," she said. "You`ll see. It`ll all work out for the best in the end."

Daniel took him to see his superintendent, David Monroe, and John repeated his story and outlined his plans. Like the other two men, Monroe had also come up from the Metropolitan Police. In fact he had been one of the original Peelers who took to the streets in September 1829. He was a kindly disposed man and more than happy to offer John his help.

All too soon the meeting finished, and it was time for John to think about returning to Warwick. He declined further refreshment with Daniel, as there was somewhere else he had to visit. As the friends parted company, he asked Daniel where to find a certain premises. With an all knowing smile, Daniel told him.

On the way back to Curzon Street station, John found the premises he sought and went inside.

☙☙

Major Charles Pearson was in a violent temper, having discovered his trousers had vanished during the night, in spite of being kept with him, in a locked room. His first thought was one of his troopers had hidden them for a joke. By the time he had finished threatening them with all manner of punishments, if the trousers were not returned, it soon became clear, they were not responsible.

To make matters worse, the landlord thought it was most amusing and so did his staff. Faced with no alternative, he stormed across to the police station. Mathew saw him coming.

"Where's Mayfield?" shouted Pearson.

"I'm afraid Superintendent Mayfield is not here today, major. He's gone to London. I think he's looking to go back there."

Pearson stopped. Had he heard right? Had they got rid of Mayfield at last? Suddenly the loss of his trousers was not quite so important. He explained to Mathew what had happened, and was forced to wait whilst the sergeant slowly recorded everything in a ledger, which included a complete description of the trousers, with special emphasis on the braiding at the knees.

At last the sergeant finished and handed the pen to Pearson to sign the entry in the book. Pearson did so, silently cursing the sergeant for being such a slow, witless dolt, and left the station. His temper only slightly improved by the knowledge Mayfield was probably preparing to leave Warwick.

He would have thought differently had he seen the satisfied look on Mathew's face. The trousers had been identified by Carter, and now by Pearson himself. The major had been thrown off guard by his comment about the Guv'nor going back to London and walked into Mathew's trap. Yes, the hangman's noose was now getting a little bit nearer to the phantom major's neck.

Mathew went back into the charge office and found a forlorn looking Samuel waiting for him.

"Tell me it's not true?" Samuel said, without any preamble. "The Guv'nor's not really going back to London, is he?"

"No, it's all part of his strategy to make the opposition careless. And this was an excellent time to set the rumour going. But, if anyone asks, he's gone to London, to try and get his old job back. Now I've got to go and and swear out some warrants."

"Of course, sergeant," grinned Samuel.

Two hours later, Pearson now in civilian dress, still had not found his trousers. Nobody dared to go anywhere near him, as he fumed in his room, irritated by the sounds of laughter coming from the taproom, no doubt at his expense. There came a knock at his door.

"Yes!" he called impatiently.

A small man, whom he had never seen before, came into the room. "I`m looking for a Major Pearson. Do you know where he is, sir?" he asked nervously.

"I`m he. Why do you want to know?"

The man looked hesitantly back at him. "I was told to look for a military man."

"I`m he!" snapped Pearson. "What do you want?"

"To give you this sir." He held out an envelope.

Pearson took it and waved the man away. He recognised the writing and quickly tore it open, and took out the letter. Reading it, his blood ran cold.

Charles
Mayfield plans to arrest you early tomorrow morning, in the Green Dragon, for Monk`s murder. I`ve just signed the warrant.

It was not signed, but he knew who it was from. Something was going on but he could not see what. Perhaps that sergeant was not so stupid after all. But, how could they know he had murdered Monk? Nobody had said anything about it being a murder. He`d made it look like suicide, just as he`d done before. "Bloody Jerry Carter must have seen me," he said aloud.

Quickly he regained his composure. Packing his few belongings would not not take long. Shouting for his orderly, Pearson gave the order to pack and prepare to move out. Twenty minutes later, he and his men left the *Green Dragon* and rode out towards the Birmingham Road. James Cooper would have to put them up for the next few days. He had the room.

None of them noticed young James Harrison go running into the police station, where Mathew was waiting for him.

"Pa," gasped James. "They`ve gone down the Birmingham Road, complete with their baggage horses."

"Good lad. Here`s the twopence I promised. But, don`t tell anybody what you`ve done. Especially your ma." Mathew proudly watched his son leave the station.

Some half an hour later, his other son, Edward arrived. "Pa, they`ve gone into the White House," he gasped, having run all the way.

Mathew gave him two pennies and also warned the boy about not telling his ma. They had done a good job watching the *Green Dragon* and the White House. He knew he should not have used them, but no one would suspect the boys of working for the police.

In any case, both wanted to follow in their father`s footsteps, so Mathew had looked upon it as giving them a taste of their future career. He just hoped his wife never find out. The Guv`nor would be pleased to know his plan was working. At long last things were now going their way. And he was fairly certain he knew who was giving all their secrets away.

✧

It was a tired, but fairly relaxed John who returned to the *Woolpack*, in the early evening. After stabling his horse, he went across to the police station, and was not at all surprised to find both Mathew and Samuel waiting for him. He was delighted over the affair of Pearson`s trousers, but was unsure how they could get round the fact the clothing had been stolen. But then, so had Cooper`s notebook been stolen: he was under no illusions there.

He just hoped the gang would not be frightened into abandoning their plans for Saturday night. Only one person might be able to find that out, and it would be another chance to see Kate. But he could never bring himself to put her in any further danger; he would just have to take a chance.

After Samuel had gone, Mathew confessed to having taken him into his confidence and John agreed it was the right thing to do. Tomorrow he would brief Robert Andrew and then lay careful plans for catching the rogue magistrate, now they were fairly certain they knew who he was.

John spent some time going over his recently acquired paperwork. He saw a note from Thomas asking him to call round, on his return. Although tempted, especially as there was always the chance of seeing Harriet, he put the note on one side. He knew he owed Harriet his life, but needed some more time to himself to complete the plans for Saturday.

John left the station and went across to the *Woolpack*. The idea of having a drink appealed, but he decided against it, and went straight up to his room. The lack of sleep the previous night, plus his energetic afternoon, began to tell on him. Without any further delay, he undressed and got into bed, hoping for a quiet night. He slept well.

❧

Samuel Perkins was also feeling tired. He had been working a double shift and, like John, had not slept much the previous night. Patrolling along High Street, on the area known as High Pavement, towards West Street, yawning, he became aware of being followed. Suddenly all his tiredness left him, although he continued pretending to yawn.

Very slowly, he moved his right hand round to his staff, and loosened it from its frog. As he turned the corner towards Castle Lane, they ran at him.

"Let's do the bastard, now," came the familiar snarl from George Kent, the Castle boatman.

The man broke the bottle he was carrying, on a nearby wall, and charged at the policeman. Then he stopped. "It's the wrong crusher," he shouted.

"Never mind," came the curt reply from one of the others. "Let's do him all the same."

"Yeah, I owe him," agreed Kent and renewed his attack.

Samuel was ready for him, and ducked at the last moment. Spinning round, he rammed his staff into the boatman's face and broke his jaw. As the man staggered, Samuel rammed his staff into Kent's stomach. Winded, the man staggered backwards against the wooden railings, which gave way under his weight. Kent landed heavily, in Leycester Place with a sickening thud, a few feet below and lay still.

Undeterred, the second man lunged at Samuel with the knife he carried. Samuel parried the blow with his staff, and kicked the man`s kneecap with his heavy duty boot. The man`s impetus kept him coming forwards, in spite of his injury. As he did so, Samuel stepped to one side and swung his staff at the man`s head. It hit him just over the ear, and he fell to the ground, and lay still.

The third man, having seen what had happened to his mates, stopped, and backed away from Samuel. He too had a large knife in his right hand. With his left, he beckoned Samuel towards him. Samuel stood his ground and waited, which was not what his assailant had expected.

Already things had gone seriously wrong. This wasn`t the crusher they were expecting. He was a good fighter, as he had just proved. But, all the same, he was confident he could finish it.

"Are you frightened, crusher?" he taunted, slashing the air, with his knife. As he moved, his coat fell open and Samuel recognised the uniform of one of Major Pearson`s men.

"What are you after, trooper?" he answered, mildly. "Can`t the major do his own dirty work?"

The man ignored his remarks, and continued slashing the air. Slowly, Samuel inched closer to him.

"Come on , trooper," he taunted. "What are you frightened of? I hope you were paid enough by the major."

He kept inching towards the other man. For all his bravado, the soldier did not come any closer to the policeman.

"Fancy coming out with only a knife. I`d have thought a sabre was more your weapon."

Samuel suddenly lunged at the man. His charge caught the man off guard. The first thing he knew was when Samuel`s staff smashed down on his hand, breaking his fingers. Shrieking with pain, he dropped the knife, then his cry was stifled as Samuel drove the tip of his staff into the soldier`s stomach, bayonet fashion.

As he gasped, the other end of Samuel`s staff was thrust up into his jaw. Dropping to his knees, he was barely aware of the rabbit punch Samuel gave him, before everything went black.

Samuel leaned back against the wall of a nearby house, and surveyed his handiwork, only vaguely aware of a small crowd which had gathered round, and who now quietly applauded him.

"Well done lad!"

"We saw it all, they attacked you first."

With their help, Samuel managed to get the last two assailants, both of whom were soldiers, back to the police station and sent someone to fetch Sergeant Harrison. George Kent, however, was a different problem.

The fall had rendered him deeply unconscious, with a severe head injury. Samuel sent for Dr Waldren, but it was Dr Hopper who came as it seemed Dr Waldren was already out on a call. Dr Hopper diagnosed a fractured skull, amongst other injuries. However, he was soon reassured that Samuel had acted in self defence.

Back at the police station, Mathew Harrison had appeared and been told about what had happened. He fully supported Samuel`s actions, even more so when some of the witnesses agreed to testify against the two soldiers. Both men would be kept in custody and charged with the attack.

Samuel had no doubt at all they had been tasked with the attack by Pearson, but if it was not meant for him, who was the intended target? Probably Robert Andrew. Whether they could ever prove it would be another matter. But, it meant another one of Cooper and Pearson`s carefully laid plans had gone astray.

They were interrupted by the arrival of Dr Hopper. Gravely, he shook his head and explained about the boatman.

"He has a badly fractured skull, and there`s not much I can do about it. I`ve had him taken home and we`ll see what happens. I`ve done all I can."

" I didn`t have any real option," said Samuel. "They meant to really hurt or even kill me."

"I know." Dr Hopper raised a hand. "You`ve plenty of witnesses on your side. And, just between the three of us, Kent`s a nasty piece of work. If he dies, he won`t be missed. After the beatings he gives his wife, she`ll probably come and thank you."

❧

At the White House, James Cooper, Charles Pearson and their leader, sat and waited impatiently for the troopers to return. It was getting late, after midnight and they should have returned before now.

"Are you sure it was a good idea to send them out after that man, Andrew?" queried the leader.

"Yes," stressed Pearson. "The other one`s just too handy in a fight. My men will find a willing pair of hands, and do Andrew over. They`re the best I`ve got and have never lost a fight yet. Then they`ll leave the hired help to take the blame. Stupid sod."

"What if they kill him?" queried the leader.

"Too bad. We`ve got to finish Mayfield, one way or another. Three of them will never be able to run this town."

"Incidentally," asked Cooper. "How did they find out about your role in Monk`s death?"

"That fool Carter must have recognised my uniform trousers, and told Mayfield."

"I can`t understand why you wore them. After all, you`re not doing so now," commented Cooper.

"That`s because they seem to have vanished," came Pearson`s embarrassed reply.

"Vanished?" cried the other two. "How?"

"I don`t know. They disappeared from my room, in the *Green Dragon*, last night."

"That settles it," said the leader. "We disband after Saturday night. You`ll have to leave the country, Charles. It won`t take Mayfield too long to make enquiries with your Regiment and then discover the truth. If Mayfield was any good, he would have done that already."

"But he isn`t any good, is he?" sneered Pearson.

"If I were you, I would not underestimate him," said the leader. "Nobody knows for sure where he`s been today. Supposedly in London, seeing about getting his old job back, but he could just of easily have gone to your late Regiment."

"Can`t you get my warrant cancelled?"

"Possibly. I don`t doubt James`s judge friend could do that for us, but it will take a bit of time. It would be easier to just pay off Carter."

"I can soon arrange an accident for him," suggested Cooper.

"No, I forbid it," instructed the leader. "There have been too many deaths already. Besides, he hasn`t been seen recently. He must be hidden away somewhere. No Charles. The best thing is for you to leave the country and wait until things have quietened down and we`ll be in touch."

Further conversation was interrupted by a knock at the door. "Yes," shouted Cooper impatiently.

A footman entered and silently handed him a note. Cooper took it, nodded at the man, who promptly left. He flicked the note open, one handed and began to read. The colour drained from his face.

"What is it?" asked Pearson.

Cooper handed the note to the leader.

"Your best men, eh Charles?" sneered Cooper. "Going to leave the hired help to carry the can? The stupid sods picked on the wrong crusher. Perkins had changed shifts with Andrew. He laid all three of them out. The hired help has a fractured skull and may not live."

"Then we`ll have Perkins for murder," countered Pearson.

"Wrong," snarled Cooper. "Your best men attacked Perkins in front of several respectable witnesses, who will say the crusher acted in self-defence." He stopped and raised his hand to Pearson.

"And before you suggest it, don`t bother. They`re not the type of witness who can be bought off. And your best men, were wearing their uniforms. If these were your best men, I shudder to think what your worst are like."

"Where are they now?"

"Locked up in the police station. Where do you think?"

"Will they talk?" queried the leader.

Pearson shook his head.

"No. They know only too well what will happen to them if they do. We`ll get them out on Saturday after we`ve finished."

"And, if we can`t?" queried the leader.

"Then we make sure they never talk," came Pearson`s blunt reply.

CHAPTER TWENTY ONE

Friday

Initially John was annoyed at not having been called out following the attack on Samuel. But Mathew was adamant.

"I`m sorry Guv`nor, but there was no need. Everything was taken care of last night. There was nothing for you to do. Dr Hopper was very supportive."

"You`re right. And the sleep did me good. But you go off duty now for a few hours. Then, we`ll go and visit Ezra Crane, the carrier."

Crane had been quoted in Cooper`s notebook, as being the carrier the foundry man always used. He had also been the most unhelpful of all the carriers interviewed earlier that week. Visiting him should tie-up his special deliveries to Cooper`s house, late at night. Once they had Crane`s records, and there would have to be some, it would then be a matter of contacting the police in the affected towns to check on burglaries and Major Pearson`s so-called recruiting drives.

It had just gone 11.15am when John and Mathew went into Crane`s yard, situated midway down Friars Street. For a supposed bustling carrier`s business, there was not much activity taking place. The yard was dirty with paint peeling off the window frames and doors. One or two workers lounged about drinking tea, making no effort to clean up the yard.

Several piles of horse manure littered the yard, which seemed to have been there for a few days. They established, from a surly passing stable hand, that Ezra Crane was upstairs in his office. John followed his sergeant up some rickety stairs, which led onto a small landing. One door was open and they saw a small man bustling around inside, whom John took to be Crane.

Mathew entered first. "Morning, Ezra. How are you today?" Although the words were polite, John noticed a lack of warmth in the way Mathew said them.

"I`ve no time to waste on you lot. I`ve already had one of the other crushers in here this week. And I`m telling you the same. I`ve nothing to tell you. I`m too busy! So clear off." The carrier was not at all pleased to see them.

Ezra Crane was a thin, bent man, aged about 50 years old. Turning his back on the officers, he walked away. Mathew followed him quickly, and catching hold of his shoulder, stopped Crane, who turned his sallow, hate filled face to the sergeant, and his pale blue eyes glared defiance.

"What about some manners, Ezra?" asked Mathew. "Mr Mayfield here is dying to meet you, and ask a few questions. And you don`t know what he wants to ask you yet. Do you?"

Crane tried to twist out of Mathew`s grip, but he was held too tightly. John saw a thin film of sweat appear on the man`s upper lip, and on his bald head.

"I don`t speak to the likes of you," Crane snarled, spitting on the floor.

"Well that`s a shame," commented John. "Because we will have to arrest you and close your business for the day. Possibly even for longer. I`m sure your customers won`t like that, will they?" He looked around. "At least, I suppose you do still have some customers?"

"What do you want?" Crane sounded resigned, and some of his truculence had gone, but not all of it.

John gave him the dates he had found in Cooper`s notebook, and asked to inspect the carrier`s consignment records. Very unwillingly, Crane led them into a filthy room and pointed to a pile of dusty ledgers in one corner.

"In there," he snarled. "I haven`t time to check them."

"That`s all right," said John. "We`ll do that for you, but you can wait here whilst we go through them."

Crane looked like he would argue again, but a closer look at the superintendent persuaded him it might not be such a good idea. He had heard about this man, and, if the truth was known, was not a little scared by his reputation, and the burns on his face made him look even more frightening. Mathew sorted out several ledgers, and put them on one side.

"We`ll take these," announced John, when Mathew had finished and proceeded to write out a receipt.

"Like hell you will!" shouted Crane. "They stay here. You`re taking nothing."

"You have two choices, Ezra," came Mathew`s silky voice. "Either you give them to us voluntarily, or Mr Mayfield will go and get a warrant to seize them. Whilst he`s gone, I`ll stay with you, and see what else Mr Cooper has been up to."

Both officers studied Crane intently, and were rewarded by the look of fear that suddenly came over Crane`s face. It had been part of their ploy to let him know how interested they were in Cooper`s business affairs.

"What`s it to be Ezra?" John said.

"Take them."

Crane watched as they removed his ledgers. After nodding politely, they gave him a receipt, went downstairs and left the building. He ran his hand over one of the dirty office windows, to clean a space and watched them go, waiting until they were out of sight, before crossing to his cluttered desk.

Clearing a space, he took a sheet of note paper and wrote a short letter to James Cooper, telling him what had happened. He sealed it in an envelope and went downstairs into his yard. Grabbing the first of his employees he could find, Crane gave him the note and instructions to deliver it to the White House as quickly as possible.

It was a worried Ezra Crane who watched his messenger depart. He had suspected, only too well, there was something special, and probably illegal, in those consignments. But, he had enjoyed being well paid for his trouble.

Cooper`s money helped to keep his failing business afloat. Now, he hoped and prayed Cooper would understand he had been given no alternative but to part with the ledgers. He, along with others, knew only too well, just how vindictive Cooper could be.

That thought bothered him. Perhaps it was time to be thinking about disappearing for a while. Leaving the yard, he went back up into is office and locked the door. Taking a carpet bag from a cupboard,

Ezra Crane began filling it with all the money he could find, and anything else which had any value.

Once he was satisfied he had everything, Crane took a last look round the office, and went out, locking the door behind him. Going down the stairs, through the yard and out into Friars Street, he intended making his way to the stables, next door but one.

"Going somewhere Ezra?"

Crane squeaked with fear and turned towards the voice and saw Mathew Harrison standing behind him. For a moment he contemplated running, but, looking away from Mathew, he saw Samuel watching him a little further up the street. Already Samuel`s reputation had spread and Crane knew he was trapped.

"Mr Mayfield wants a few words, Ezra. It seems you have been a naughty boy. Carrying all sorts of stolen property. Tut! Tut!" Mathew paused. "But I`m told Australia can be quite nice at this time of year."

A sobbing noise came from Crane as he slid slowly down the wall and on to the ground. It was over.

"Can we make a deal?" he pleaded.

"That depends on what you can tell us, Ezra. Let`s go and speak to Mr Mayfield, shall we?"

❧

James Cooper was not a happy man. He had just received the note from Ezra Crane following John`s visit. Having read and re-read it several times, he screwed the note up. "Damn Mayfield! Damn him! Damn him! Damn him!" he cursed and threw the paper in the fire.

"What is it?" asked Pearson.

Cooper told him. For a moment both men were silent.

"What do his books say?" queried Pearson. "I can`t see how they will really help Mayfield."

"You`re probably right. But, if he`s clever enough, Mayfield will be able to check on the various places, where your men have sent the goods to me. If the crushers do their job properly, they will soon associate your being in the area at the same time as their burglaries."

"In many places, they didn`t have crushers, only the local witless parish constables. Most of them don`t pose a threat. Anyway, it`ll take some time for Mayfield to find it all out." Pearson chuckled.

They were interrupted by the sudden arrival of their leader, and he was clearly agitated. "Have you heard about Crane?" he asked.

"Yes," replied Cooper. "One of his lads brought me a note an hour or so ago. We were just talking about it. There`s nothing to worry about. It will take Mayfield some time to go through the ledgers and get his enquiries in the post. Knowing Crane, he`ll probably lie low for a while. He certainly will, and keep quiet, if he knows what`s good for him."

"Quite clearly you haven`t heard about Crane," snorted the leader. "Forget about Mayfield going through the books. He`s arrested Crane. The man`s in custody!"

"Will he squeal?" asked Pearson, now feeling less confident.

"Probably," replied Cooper. "But what does he know?"

"Enough to send you to Australia on a one way ticket," replied the leader. "We can`t wait till tomorrow night. We`ll have to make the coins tonight. Then tomorrow, we can scatter until I can find a way of ensuring Crane`s evidence cannot be used in court."

"Think!" retorted Cooper. "Yes he knows we had special delivery arrangements and he was well paid well for his part in them. If Crane shows Mayfield all the transactions, he can do nothing without the evidence from where these consignments started. Even if his letters get on the late London train from Coventry tonight, by the time they are delivered, Mayfield cannot get a reply before Monday at the earliest." He paused. "And there`s no way we can make the coins tonight."

"Why not?"

"Because, my dear Charles, I cannot have the furnaces ready in time. They are special ones and take many hours to heat up properly. No. It has to be tomorrow night. It cannot possibly be done any sooner."

Pearson turned to the leader. "Can`t you get Crane released from custody?"

"I`m a magistrate, not a lawyer. But I think James is right. Mayfield cannot get any proof before next week and by then it will all be over. We just have to sit tight for the next few hours and wait."

"I wonder," mused Cooper. "It`ll take Mayfield some time to get his letters written. He`s unlikely to get any away before the last train from Coventry. What if someone watches the police station and waits for the letters to go. Then we intercept them, and ensure they go nowhere?"

"Good idea," replied Pearson. "I'm sure my remaining troopers will leap at the opportunity. Perhaps the errand boy crusher, could meet with a little accident as well."

He and Cooper chuckled. Their leader was not so amused.

❧

Back in the police station, Ezra Crane was being very helpful, and showed John all the dubious transactions. He admitted knowing there was something suspicious about them, because delivery had to be at night and to the White House. Cooper had paid him well, which had only added to his suspicions.

Meanwhile, Robert Andrew had been fetched back into the station, and was busy writing to the towns where these packages had originated. It was a thankless task, but Robert was happy to get on with it. He already knew which towns had proper police forces and he wrote to these first.

The ones still operating the old parish constable system would have to wait. Depending what happened the following night, it might not be so urgent to contact them. It was late evening when he had finished and they were faced with the necessity of taking the letters to Coventry for the late train to London.

When Mathew returned to duty, he and Samuel hired a cab to take them to Coventry. By mutual consent, it was agreed the driver should remain in Warwick. Initially he was not exactly happy at this prospect, but soon changed his mind when he realised the journey might be dangerous.

"I'm sending both of you as a precaution," explained John, as he gave them a small satchel. "There has to be the very real possibility Cooper now knows about Crane, although he will be our guest for some time yet. If he does, he will also suspect what we have done and will almost certainly try to delay matters by intercepting the letters."

The officers nodded in agreement. He crossed to his safe and took out one of his two revolvers, which he gave to Mathew.

"Do not hesitate to use it if you have to," he instructed. "Be on your guard all the time, and be aware that if you are attacked, just taking the letters may not satisfy them. Remember, we have two of their lot in custody, and they will be out for revenge and seeking to weaken us further."

He gave both men some further instructions, before wishing them good luck. Mathew had already taken the weapon, checked it was loaded and put it in his belt. John watched them leave the station and climb into the cab, where Mathew took the reins.

"Walk on!" he commanded the horse, and at the same time flicked the reins slightly. The animal obeyed and Mathew drove the cab up into the Market Place, and headed towards Coventry.

Somebody else saw them leave.

℃℈

By the time they had left Warwick, both men were aware they were being followed by three riders, who made no attempt to overtake, but just kept the cab in sight.

"I doubt they`ll attack us this side of Kenilworth," said Mathew, breaking the silence. "It`s too busy. After Kenilworth, it becomes much more deserted." He made sure his revolver was within easy reach.

"How well can you use it?" asked Samuel, pointing at the weapon.

"Well enough, I hope. It`s a pity Mrs Foxton isn`t with us. She certainly can shoot."

"And more attractive than me?" chuckled Samuel. "Seriously though, I`ve never used one before. But I have got this."

He reached under the seat and produced an old fashioned flintlock blunderbuss with a brass barrel.

"Where did you get that?" whistled Mathew. "I haven`t seen one of those for ages."

"My pa used to a be guard on the mail coaches, but he works the trains now. He taught me how to use it. I`ve only half charged it, but it still packs one hell of a punch."

They said nothing for a while.

Passing through Kenilworth, the three riders overtook them, without so much as a glance in their direction.

"As I thought," said Mathew. "They`ll wait for us somewhere the other side of town. Did you recognise them?"

"Oh yes. Some of Pearson`s men."

All too soon, they left the shelter of Kenilworth and headed towards Wainbody Woods.

"They will attack us somewhere in the woods, I should think," said Mathew. "It's where I would. Now the interesting thing is will they be masked or not?"

"What difference will that make? We know who they are."

"But they may not know that. If they're masked, then they'll probably be happy with just the letters, knowing they can't be recognized. If they're not, then it means they are not worried about what happens to us." Mathew paused. "We've got what they want and have some of their friends locked up. And we have caused them a lot of trouble. If they're not masked, it means we will have a serious fight on our hands, and they will not worry about killing us."

They entered the woods, as Mathew was talking. Samuel was watching all round, but the road was dark and no moonlight penetrated through the trees. They had not gone very far into the woods, when the attack came. The three riders came at them from different sides.

Zeb Hopkins, was directly in front, pointing a carbine at Mathew. Nat Hale and Dick Bolton stayed on either side of the cab. None of them wore masks.

"STAND!" shouted Hopkins at the front.

With a vicious back handed slash, Mathew hit out with the whip, at Nat Hale, the rider on his right. Hale pulled his horse to one side to avoid it. At the same time, Mathew flicked the reins making their horse break into a fast trot and head straight for Hopkins.

"Down!" he cried at Samuel, just as Hopkins fired.

The shot went wide, but frightened the cab horse, which began to rear and jerked the cab towards one side. Whilst the animal's thrashing hooves kept Hopkins at bay, Dick Bolton jumped onto the cab and quickly fastened his hands Samuel's throat. Samuel struggled, but letting go of his hold in the carriage, both men fell into the road.

Bolton was much heavier than Samuel and now knelt over him, squeezing hard. Samuel could not dislodge him, and realized he was slowly being strangled.

Suddenly he felt Bolton's grip slacken and heard him scream, which quickly became a gurgle, as Mathew's whip coiled round his throat. Unfortunately, in doing so, Mathew lost his hold on the whip.

Struggling to his feet, Samuel pulled the whip tighter round Bolton's throat and turned back towards Mathew.

Meanwhile, Hale had climbed onto the cab. Mathew kicked him off, but lost his own balance in doing so and fell into the road. He landed heavily and lay still, momentarily stunned and winded. Seeing him lying there apparently helpless, Hale and Hopkins moved towards him. The cab horse had stopped rearing and was standing still.

Hopkins took out a knife. "I'm going to cut the bastard into little pieces," he gloated. "He'll never whip anyone else again. Even his widow won't know him by the time I've finished."

Samuel saw Mathew's predicament, and staggered towards the cab. Seeing, the mail bag, he picked it up, and threw it with all his strength at Hopkins. It was a good aim and hit the soldier full in the face.

On its way, the bag deflected the knife upwards and into the man's face. It only stopped Hopkins for a few seconds, but it was enough for Mathew, who had recovered a little, to make his way back to Samuel at the cab. Together they waited for the next attack.

All three troopers now had knives in their hands. Mathew was breathing heavily and his head was still ringing from the fall, and knew he was not in the best of shape for a close fight especially against men armed with knives. The three attackers spread out slightly. Samuel retreated closer to the cab, whose horse was now waiting patiently. Mathew reached for his revolver, only to find it was not there. He must have lost it when he fell.

As if reading his mind, Hale produced the revolver and waved it at him "Is this what you've lost, crusher?" he taunted.

He and the others advanced and it was clear murder was in their minds. Samuel leaned back into the cab. His searching hands quickly found what he sought.

"GET BACK!" he shouted, cocking the hammer and waving the blunderbuss at them.

A shriek of derisive laughter greeted him.

"I warn you," said Samuel calmly. "And I won't warn you again."

"GET 'EM!"

The men charged and Samuel pulled the trigger.

It sounded like a small cannon being fired, and for a moment he could see nothing for the huge cloud of smoke swirling round.

A sudden silence followed the tremendous explosion, which was quickly replaced by screaming. Two of the soldiers were writhing on the ground, in some degree of pain. The third, Nat Hale, stood bewildered, blood streaming down his face.

"You`ll all live," Samuel informed them. "I wouldn`t want to do the hangman out of a job."

Picking up Mathew`s missing revolver, he backed towards the cab and climbed on board. Mathew was there already, after having picked up the whip. The horse seemed only too glad to be leaving the woods, and heading for Coventry.

The mail bag was left behind.

❧

It was a sorry trio who made their back to Cooper`s House. All three were suffering from wounds of one sort or another. Hale, still with a bleeding face, handed Pearson the mail bag.

"They were in such a hurry to get away, they left it behind. It was a stroke of luck."

Pearson emptied the bag and looked at some of the envelopes. He nodded. They were all addressed to the chief of police at various towns.

Cooper picked one up. "I wonder what he`s written. Let`s have a look shall we?"

"Careful James," warned Pearson. Isn`t that a criminal offence?"

They laughed and Cooper opened one of the envelopes.

His laughter suddenly stopped, when he saw the envelope only contained old pieces of newspaper. Quickly they opened the others. They too contained nothing but newspaper.

"You bungling fools," shouted Pearson at his troopers. "A stroke of luck was it? They meant you to have them. The real ones will be well on the way to London by now!"

Somewhat belatedly, he was beginning to understand. Their leader was right, Mayfield should not have been underestimated. Strangely, he felt something of a grudging respect for the man. He really was becoming a dangerous adversary, who made the rules up as he went along. Still it would all be over tomorrow night.

After the coins had been made tomorrow, he had one or two things to take care of; such as the elimination of a few witnesses and partners. Then it was off to America and never have to work again. He might call for his young wife to join him, but probably not. It would be time to make a clean and fresh start. Tomorrow night, or rather tonight`s work, would be the end of it.

And there was no way Mayfield could know anything about that. Up till now, it had just been luck on Mayfield`s part. But not any more. After tonight he would find Mayfield and have that long relished duel. Mayfield would not stand a chance. How he was looking forward to it. It would be a special bonus.

"Enjoy your last night on Earth, Mr Mayfield!" he whispered.

❧

Back in Warwick, a bruised Mathew and Samuel dismounted stiffly from their cab, handed it back to its owner and made their way into the station. Both John and Robert were there, waiting for them.

"Well?" asked John.

"Safely on the train. And, as for the others, hopefully with Mr James Cooper. But it was a close thing," answered Mathew. "Samuel saved the day."

He gave a full account of the fight in Wainbody Wood.

"I`d love to be there when Cooper discovers he`s been tricked," chuckled Samuel. "It makes these bruises all worth while."

CHAPTER TWENTY TWO

Saturday

Saturday morning was always a busy time, when the weekly market was held, and meant an influx of strangers into the town. Whilst situated mainly in the Market Place, some stalls spilled out into the adjoining streets, and made it an ideal opportunity for pickpockets and other criminals to operate. Samuel had agreed to patrol this particular event, and John went with him.

It was a very busy and bustling scene. Samuel knew most of the stall holders by sight, and several by name. He introduced John to them, whenever he could. Walking around with Samuel, John had the feeling he was being watched, but could not see who was doing it. In fact, his secret watcher was Kate Whiting.

She had supposed, rightly, that John would be at the market and wanted to make sure he was still alright. Casually she made her way closer to him, trying to think of an excuse just to brush against him. It would be extreme folly for both of them, to indulge in anything else, in such a busy place.

Kate knew what she was doing was wrong. Her conscience kept reminding her that she was married, and loved Silas, but at the same time, she wanted John. To make matters worse, she knew he felt the same way about her.

She had wanted him so badly the other night, and had respected and loved him all the more, for his not taking her. Deep down she was convinced it would happen sometime, Silas or no Silas. But when it did, it would be done properly, in nice surroundings and not just a quick fumble in the dark. Kate knew she ought to be ashamed of such thoughts, but she wasn`t.

Gradually the idea grew in her mind. If she was to drop something in front of him, he would automatically bend down and pick it up, and hand it back to her. Their eyes would meet and possibly their fingers might touch, albeit just for a moment. He was easy to spot, in his uniform and was walking in her direction. Slowly she moved into position and waited.

John was making his way back to the station. Although he was seeing what was going on around him, his mind was really on the coming night. For the moment, it was important for any watchers to see he and his men were acting normally.

As he approached the last market stall in the row, Kate moved and dropped the packet she was carrying. John saw it fall and bent down to pick it up.

"How nice to see a gentleman at work," came a familiar bantering voice.

John looked up and saw Harriet standing alongside him. Her beauty was enhanced by the autumnal sun shining on her glorious hair. He saw her mischievous twinkling green eyes were fixed firmly on his, almost making him lost for words. Harriet laughed, her gay infectious laugh, and touched him lightly on his arm.

"Ooh," she chuckled. "I shouldn`t have done that. Should I? That`s assault, isn`t it?"

"Never, in your case, my dear Harriet."

Suddenly John remembered he was holding the fallen packet, and turned to hand it back, but stopped dead on seeing Kate standing there, her face a picture of misery.

She snatched the packet, glowered at Harriet and ran off, with tears streaming down her face. What horribly wrong timing! The red-headed woman must have been Dr Waldren`s niece, whom she had heard about. Kate had to admit the woman was attractive and clearly very fond of John. How could she compete against such a beauty?

"How strange," remarked Harriet, looking at John, as he watched the fleeing woman. "She could at least have said thank you. Do you know who she was?"

"Er no."

Harriet knew he was lying. He did know that woman, but who was she? She had been cleanly turned out, but was obviously just a working class girl, albeit a good looking one. Harriet knew she have to make some enquiries.

"I`m glad I`ve seen you, John," she changed the subject. "Aunt Sarah wants to know if you can come for supper tonight? Uncle Thomas will be back late, and we`d like your company."

John`s heart sank. Much as he relished the thoughts of Harriet`s company, it could not be tonight, of all nights.

"I`d love to," his brain worked overtime. "But I`m afraid I`m already seeing somebody else in Leamington."

Harriet`s face fell. "Can`t you put it off?"

"Not really. It`s with the Leamington Police Superintendent. It`s the only time he can see me. In fact I`m dining with him." He was telling some of the truth.

"Oh, that`s alright. For a moment I thought you had been going to a secret assignation with another woman, like the one who dropped her packet," Harriet teased. "Never mind, we`ll invite William Slattery instead. He`s such a nice man."

In fact, Sarah had not invited John, and knew nothing about her niece`s plans. It had been Harriet`s idea, and only when John had accepted, would she have told Sarah. She had hoped to see him in the market and had been wandering around for some time, just on that very chance. John`s refusal had not been expected.

Although she liked Slattery, she had no intention of inviting him, and merely mentioned his name, just to make John jealous. Yet, it seemed as her ploys had failed. She could see John`s mind was clearly on something else. Was it that other woman? she thought.

They made small talk for a while, before John excused himself. He knew he was not being very good company, but so much depended on what happened that night, for him to really think about anything else. As they parted, Harriet wondered just where he was really going that night, and decided to follow him and find out.

The remainder of the day passed slowly. Mathew and Robert came on duty and went about their normal business and patrols.

At last night fell and the market packed up until the following week. John wondered if he would still be around to see it. He still had another four hours to wait until his plan could swing into operation, but he needed to go to Leamington first. Time hung heavy on his hands. By now he had lost count of the times he had gone over and over the plans.

They were as tight as he could make them. Nevertheless, he went over them yet again. There was always the chance of the unexpected, but if it happened, then it happened, and he would deal with it accordingly. At last it was time to go.

John went back to the *Woolpack* and changed out of his uniform into more casual clothes. Hiring a horse from there, he mounted it and rode off towards Leamington. At last things were moving and he had the comforting feel of a revolver tucked into his belt.

He was totally unaware of Harriet following him.

Kate had spent a miserable day, after leaving the market. Deep down she thought she loved Silas, but now had serious doubts. Did she really love John Mayfield, a man she hardly knew, or was it just sheer animal lust? It was a question she could not answer and had nobody to ask.

It was clear the red-headed woman had feelings for him. That was obvious from her body language and the warning look she had given Kate. Yet, she drew some comfort from the confused look on John`s face, when he saw her. Being realistic, Kate knew there could be no future for them, and she would be better to forget about him.

But then she remembered how close they had been in the herdsman`s hut. He had not shied away or flinched when she told him about Cooper, but had held her tighter. In his arms she felt a security, that was not there with Silas.

"What am I going to do?" she moaned aloud, to herself and started to cry. Luckily Edward was out.

Suddenly she brightened. She knew where John would be tonight, and would go along to watch. It would give her the chance to see him again and, hopefully, see Cooper arrested and taken away. Knowing Cooper would not start work until after 10 o`clock, it would be a long afternoon.

Harriet kept a respectable distance behind John and was glad to find the road was quite busy. He had ridden out on the Myton Road, being quieter than using the Emscote, Road, which was where Cooper had his foundry. On arriving in Leamington, John went to the *Bath Hotel*, which was not quite where Harriet had expected. Having tethered his horse outside, he entered.

She was intrigued. Apart from it not where she had expected him to go, to meet his opposite number, she had expected him to be smartly dressed: but he was not. If anything, he was almost scruffy.

That knowledge gave her some comfort. It was not what she would have expected him to wear, if going to see another woman. Yet, he certainly gave the impression of almost being in disguise. She decided to wait and hoped it would not be too long.

The night grew colder and Harriet was glad she had taken the precaution of wearing a heavy coat. Inwardly she chuckled, and thought how shocked Aunt Sarah would be, to see she had taken off her dress and was wearing trousers! Somehow she had managed to hide her long hair under a hat. She heard All Saints Church clock strike 10 o`clock, quarter past, and then half past.

By now her mind was working overtime, as she tried not to imagine John having an assignation with some woman. Harriet was so wrapped in her thoughts, she almost missed John leaving the hotel. It was only as he passed her, that she realised and set out to follow him.

She was curious to see he took the Emscote Road now, and not the Myton Road. Her curiosity was even more aroused when he stopped his horse by the canal bridge, dismounted and quietly made his way down onto the towpath towards Cooper`s foundry.

❣

John crept quietly along the towpath, keeping to the shadows. His eyes had long since become accustomed to the dark and it did not take him too long to locate Cooper`s guards. There were three of them. Two on the far side and one on his. For a moment, he was back in the army, and going on a raid. Running his tongue over dry lips, he felt the familiar butterflies in his stomach.

What happened in the next hour or so, would determine his future career, one way or another.

Whilst he had every faith in Kate Whiting, and the information she had given him, yet suppose, just suppose, it was all part of an elaborate trap to finish him completely?

He quickly dismissed the idea, recalling the fight Mathew and Samuel had survived the night before. And, why were there sentries around the foundry? No, the information had to be correct, and he needed to get closer. Quietly he removed the cudgel he had up his sleeve, and crept towards the nearest sentry.

The man never saw or heard him approach. John had not lost his army skills. His cudgel hit the man, just above the ear. Letting his cudgel swing on its lanyard, John caught the man as he fell and lowered him quietly to the towpath. Taking some rope out of his pocket, he tied the man up and thrust a gag in his mouth, before pulling him into the undergrowth.

The way was clear now for him to get closer to the foundry.

Kate had left it until just after half-past ten before she left her lodgings. She had taken the precaution of dressing in a mixture of her oldest clothes, and some of her husband`s. Not that it made much difference, in her case, as she could barely manage two changes. Luckily, she did not have to pass the barrage of Phoebe Morris and her cronies. If only they knew what she was really doing.

Nearly twenty-five minutes later, she arrived at the canal bridge on the Emscote Road and crept down onto the towpath. Harriet saw her go. Although, she was dressed as a man, Harriet recognised her as the woman in the Market Place, earlier that morning. And, she was going the way as John had gone. Pangs of jealousy now hit Harriet, and she climbed down onto the towpath and went after her.

She had no idea why. Was it to catch John out? To challenge him? But, she countered, it was his life. They were not committed to each other. For a moment, she hesitated and almost went back to her horse. Then, with her mind made up, and ready for any confrontation, she went after Kate.

Meanwhile, John had crept up to the building, and looked through a window. Although dirty, he was able to see was happening inside the foundry, where there was a hive of activity. In one part, some small furnaces blazed away, with several men attending to them.

From time to time, they removed large ladles, from which they poured a molten metal into what looked like moulds. As soon as these had cooled, they were opened and small metal discs fell out. John surmised, correctly, that these were base metal coins.

These were removed and taken to another part of the foundry, where piles of gold and silver cutlery, plates, tea, coffee and chocolate pots, were being melted down. Here there was a separate ladle for gold and another one for silver.

This new molten metal was then used to plate the newly made coins. Such was the fate of all the stolen silver and gold. It was being melted down and turning base metal discs into coins. Kate's information was correct.

Cooper and Pearson watched the opening of the moulds and the bagging up of the coins. Once bagged they were loaded onto a small trolley, which was wheeled out of another door, and loaded onto a narrow boat moored alongside the canal. Other men then took the empty moulds, re-assembled them and began the process all over again.

John heard a slight scuffling behind him, accompanied by a muffled cry. He sank further back into the shadows, as two figures passed him, struggling with a third. They went into the foundry and John returned to his window and looked in. His heart sank, when he recognised the captive.

It was Kate Whiting. Why hadn't she stayed at home as he had instructed?

As he looked, trying to think of what to do, he saw Cooper cross to her. Clearly furious, he started to punch her on the body and in the face. She reeled back, but the two captors held her tightly. Their hands enjoying groping her body as they did so. Cooper's face was a mask of hatred, whilst Pearson looked on impassively.

Kate was sinking to her knees with blood pouring all down her lovely face, and John could not bear to watch her being hurt any more.

Taking out his revolver, he burst into the foundry.

Harriet was several yards behind Kate, when she saw two men spring out of the shadows and grab her. Although she struggled, Kate was no match for them, and by the time Harriet realized what had happened, the men were pushing Kate towards the foundry. She now began to suspect John was not here for any assignation, but for something far more serious.

Taking out her revolver, which she had only taken as an afterthought, Harriet crept towards the foundry. She was almost there when she saw a figure move, from outside a window, and go into the foundry. Too late, she saw it was John.

She moved to the window and looked in.

Kate Whiting was down on her knees and seemed barely conscious. John kept his revolver firmly fixed on Cooper. All work had stopped, whilst everybody looked at John. Then she saw a door open behind him, and was relieved to see a familiar figure emerge, also holding a revolver.

Her relief was short-lived as he walked up to John and pointed his revolver at Kate`s head: his meaning was obvious. Either John surrendered or he would kill Kate. There was nothing John could do, so he surrendered his gun to Cooper.

Harriet needed no telling this was a serious matter. She could go for help, but who could she get at this hour of the night? Alternatively she could try and rescue John, although it was unlikely he would leave without Kate. But could she do it, and would they have enough time to get clear?

She saw Cooper give Kate another kick. John struggled in frustrated anger and was rewarded with a hefty punch in the stomach from Pearson. Harriet felt desperately sorry for Kate and knew she must act quickly. As she tried to decide what to do, the decision was made for her.

Suddenly her revolver hand was grasped in a vice like grip, and another hand clamped over her mouth, and she was pulled away from the window.

CHAPTER TWENTY THREE

The Foundry

John pushed open the foundry door and rushed in. His entrance took everyone by surprise. "Let her go!" he instructed.

Pointing his revolver at Cooper, he made it quite clear who his target was, unless Kate was released. He was aware of the workers beginning to gather round, and knew his advantage would soon be lost. Too late he saw the gang`s leader walk by him and point a revolver at Kate`s head.

"Although I`m opposed to violence, and I don`t approve of this," he pointed at Kate`s injuries. "Please be under no doubt I will shoot her if you do not surrender your gun."

"So it was you," said John. "We were fairly certain it was. Someone close to me was warning the others."

"The gun!"

"What guarantee do I have that you still won`t shoot her?"

"You don`t. But this is the best chance you`ve got."

"Don`t do it John," came Kate`s wheezy voice.

"I can`t risk it."

John handed over his revolver to Cooper. Then bending down he went to help Kate up, but Cooper was too quick for him. He kicked her once again. As John moved towards him, he received a massive blow in his stomach, from Pearson.

John sank to his knees besides Kate. She turned her tear and bloodstained face towards him. "I`m so sorry, my love. So, so, sorry, but I had to make sure you were safe."

"How touching," sneered Pearson. "She`ll provide good entertainment for the men when they`ve finished. We`ll even keep you alive just long enough to watch."

"You bastard!"

Pearson hit him again, this time in the face. "In fact, after they've had her, she can watch me cut you up into little pieces. That will really be a nice end to tonight. Then you'll both be found in the canal. It'll look just like a suicide. Two lovers caught out and unable to face the scandal"

"Take heart," whispered John. "We're not dead yet."

"Is all this violence really necessary?" asked the leader. "I absolutely forbid it."

"You forbid me nothing!" snarled Pearson. "I'm cutting Mayfield up, although he's not a gentleman. But he will be taught a lesson. The only problem is he won't live long enough to appreciate it."

"On the subject of gentlemen," said John. "Can you tell me what right a cashiered army officer has to that title? Let me see, fraud, larceny and cheating at cards wasn't it? Do you think we didn't find out? We've known about you for a week."

"I warned you not to underestimate him," said the leader. "Have you even thought why he's here tonight?"

"Because of that bitch," Cooper pointed at Kate. "You told him. Didn't you, bitch?"

"Yes, she did," answered John. "It's pointless denying it. She told me all about you as well. Mind you, I'd realised you were a bastard before then. A typical coward and a bully. I've met your sort before. You're finished here, irrespective of what happens to us."

"But you're not that clever, are you Mayfield? Because if you were and had listened to her, you would have known better than to come here alone."

John sighed. "You're right there. I had an ambush all lined up for you, but they were unable to come in the end. So, I just came to see for myself."

Cooper, Pearson and the leader visibly relaxed.

"As we will clearly be dead, before long, allow me to tell you what I found," said John. "Your big mistake was not just drawing attention to yourself, by antagonizing me, but in killing Thompson. By the way, was it Monk who did it?"

The leader nodded.

"You see, had you been a real major, you would have noticed his spurs and sabre were missing. And you never searched his uniform before putting him in the river. Had you done so, then you would have found a snuff box, bearing the initials **W T.** in one of his pockets. He had stolen it from a house in Aylesbury, along with all the other silver and what have you."

Cooper, Pearson and the leader looked at each other.

"Then murdering Monk nearly succeeded. It would have done so if you had used another piece of rope. I suspect you had to do it in a hurry, knowing we would soon be coming for him. You were a little unlucky with the way you slid the bolt." John paused. "You see, I came across an identical case only a few months ago. And Carter recognised your uniform. By the way, we have the trousers, you lost."

John stopped for a moment and gave a Kate a re-assuring squeeze, which the others did not notice. She responded, but had no idea how they would escape.

"Ezra Crane told us a lot," he continued. "So have your two men in custody. Did you enjoy reading all those letters last night?"

Pearson punched him again.

Gasping for breath, John looked at the leader. "As for you, you were not so easy to discover. You always seemed to be around and very eager to help, as a magistrate should be. But thanks to Kate here," he squeezed her again. "She put me on my guard. To be correct, she did not actually recognise you, but thought you were a magistrate. That narrowed the choice down to two of the people I trusted. So I set a little trap."

John paused a moment, and was aware of the charged atmosphere in the foundry. Every man in there was listening to him.

"Sergeant Harrison got me two arrest warrants for Pearson here. One was for him to be arrested yesterday morning, and another one for today," he continued. "You couldn`t leave the *Green Dragon* quickly enough, could you Pearson?"

None of the three said anything.

"Now, tell me please. Am I right?"

"Absolutely correct," replied William Slattery. "I told them not to underestimate you."

"What a pity there`ll be no evidence to convict any of us, after you're dead," smiled Cooper. "We shall all be safe."

"Wrong, Mr Cooper. There is the matter of your special note book. I suspect you haven`t been able to find it lately, eh?"

"You fool," hissed Pearson. "Where is it?" he snapped at John.

"You bitch," snarled Cooper aiming another punch at Kate. She flinched, but John moved in front of her and took it instead.

"For your information," he gasped. "By now it will be with the Bank of England, along with my report and written statements from all the witnesses. You`ll have to run far and fast to escape the hangman." John laughed wheezily.

The three men started arguing amongst themselves, whilst the workers at the furnace were now showing far less enthusiasm than before, and had not started work again.

"Here`s the deal," said John. "You all go now and leave us here. That way you get a head start, in return for our lives."

"Ha! Ha! Ha!" sneered Cooper. "Do you seriously think there`s the slightest chance of your getting out of here alive?"

"Apart from knowing too much, you`ve also been responsible for ruining this very profitable scheme," added Pearson.

"I don`t see why we can`t do as he suggests," said Slattery. "After all I`ve got just as much to lose as you have. I say let them live."

"Your views don`t matter any more," hissed Pearson. "With a careful defence and a sympathetic jury, bearing in mind all your noble works, you`ll probably get away with being transported. But he knows I killed Monk, don`t you, Mayfield?" snapped Pearson.

"So you admit to killing Monk, do you?" asked John.

"Of course I killed him, just as I`m going to kill you."

"And, I take it you were behind the attack on me and Sergeant Harrison when we came to the White House?"

"Not entirely," corrected Pearson. "It was James`s idea, and a good one too. It nearly worked. And would have done if it hadn`t been for Waldren`s niece. If I get the time, I`ll see she gets it."

"He`ll kill you too, Slattery. You know that." said John. "Give me your gun, and I`ll speak up for you at the trial."

Slattery shook his head. "It`s not even loaded."

Cooper burst out laughing. "What a laugh! The oh so clever Superintendent Mayfield, was captured with an unloaded gun, when he tried to save his whore. How touching."

"Tell me just one more thing?" asked John. "Whose idea was it to use stolen gold and silver to plate basely made coins?"

"I`m afraid I must take the credit for that," said Slattery. "You see, I carry out all manner of charitable works, and did not have enough money to do all that I wanted. As a jeweller, it was a simple matter for me to make the moulds: make the coins out of base metal, approximately of a similar weight, and then plate them."

"And a bonus was actually acting as an adviser to the Bank of England and the Royal Mint in this affair."

"Correct." Slattery paused. "But, how did you know about that?"

"From a friend of mine in the Birmingham Police."

"ENOUGH!" shouted Cooper. "Take the woman, men. She`s all yours."

The men grinned, put down their tools and surged forward. Kate held on tightly to John`s arm, surprised to see him smile.

"DANIEL! MATHEW!" he shouted.

All at once the foundry doors were thrust open and armed men surged inside. As this happened, other men outside, broke the windows and pushed their muskets through, all aimed at Cooper, Pearson, Slattery and the foundry workers. The latter men looked wildly around, but every exit was covered. Slowly, they raised their hands over their heads.

"Thank God, you`ve come," shouted Cooper. "I just came in and found all this going on. I know absolutely nothing about it."

"Don`t lie," answered Daniel Roberts. "We`ve been outside listening to everything, ever since John came in. And it`s all been written down."

A shocked silence followed his words.

"Let me introduce you to Superintendent Monroe and Inspector Roberts from Birmingham," announced John. "But, Mr Slattery, you already know my good friend Daniel Roberts. These other police officers are all from there or Leamington, except the two men in black, who are from the Bank of England. The young lady, Miss Penrose, is an artist employed by the Bank, to sketch scenes such as this, for Court purposes. The constable guarding her is Samuel Perkins. No doubt you have heard of him? After all you have tried to have him killed twice."

As John spoke, Lucy Penrose gripped Samuel`s arm, and gave a small gasp. "It`s all right, Lucy," reassured Samuel and patted her hand, but made no effort to remove it.

John smothered a small chuckle as he witnessed the scene. Miss Lucy Penrose was an attractive young woman, and clearly taken by Samuel. It seemed the feeling was mutual.

"In that case then I`ll turn Queen`s Evidence. I`ll tell you everything you want to know. It was............" Cooper broke off, as Pearson shot him twice in the chest.

David Monroe knelt beside him. "He`s dead. You`ve killed him, Pearson. We all saw it," he stated.

In the stunned silence that followed, Pearson grabbed Kate by the hair and pulled her towards him. Holding his revolver to her head he backed towards the door.

"Mayfield!" he shouted. "Tell your men to back off or I shoot the woman."

"Keep back, men!" called John.

"Can we trust this bastard?" whispered Daniel.

"For the moment, yes. She`s in serious danger, but it`s me he really wants."

"Pearson," called John. "They`ve backed off. I know it`s me you want. Let her go and take me instead."

"No!" He made his way to the door. "If any of you try to follow me, I`ll shoot her. Understand, Mayfield?"

"Yes."

"But you can follow in five minutes time, but nobody else. You know where I will be. I`ll have the swords ready."

With that, he was through the door, forcing Kate in front of him. Moments later, they heard his horse gallop off.

"Oh John, what are you going to do?"

John turned, amazed to see Harriet standing behind him. "What are you doing here?"

"I followed you, saw you captured and was about to try and rescue you." Harriet rubbed her face gently. "But Daniel here stopped me."

"My humblest apologies, ma`am," smiled Daniel. "But we couldn`t let you spoil things."

"I`m glad he did. It was vital for Cooper and his gang to be caught in the act, and getting a confession was a bonus. We needed to definitely link Slattery here with the gang, so I agreed to be captured."

"You deliberately got yourself captured?" Harriet was aghast.

"Sadly yes, but not as it happened. Kate was not supposed to be here. Still, it worked. Now, I must go after Pearson."

"Where are you going, Guv`nor?" asked Mathew. "The White House?"

"Yes. Give me a few minutes start and then come after me with some of the men. See if you can pick up Dr Waldren on the way. I think he`ll be needed."

John left the foundry, mounted his horse and set off in the direction of the White House.

Back in the foundry, Harriet looked angrily at Mathew and Daniel. "What did Pearson mean by having the swords ready?"

"He wants to fight John, man to man, with swords, in a duel," replied Daniel slowly. "But don`t worry, John can take care of himself."

Harriet did not answer, but ran out of the foundry, out on the towpath and recovered her horse. Seconds later she was galloping after John.

CHAPTER TWENTY FOUR

The White House

Kate Whiting did not struggle, knowing there was no point, so she let herself be bundled onto Pearson`s horse. He climbed up behind her and the animal trotted off, then broke into a canter and soon into a gallop, as it felt Pearson`s spurs. It took most of her strength just to hang on. Pearson held the reins in one hand, whilst he rammed his revolver into her side with the other. She barely noticed the pain, amongst all the other injuries she had received.

Any hopes she might have had of trying to escape in town, were quickly dashed, as Pearson kept to the canal towpath. But such an uneven route, full of unseen hazards such as mooring ropes, slowed him down and he was forced to rein in his horse to just a trot. Kate did not worry too much about herself now. Her beloved, John who had come to her rescue was safe, at least for the moment.

Yet she knew Pearson was a killer and intended John should be his next victim, before killing her as well. Kate felt she could die happy, if John was safe, but suddenly she thought about Edward and Silas and the tears ran slowly and quietly down her face.

She barely noticed they had left the towpath, and were trotting up the Birmingham Road and into the drive of the White House. Pearson reined in his horse by the front door, which was opened as he knocked.

"Get out!" he snapped at the bleary eyed servant, who was only too happy to oblige. "Come along, bitch."

Pearson pulled Kate, by the hair, into the hallway, and headed for the stairs.

She pulled back and began to fight. Her nails went for his eyes, but he was too quick for her and jerked back his head. At the same time he punched her hard in the face, then the chest. Semi-conscious, she sank, sobbing to the floor. Pearson, gave her a hard kick, and Kate mercifully lapsed into unconsciousness.

She never knew how long she lay there, but when she recovered, the front door had opened and John was in the house. Pearson stood on the stairs, with two rapiers in his hands.

"Well," he said. "I never thought you'd come to your death so easily."

John ignored him, and knelt by Kate, relieved to see her eyes flutter open, and that she was breathing. Pearson stood impatiently on the stairs.

"When you've finished ministering to that whore," he sneered. "You can face me. Oh, I must apologize. Of course, you're saying goodbye to her. You won't be apart long. She'll be joining you soon."

"We'll see about that!" came a female voice."

Nobody had seen Harriet enter the house. She stood with her revolver pointing directly at Pearson.

"I might have guessed," he said. "You haven't really got the nerve to fight me properly. You have to bring your pet watchdog with you."

John stood up from Kate. "Please Harriet. This is between Pearson and me."

"No!"

"Yes! I have to do this or run for the rest of my life. And I can't do that."

For a few seconds they glared at each other, before Harriet lowered her gun, reluctantly, biting back her anger, frustration and pain. Deep down she knew it was something that men had to do. She would wait and see what happened. They all heard horses arriving outside, and Mathew and Daniel Roberts entered, both carrying their revolvers.

"Put them away please," said John quietly. "This is the deal. If Pearson kills me, he goes free. Understood?"

"You can't do that Guv'nor," said Mathew. "Mr Roberts. Stop him!"

Daniel shook his head. "No. Let matters take their course."

"And I thought you were his friend!" snapped Harriet, as Mathew turned away in disgust.

Further discussion was averted by the arrival of Thomas Waldren. He said nothing but went straight to Kate, and opened up his medical bag. John took off his coat and accepted one of the swords Pearson offered him. He wrapped his hand around the hilt, as he would have done to a cutlass.

Pearson laughed scornfully. "This isn`t a cutlass drill, Mayfield. It`s a gentleman`s weapon, which you obviously know nothing about. Look, you hold it like this." He took John`s hand and put it into the correct position on the hilt.

"Oh yes, I remember now," said John. "I went for some practice the other afternoon."

Pearson ignored John`s comments and stood him in the correct *en garde* position. "Now we`ve got you standing right, we`ll begin the lesson. Don`t ever let it be said I never gave you a chance. What you have to do," he explained sarcastically. "Is to try and hit me, with the point of your sword, whilst stopping me doing the same to you. Understand?"

John nodded.

"Also," continued Pearson. "There`s no purpose in trying to slash me with the edge, because it is a pointed weapon only. Shall we begin?"

Harriet and Mathew tensed as John nodded his agreement. Kate had brushed aside Thomas`s ministrations, and watched fearfully as the two men faced up to each other. Harriet slowly moved her hand back to the pocket, where she had put her revolver. She would let John fight for a while, or for however long it took, for him to satisfy his honour, but Pearson would never kill him. Or, if he did, she would still shoot him.

Kate saw her and realised what she was doing. She prayed the red-headed woman was as good a shot with the revolver, as she was reputed to be.

"Now, Mayfield," taunted Pearson. "I`m going to lunge at you and you must parry my blade. That means you have to prevent it from hitting you."

He lunged gently and slowly at John, who fiercely knocked his blade away. "Yes, that`s the idea."

Pearson lunged again, but John merely retreated out of range.

He tried again, but John retreated once more.

"Enough of this foolery," snarled Pearson. "You`re meant to stand and fight, not run away. This time it`s for real. I`ll just nick your right cheek and we`ll take it from there."

He lunged at John, who stood his ground, this time, and neatly parried his opponent`s blade.

"Beginner`s luck. But I`m impressed. You`re a quick learner," chortled Pearson. "Let`s go for the left cheek this time."

He lunged again, and was a little surprised to find John parried this attack as well.

In the room, the atmosphere was electric.

Pearson circled John and lunged once more. It was a feint and he changed the direction of his attack at the last moment. Harriet and Kate gasped, but John parried this attack, with apparent ease. Pearson was puzzled. Mayfield was not bad for an absolute novice. He continued with his attacks, but still found himself unable to get through John`s guard.

Whichever way he attacked, his lunges were always parried. Pearson tried again and again. Regardless of how he attacked, he could not get through the policeman`s guard. Pearson was puzzling over what attack to do next, when John suddenly moved from pure defensive actions to a riposte and attacked him.

The move took Pearson completely by surprise and he found himself retreating, something he very rarely, if ever, did when fencing. He was even more puzzled by his failure to get through John`s guard. Then, looking up into John`s eyes, he was horrified by what he found.

He saw a pair of hard steely blue eyes boring into his own, with a cold determined look to them. At the same time, John began to attack him in earnest. Slowly realization had dawned on Pearson. His opponent was not a novice at all with the sword. In fact he was a very capable swordsman, something Pearson had never expected. The more they fought, the harder he found it to resist the policeman`s attacks.

The spectators had relaxed slightly as the duel progressed, although Harriet still held her revolver. She looked at Daniel and saw him smile knowingly when he saw Pearson realise how he had met his match. No wonder Daniel had been so indifferent to their pleas about stopping the fight.

He obviously knew of John`s prowess with a sword, and had never really been worried for his friend. But, he had not dared to say anything to the others, in case Pearson discovered it too quickly. Having witnessed how the man had attacked Kate, he was content to see him being taught a lesson.

Pearson began sweating profusely and his breath was coming in gasps. To make matters worse he saw John hardly seemed out of breath. He was coming to the end of his strength, whilst John was clearly very much in charge. The man was playing him at his own game, and Pearson did not like it, but still had one last trick to play.

Retreating after a vicious engagement, he opened his hand and dropped his sword. Quickly catching it, with his hand in front of the hilt, Pearson aimed it like a dart and threw it at John. The watchers held their breath and Harriet tightened her grip on her revolver. They need not have worried.

John beat the sword down, where it stuck quivering in the floor at his feet. Without taking his eyes off Pearson, he pulled it free and tossed it back to his opponent. "Yours, I believe," he said drily.

It was what Pearson had wanted him to do. Gripping the sword, he launched a *fleche* attack on John by running at him, hoping to catch the policeman off guard. As the attack arrived, John sank to one knee, and Pearson`s sword passed harmlessly over him. Pearson came to a halt, only to find John was behind him. Desperately he ran for the stairs, jumped up several and turned to face John.

But, he was too late. Even as he turned, John twisted his sword round the other man`s blade. With a flick of his wrist, John sent Pearson`s sword over the balustrade, where it stuck, point first, quivering in the floor, well out of reach. The point of John`s sword was now at Pearson`s throat.

"On your knees!" he instructed. "I don`t give a damn for the hurt you`ve caused me. But you will apologize to Mrs Whiting for the insults and the beatings you`ve given her tonight. Apologize!"

"I....I....apologize, Mrs Whiting."

"Thank you. Your prisoner, gentlemen." John turned to walk downstairs.

"JOHN!" screamed Harriet and Kate together.

"NO!" cried John as he saw Harriet aim her revolver and fire. He felt the bullet whistle past his ear, and heard a cry from Pearson followed by a slight thud. Spinning round, he saw Pearson, still on his knees, clutching a bleeding hand. A small pistol lay on the floor in front of him.

Harriet had saved John's life yet again.

Mathew and Daniel ran past him and seized the now whimpering Pearson. It took them only seconds to put manacles on his wrists before letting Thomas have a look at him.

"You stupid, stupid bastard!" cried Harriet. "You stupid, stupid bastard! I could have lost you." She started to sob and flew at John, hitting him with her fists.

"And I already have," said Kate, wistfully, to herself, also sobbing. John held Harriet with one arm, went over to Kate and helped her up with his other. Then he held both women to him as they sobbed.

"I don't know how to thank both of you," he said, his mind in an absolute turmoil.

Harriet had saved his life, again, whilst Kate had saved his career. He found he loved them both, and did not know what to do or say. Whatever he did would please one and hurt the other. It was hardly the way to thank them. John was so wrapped up in his own thoughts, he was unaware of other police officers now arriving.

Ironically, he was saved, certainly for the moment, by an unexpected source.

"A question, Mr Mayfield, if I may?" The speaker was a very subdued and polite Charles Pearson. "Where did you learn to handle a sword like that?"

"In your military days, and a swordsman like you, did you ever come across the Army champion fencer, Lieutenant William Mayfield?"

"Yes."

"My father. He taught me all he knew and I was rated better than him."

Pearson sighed. "You're Billy Mayfield's son! I should have made the connection."

After Pearson had been removed, Harriet helped John carry Kate over to a sofa, supervised by Thomas. John left uncle and niece tenderly examining the now semi-conscious Kate, and gratefully applied himself to work, of which there was now no shortage.

The rest of the night passed in a blur for him. By daybreak, all of Cooper's remaining servants were in custody, and coupled with those arrested at the foundry caused a major problem. Where to put them all?

As it happened, the White House had several cellars, which sufficed as temporary accommodation. The Bank of England staff decided to take the house over as their temporary headquarters, especially as more staff arrived during the following day. They asked for a liaison officer, especially to act as escort for Miss Lucy Penrose and Samuel`s face lit up, when he was given the job.

CHAPTER TWENTY FIVE

The Assizes

The Lent Assizes were the largest held in Warwick for many years, and John had his work cut out just making sure they passed off with the minimum of problems. Ben Underwood and Caleb Young who replaced Elijah Snow and Patrick Monk, had the makings of becoming useful officers, although John had reservations about Underwood.

Not about his ability, but whether Warwick was challenging enough for him, as the youngster had ambitions. Even with these two extra men, they were not enough, and it had been necessary to to swear-in several special constables.

The highlights would be the trials of William Slattery and his gang, followed by Charles Pearson. Somewhere in the calendar, Silas Whiting would also appear, when an application would be made to have the charge against him dropped. Whilst John expected this to only be a formality, there was always the risk of something going wrong.

Not everybody who wanted to, could get into the Court for the trial of William Slattery and his remaining associates. Although he had offered to turn Queen`s Evidence, the Bank of England declined. It was felt the part he had played was far too serious for him to be allowed to escape justice.

They all pleaded not guilty, but there was more than enough evidence to convict the whole gang, several times over. The jury never even bothered to retire before pronouncing guilty verdicts on all of them.

In some respects they were fortunate, as coining offences no longer carried the death penalty. The remainder of the gang received terms of transportation, varying from seven to fourteen years. Slattery was not so lucky. In spite of his having used the money for charitable purposes, instead of personal gain, he found himself transported for life.

As expected, Charles Pearson stood indicted for the murder of James Cooper, which had happened in front of numerous witnesses.

Although he pleaded not guilty, the jury took less than five minutes to convict him. He showed no emotion as the Judge solemnly put on his black hat, and sentenced him to death. The watchers booed and hissed as he was taken down from the court. When order had been restored, Silas was called.

John could see Kate up in the public gallery. He had not seen her when she had arrived, and left Edward at the police station. It was the first time he had seen her since that night at the White House. In view of her involvement in the affair, there had been concerns for her safety, and Superintendent Monroe had taken her and Edward back to Birmingham.

At a special hearing the next day, Silas had been released on bail and taken there as well, to be re-united with his family. The Bank of England had stood bail for him, and one of their barristers, Joseph Beale now acted on his behalf.

Kate looked pale, but apparently none the worse for the beating she had received. She was wearing a blue silk dress, covered by a black velvet cloak and hood. Her hair was parted in the middle and she had put on some weight, clearly as a result from now having enough to eat.

John could not believe the difference in her appearance. He had ensured she benefited from the reward put out by the Bank of England, and clearly she had spent wisely. Suddenly she saw him and smiled, her heart fluttering at the same time.

Beale addressed the court before the charge was put to Silas. He asked for the case to be dismissed, and called John as his one and only witness. John entered the witness box, took the oath and and identified himself. He explained how the arresting officer had since been murdered and there was now no evidence to connect Silas with the stolen meat. The butcher had not seen the meat taken, and only saw Silas being savagely attacked by Monk, and the stolen joints of meat lying between them.

The Judge had been appraised of the facts before the hearing, including the part Kate had played in bringing Slattery's gang to trial, but gave the impression of finding the whole affair unusual. He was clearly most unhappy about an important London barrister defending such a case, and trying to take charge of his court. He began asking John all manner of seemingly trivial questions, mainly concerning Monk's death.

John felt the Judge was stalling and waiting for something to happen. Beale steadfastly avoided meeting John's eyes. Several minutes later, a man entered the court and handed a note to the clerk, who passed it to the judge

"I'm going to retire and think about this case," he announced, after reading the note. "Meanwhile, take Whiting down the steps for the time being. His bail is rescinded."

There was an audible gasp from Kate at this announcement. John went pale with anger, but knew better than to object. The court rose as the Judge retired. Beale called John over to him.

"I hadn't expected this. It looks like the old fool wants to convict him. Are you sure the butcher cannot identify Whiting as having stolen the meat?"

"Yes," lied John, feeling his ears redden.

In reality, the man had not needed very much persuasion to change his evidence. After only a token resistance, he agreed and John handed over an envelope containing a few shillings, much more than the value of the meat.

Strictly speaking, he knew it was perverting the course of justice, but he had done it for Kate's sake and her future happiness. If the truth ever came out, he would not only be out of a job, but joining Slattery in Australia. His reverie was interrupted by a court usher summoning him and the barrister to the Judge's chambers.

"Let me do the talking," hissed the barrister. "I think I may have a way around this."

They were shown into the Judge's chambers, where he sat at a desk with his wig off and robes open, and was clearly not in the best of moods. Standing in front of him was Arthur Webb, the butcher, and John feared the worst.

Webb was clearly worried, and kept turning his hat round and round with shaking hands. Sweat glistened all over his face, and

John`s heart sank. He knew only too well, that he could not rely on the man not to tell the truth. It would be an inglorious end to all he had achieved recently. All for an act of stupidity involving a married woman, whom he loved. And, not any married woman, but the husband of the man they were discussing. They all waited.

"Well," snapped the judge. "As I can`t interview this man Monk, I`ve had the butcher brought here, where I propose to question him about what really happened, and how much he`s been paid. What have you got to say about that, eh?"

"You could do so," replied Beale. "But, may I remind you I am retained, in this case, just as in the Slattery trial, by the Bank of England. Mrs Whiting provided us with the evidence to bring Slattery and his gang to justice. She did so at great personal risk to herself, and was very nearly murdered in the process."

"And, just how did she come by this information, eh?"

He paused and looked at John. "I don`t believe, for one moment, that she just happened to find it. I suspect she stole it, so it can`t be used in evidence, can it? What was she doing in the house, eh? Selling her body, no doubt, to James Cooper? And just who put her up to it? You, Mr Mayfield?"

John noticed the judge`s sudden use of Cooper`s full name. Did that mean he was friendly with Cooper, he wondered. Is this what it was all about? He looked towards Beale, who did not acknowledge his look.

"I don`t give a damn about what she did or did not do to bring this gang to justice. What I am interested in is this man Whiting, who is charged with a felony. I refuse to believe it has any bearing on the earlier cases. Are you trying to tell me, this Whiting woman was solely responsible for the gang appearing here in court?"

"My lord........." began Beale.

"I`m not speaking to you. Be quiet. Mayfield, answer the question!"

"That is correct," John confirmed. "If it had not been for her, I doubt the gang would have been arrested. I should add, Mrs Whiting was seriously assaulted in the process."

"I think I can safely say," added Beale. "That the Bank will not be impressed if Whiting is not released today. Words will be said in high places."

The Judge glowered at him.

"Mayfield," Beale continued. "Would you and Webb leave us alone please. But, don`t go too far away."

John and Arthur Webb thankfully left the Judge`s chambers.

"You told me I wouldn`t have to come to court," whined Webb, the moment they were outside.

"Shut up! That`s what I thought. Now listen. And listen carefully. You did not see Whiting with your meat. And you`ve had back more money than the meat was worth. Understand?"

Webb nodded.

"And understand this. If you change your story, you and me will both end up in Australia." John pointed at Webb and himself as he spoke. "Understand?"

Webb nodded miserably.

It was nearly half an hour later before a smiling Beale re-appeared. After telling Webb he was free to leave, Beale took John on one side.

"The Judge will be a few minutes yet, and we have to wait for him to enter first. But, we have a result."

"Thank you."

"However, a word. His lordship is convinced something is going on between you and Mrs Whiting, and suspects you have been not telling him the whole truth." He held his hand up. "No, don`t deny it. I was there remember. So, he will always treat you with suspicion. Be very careful, in future, with any cases you may have before him. If they are not absolutely correct in every detail, he`ll throw them out." Beale paused and looked meaningfully at John. "I`m afraid you`ve made a bad enemy my friend. However, I think he will apply to leave this Circuit, after our little chat, and may even retire."

"But why the animosity? I`ve never met him before."

"He has, on several occasions, hunted with a certain Mr James Cooper. He invested heavily in Cooper`s business. But, with Cooper`s death and everything else, the Government has seized all the assets, to the detriment of the investors, including his lordship, who has now lost a considerable amount of money, which he could not afford to lose. And he is looking for revenge. It seems, he was the main sponsor trying to get Cooper a knighthood, and Cooper paid him a handsome retainer for these services, all of which have now ceased."

Beale paused again and looked back towards the Judge's chambers. There was as yet no movement.

"I found the evidence back at the White House and reminded him of it," Beale continued. "You, my friend, were responsible for uncovering the truth about Cooper, which he couldn't or more likely wouldn't see."

"So he considers me responsible for his financial problems?"

"Correct. Once word gets out, as it surely will, he will not be allowed to forget it, and neither will you. For what it's worth, I hope I never have to plead a case before him again. He is a very vindictive man."

Just how vindictive, they would soon discover.

"My thanks."

"A last bit of advice, my friend. Next time you buy a witness off, make absolutely sure he won't go back on his word. Webb is a poor liar." He paused. "And so are you."

Further conversation was stopped by the usher calling them back into court. By the time they arrived, Silas was stood again in the dock. John looked up at Kate, but she was looking at her husband.

"After due consideration of this case," began the judge. "I have come to a decision, which I am not convinced is the right one. The prisoner stands indicted on matters not concerned with the previous forgery and murder cases."

He paused for effect, pretended to consult his notes, then he took out a handkerchief and blew his nose. "In the public gallery, today, is the wife of this man." He pointed to the gallery. Whilst he did not know Kate by sight, other women in the gallery did.

John went cold, wondering what the judge would say next. He looked at Beale, whose mouth was tightly closed, in anger. It had long been agreed to keep Kate's identity out of the whole affair.

"My lord," interrupted Beale. "This is most improper!"

"BE SILENT SIR! Or I will have you removed. This is my court."

The judge looked at his notes and continued. "It would seem Mrs Whiting was responsible for the forgers being brought to Justice, and her husband is to be acquitted, of this charge, as a reward for her informing on people, who were her betters and even her equals. How she came across this information, I will leave to your imagination."

He paused. "Her actions have resulted in the foundry being closed, several men being transported and others losing their jobs."

"MY LORD! I MUST PROTEST!" Beale had to shout to make himself heard in the following uproar, among the the public, in the gallery.

John ran out of the court and up the stairs to the public gallery. On the way he saw Robert Andrew and Caleb Young who were already on their way to the gallery, after hearing the noise. Together they ran up the stairs.

John was first though the doors. Kate was walking towards him, with a tight face, and tears already trickling down her cheeks. Any chance now of a new life in Warwick had gone.

Many of the spectators in the gallery, had seen their menfolk sentenced for their involvement with Slattery`s gang. Whilst they had no feelings for Cooper`s death, nor the law, they did not appreciate Kate`s role in the affair. Others were there because they wanted to see why their menfolk had lost their jobs. Now they knew and were not very happy, and Kate was their obvious target.

The three officers surrounded Kate and took her out just as the spectators moved towards her. Her hood had fallen onto her shoulders and a woman`s hand made a grab for her hair.

She yelped in pain, as Robert`s staff crashed onto her knuckles. For a moment, the other women hung back, which gave the policemen time to get Kate out of the gallery. By now, several of the special constables had arrived and slowly order was restored.

"Take Mrs Whiting to the police station," instructed John. "I`m going for her husband."

John went back into the court, but the judge had gone. He found a bewildered Silas Whiting sitting alongside Joseph Beale, obviously the charge had been withdrawn.

"Is Kate alright?" asked Silas.

"Yes. She`s at the police station and that`s where we`re going in just a moment."

"What did the judge mean by his remarks? I thought Kate had found the information in a book he had left lying about it?"

"It`s probable she might have stolen it," John replied quickly. He had never asked her how the book had been found. "I felt it best not to ask. But, remember, whatever Kate did, she did for you."

Silas seemed to believe this and John relaxed only slightly, and just hoped poor Silas never discovered the truth about his wife.

"Mayfield," said Beale. "I am appalled at what has happened. I will see a full report is sent to the Lord Chancellor. With the Bank's support, I have a feeling his lordship will not be a judge for very much longer."

Taking Silas by the arm, John took him out into the main entrance to the court where several special constables waited. Together they took Silas to the police station.

Nobody paid any attention to a slender woman, dressed in black, who was the last one to leave the Court.

❦

For a while, an angry mob gathered outside the police station. When it subsided John, Joseph Beale and the Whiting family left the station and went to the *Bath Hotel*, in Leamington, where they stayed for the night. Next morning John drove them to Coventry railway station.

Once on the platform, Joseph took Silas and Edward for a closer look at a nearby locomotive engine. John, thanked him mentally and stayed with Kate.

They sat on a bench, and Kate took his hand. Hers was very cold.

"Oh my love," she said. "What must I do? I love you and I love my husband."

John squeezed her hand. "I know my love. But only you can decide. I promise I will respect your decision, whatever it is."

"I'm glad you say that. Because...because.....much as I love you... and I do love you....I am married to Silas." She faltered.

"I know. And that has to be the right decision."

"Will you write to me?"

He shook his head. "No. That would not be proper and would do neither of us any good." He put his finger on her lips as she started to protest. In the distance a train whistle sounded.

"We have so little time," she whispered. "But we cannot part without my saying thank you for all you've done for us. Yesterday wasn't your fault. We all know that."

234

They sat in silence, not knowing what else to say.

The train drew slowly into the station and Joseph brought the bemused Silas and excited Edward back to Kate. She was the last one to board.

At the last minute, throwing convention aside, she threw her arms around John and kissed him fully on the lips. "Good bye, my darling. But, it won`t be for ever. I know we will meet again."

Then she was gone.

John watched the train until it was out of sight. He owed Kate more than he could ever repay, and loved her as well. Somehow, part of his life was now missing. Going out of the station, he returned to his carriage and then stopped.

He saw a horse was tethered to its rear and somebody was in the carriage.

His hand slipped into his pocket and fastened round the revolver he carried there. He had only put it in at the last minute, just in case they had been attacked on the journey.

"Hello John. You won`t need that," came Harriet`s cheerful voice. "I thought you might need cheering up. I take it she`s gone?" Her cheerfulness belied her real feelings. She had fallen in love with John, and recognized Kate as a serious rival. But now she was gone, and most unlikely ever to return.

"Yes," agreed John. "She`s gone."

His mood felt much lighter already. He had seen very little of Harriet after the night at the foundry and the White House. She had seemed a little aloof and even cool whenever they met by chance, and was never at home when John visited Thomas and Sarah. Now she seemed just like her old self, as she had been before Kate appeared.

❦

A few nights later, John dined with Thomas, Sarah and Harriet.

It had been a difficult day starting with Pearson`s execution.

"I hear he died well," said Thomas.

"I suppose so," replied John. "Though I find it hard to accept anyone can die well, in such circumstances."

The conversation moved on, but inevitably returned to Slattery`s gang.

"Is it true Mrs Whiting got the reward money?" asked Sarah.

"Yes," said John. "And it was substantial, more than enough for them to start a new life, probably in America. I put her in touch with my father's solicitor. He's absolutely trustworthy and has a good business head."

"One thing I've always wanted to know," said Thomas after a while. "How did you know it was Slattery who was giving all the secrets away? It could just as easily have been me."

"That was the problem," John replied slowly. "I knew it had to be one of you, but didn't know which one it was. I had my suspicions and put them to the test, and that's why I laid the trap, with the warrants for Pearson's arrest. And Slattery took the bait. If he hadn't, then it would have been academic after that weekend."

"But why did you choose him first?"

"Quite simply. Slattery came before Waldren in the alphabet."

Thomas nearly choked on his wine, whilst Sarah could not stop herself smiling. Harriet burst into laughter. Soon all four of them were laughing.

Whilst the Waldrens were enjoying their supper, a young slender woman, dressed in black, was on her knees, in front of a freshly dug grave, in St Mary's Churchyard. The grave was unmarked and would remain so.

Charles Pearson's young widow slowly got to her feet. "Good bye, my darling," she said quietly through her tears. "I promise I will avenge you. Mayfield and that whore will be made to suffer, although not for a while. Vengeance is a dish best served cold. By the time I have finished with them, they will both be pleading for death."

She walked out of the churchyard without another look back.

HISTORICAL NOTE

Mayfield is not and is never intended to be a history of the Warwick Borough Police. It is a work of fiction, although set in a real town.

The Warwick Borough Police started in 1846, not 1840, as in this story. I have had to change the date as I needed a certain time line for the trilogy.

Life for early policemen was exceptionally hard, by today`s standards. Discipline was harsh, with many supervisors coming from the Army and Navy, bringing their own exacting standards with them. There were all manner of restrictions placed on both the working and off duty lives of officers, some of which still exist today.

In many instances, towns, cities and rural areas were required, by law, to set up police forces, often against their will, usually on grounds of cost. Prior to this period, these authorities had been quite content to utilize the old-fashioned system of parish constables, and the Associations for the Prosecution of Felons, to do their policing for them. It was inefficient and had to change. However, some parish constables were good at their jobs.

Promotion within a small force, would be very slow, if ever. It would be a case of dead men`s shoes. Warwick was no exception. Being the county town meant holding the Quarter Sessions and the Assizes, all at a time when Warwickshire was much bigger than it is today. Assistance from specially sworn temporary constables and assistance from neighbouring forces, was vital on occasions. For many years, the Races were policed by Birmingham City officers, who had the advantage of knowing many of the visiting criminals.

Although *Mayfield* is a work of fiction, it is set in a real town, Warwick, where I live. I have used the modern names for the streets and roads. All the main locations still exist today: but you will not find any house which matches where Thomas and Sarah lived in High Street. Likewise, there is no *White House*.

The original police station in the Holloway, still exists. So does the *Green Dragon*, but is now called the *Tilted Wig*. Most of the old gaol has gone, but the Crown Courts (once home of the Assizes and Quarter Sessions) remain very active, albeit with an uncertain future. The *Woolpack* and *Bull's Head* no longer exist as such, although their buildings do.

With the exception of the Earl of Warwick, who plays no active part, and is only referred to by name, all the characters and events are entirely fictitious.

There was no 87th Regiment of Dragoons.

John Mayfield and his men will have many more problems to face.

ABOUT THE AUTHOR

Graham Sutherland is a retired police inspector, who is married, with three adult children and lives in Warwick. Although not born in Warwick, he has lived here for over forty years, and is currently the town's Beadle and Town Crier. He is also a blue badge tourist guide for the Heart of England Region, with special interests in Warwick, Leamington, Kenilworth, Stratford-upon-Avon, Oxford and the Cotswolds.

A keen historian, he gives numerous talks each year, mainly on social and criminal related topics. At one time he was the secretary of the Warwickshire Constabulary History Society, with a particular interest in policing in Victorian times.

A prolific writer, he is currently producing booklets to compliment the talks he gives. Mayfield is his first venture into the world of fiction.

Printed in Great Britain
by Amazon